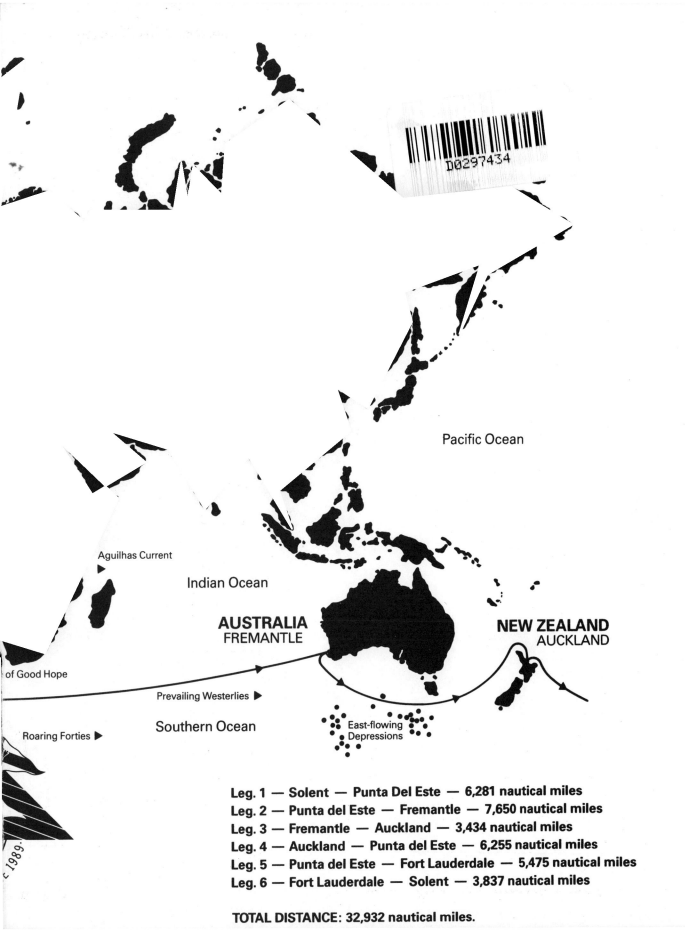

Pacific Ocean

Aguilhas Current

Indian Ocean

AUSTRALIA
FREMANTLE

NEW ZEALAND
AUCKLAND

of Good Hope

Prevailing Westerlies ▶

Roaring Forties ▶

Southern Ocean

East-flowing
Depressions

© 1989.

Leg. 1 — Solent — Punta Del Este — 6,281 nautical miles
Leg. 2 — Punta del Este — Fremantle — 7,650 nautical miles
Leg. 3 — Fremantle — Auckland — 3,434 nautical miles
Leg. 4 — Auckland — Punta del Este — 6,255 nautical miles
Leg. 5 — Punta del Este — Fort Lauderdale — 5,475 nautical miles
Leg. 6 — Fort Lauderdale — Solent — 3,837 nautical miles

TOTAL DISTANCE: 32,932 nautical miles.

Maiden

Maiden

TRACY EDWARDS

AND

TIM MADGE

SIMON & SCHUSTER

LONDON · SYDNEY · NEW YORK · TOKYO · SINGAPORE · TORONTO

First published in Great Britain by
Simon & Schuster Ltd in 1990
A Paramount Communications Company

Simon & Schuster Ltd
West Garden Place
Kendal Street
London W2 2AQ

Simon & Schuster of Australia Pty Ltd
Sydney

British Library Cataloguing-in-Publication Data available
ISBN 0-671-71027-3

Typeset in Palatino/Optima by Ace Filmsetting Limited, Frome
Reproduced by Thomas Capone, Southampton
Printed and bound in Great Britain by
Richard Clay Ltd, Bungay, Suffolk.

To

My mother and father, Patricia and Anthony Edwards, for everything.

Janne Gustavsson, the biggest and most beautiful albatross.

The crew and shore team of Maiden.

Preface

Much like the *Maiden* project, putting the book together has been an immense undertaking, spread out over two years and the entire globe. While Tracy sailed 33,000 miles, Tim travelled nearly 80,000 air miles to keep up with her.

The *Maiden* shore crew were a great asset in all this, as in most things. Howard kept both of us laughing as the author tried to write various chapters in odd corners of the world; Sarah-Jane was a tower of organisational strength abroad, as was Dee back in Hamble. Ian Bruce was an invaluable source of help with the technical drawings and details. And thanks to two crew members in particular, Tanya Visser and Angela Farrell, for taking many of the photographs in this book.

In Southern Chile David Branigan, as president of the Beagle Club, kept Tim company; he also took some of the pictures we have used. Barry Pickthall wrote a very inventive piece in *The Times* about Tim's Cape Horn trip, but we would like to thank him more for never letting Tim forget, every time he saw him, that he ought to be somewhere else – writing.

To all the skippers and crew of this Whitbread who provided background information on this and other Whitbreads, our thanks also.

In the Whitbread Race organisation, to Charles Williams, to David Pritchard-Barrett, to Charm Eberle (never yet seen in a flap in the WRTWR Press Office) and to Roger Lean-Vercoe: we are extremely grateful for all your help and advice.

British Telecom very kindly have allowed us to use all their charts and data on leg positions.

We would like to thank various people at the *Sunday Times* in London: Brian MacArthur, Mike Williams, and Nick Rufford for their support and encouragement over the duration of the Race.

In a different way, but no less important, we would like to thank Nicola Madge and the boys for putting up with the often long absences of Tim abroad.

Thank you also to Bill Hamilton at A. M. Heath for advice and help.

Finally, to all those at Simon and Schuster who have worked like Trojans to get the book out within four months of *Maiden*'s return, many, many thank yous. In particular, to our editor, Nick Brealey, who believed in the project from very early on and whose stringent attention to detail has ensured the book's success; to Fenella Smart for producing the final work; to Jeanette Graham for her work on pictures and paste-up.

Tracy Edwards, MBE and Tim Madge June 1990

Contents

Foreword

When Queen Noor and I met Tracy Edwards several years ago in the United States little did I know that she would become the first woman to skipper an all female crew in the most gruelling of all yacht races – the Whitbread Round the World Race, and that she and her gallant crew would complete the race in a most competent, able and professional manner, achieving many honours, and earning the respect and admiration of one and all. Little did I know that Tracy would in a sense become a member of our 'Jordanian Family' by carrying the name of Jordan to people throughout the world and across its oceans and seas.

Yet from the outset I was impressed by Tracy Edwards, recognising in her a genuine person with great strength of character, courage and determination to fulfil her dream. I am proud of her for having fulfilled that dream; for having risen to the challenge by no more than her own will and her unbeatable, infectious and inspiring spirit. I share this pride with the multitudes.

Tracy has done what many thought impossible and at the same time achieved one of her life's goals. I am delighted that Royal Jordanian airlines, our national carrier, in the true spirit of our people, was amongst the privileged few who sponsored *Maiden* and her gallant crew on their epic venture and that Jordan has been in a small way associated with this remarkable accomplishment.

When reading this book you will appreciate that Tracy Edwards is a very special young lady, with unique qualities. Her success is a reflection of her great fortitude and it is an inspiration to all who strive to achieve what others believe is impossible.

Hussein I
Amman, Jordan, June 1990

Cape Horn

When Tracy Edwards, at 23, and just off a racing yacht as its *cook*, announced she would enter the fifth Whitbread Round the World Race in her own yacht and with an all-woman crew, hardly anyone believed she could – or would.

But she did. Even more astonishing to the world's yachting establishment, whose scepticism had nearly sunk her project at one time, she and her crew proceeded to win the longest, most hazardous second leg from South America to Australia; and then, the third leg to New Zealand.

Now she and her 11 crew faced the fourth leg with excitement. They had nearly a whole day's lead over their nearest rival yacht, and they believed they would win it. Every woman on board was excited by the prospect of reaching Cape Horn, to sailors everywhere the place where you finally can call yourself a deep sea mariner.

Cape Horn is to sailors what Mount Everest is to mountain climbers. Both are inaccessible, wild, treacherous killers, places peopled by heroes and ghosts. Both are the settings where history is made.

Cape Horn had never been rounded by an all-women crewed yacht before. And Naomi James, who had sailed it single-handed had frequently (and generously) said that whereas when the weather got bad for her she would heave-to and wait, *Maiden* had to keep going under the worst of circumstances. As indeed she did.

Tracy's yacht, *Maiden*, finally rounded Cape Horn, at the very tip of South America, at 10.00am on February 25th, 1990. They had travelled 23,000 miles, survived a long and bitter struggle in the Southern Ocean, and emerged victorious, despite icebergs and gales and with injured crew . . .

CHAPTER 1

Tracy

Sunday, February 25th, 1990

Every sentence had Cape Horn in it today. We passed the Diego Ramirez island (in the approaches to the Horn) whilst it was still dark. Two hours later, as the sun rose, we saw it behind us. We thought the clouds might clear, but they hung determinedly on. Spotted the Hermitas islands (a group of islands just to the north-east of the Horn) soon after sunrise: monstrous mountains rearing out of the gloom.

By now excitement on board was beginning to grow – nothing drastic, just in the air. The Chilean navy vessel waiting behind the Cape was in touch on the radio. They said they'd come out to take pictures of us.

As we approached Cape Horn more of the girls scuttled up on deck. It was a grey day, but mild with a good breeze. We were travelling dead down-wind but never mind, we were moving nicely.

One for posterity and a souvenir for the girls.

Mikki (Mikaela von Koskull) uses a Finnish telescope!

When we were ten miles off we spotted the Chilean ship. They came in closer and as we got to the Horn everyone was on deck. So, out came the champagne. It is difficult not to think of all the ships under you and all the sailors who died trying to get round this most treacherous of coasts. I wasn't imagining it, there *was* a hush as we drew nearer.

Just to bring us back to earth, there were the Chileans taking pictures, and then our radar went. Still, the Chileans welcomed us to the Cape Horners Club, which was sweet, and they promised to send us the pictures for our albums.

We popped the champagne and drank a toast to Neptune and to going north, at last, out of the Southern Ocean. So this impossible epic moment in history slipped quietly by, with just the Chilean navy and the albatrosses looking on. No-one in the rest of the world was any wiser.

Twelve women sail round the Cape together after having sailed all the way through the Southern Ocean. Impossible. Captain Blythe would be turning in his grave. Oh well. Jo came up from the galley, said she'd cross it off her things to do list and went back to making bread.

The Horn is peopled by memories stretching back to the earliest voyages made to chart its fearsome storms, the desperate clash of Atlantic with Pacific Oceans. To sailors, worldwide, this is the place that marks the final exam, the one spot in millions of square miles of ocean-sailing that turns you into a 'real' sailor. It is the last rite of passage. Almost invariably, it turns a stormy, implacable face to those who venture to weather it.

For Tracy and her crew – as they stared across a few miles of seascape at the grey lumpy headland that is Cape Horn, set amidst hundreds of half-awash reefs, and islands battered by storms – the calm light air and flat seas were unnerving. It was too easy. After 23,000 miles of the Race, was this really the climax? they asked each other. Two days later they had the answer when whatever gods guard the Horn took their fee with a vengeance.

February 27th   52'13"S   61'56"W   Black Tuesday

4.00pm: We have just discovered the boat is full of water – when we are heeled it's reaching as far as the second tier of bunks. All hell has broken loose, everyone is up and trying desperately to discover where it's coming from. We decided we had to get all sails on deck which was a total nightmare. Then we had to pull all the boards up so we could check the bilges and the bottom plates.

The bilge pump wasn't working because the generator was full of salt water. So we formed a human chain passing full buckets up on deck to get the bilges emptied. (As someone once said on another Whitbread, there is no bilge pump like a bucket in the hands of a frightened sailor.) We had to take the headsail down and heaved to with three reefs in the main. Oh God, surely this isn't the end of the Race?

In the middle of all this Nancy, who had managed to stay asleep, sat up in her bunk and asked 'What sails have we got up?' Jeni, in mid-flight with a full bucket glared at her: 'the bloody mainsail, we've hove to. . .'

We got the engine pump on and kept on searching: nothing obvious. Then we were having to tack to avoid various islands in the Falklands; with all the sails on deck that was proving very difficult. There were people all over the place – the watches got totally confused. Needless to say, the wind was going round and round. We ended up with a terrible tangle in the rigging. Our speed was dreadful; all in all an absolute horror show.

Breaking waves in the Southern Ocean were a constant threat.

Looking for the leak.

Dawn estimates that about 50 gallons an hour is coming in; but from where? We have checked everything we can think of and there is no obvious place where there's a leak. You'd think we'd be able to see it – after all it's a hell of a lot of water sloshing in. One thing: it does seem to be much worse when we are on port tack. It has to be somewhere at deck level too as we have checked every possible place below the waterline.

Tracy was in constant radio contact with the Race Committee in Punta del Este in Uruguay. They were so worried by what Tracy reported they alerted the military command in the Falkland Islands. An RAF Hercules was scrambled (and overflew *Maiden*). Meanwhile HMS *Leeds Castle* steamed to within 30 miles of the yacht until Tracy reported she was not sinking.

On board, the effort of finding the cause of the leak was creating tremendous strain. More or less out of the Race for the five hours it took to pump the yacht out while they were hove to, Tracy and the crew knew they had lost any chance of winning the leg.

February 28th   Bloody Wednesday

No wind and all day our position has been getting worse. I am about as depressed as I have ever been. The girls have stopped asking how we are doing and I've stopped volunteering the information. I feel it is all my fault we're where we are now. We still can't find the leak, although we are still taking about as much water in whenever we are on a port tack. To cap it all, Tanja and Mich both nearly went over the side today. They were swept with half the crew the length of the boat. While the rest managed to hang onto something, they didn't. Both of them went right under the lifelines. Thank God they just grabbed them in time. It all seemed to fit the mood.

We are now wondering whether all this water is coming in through the mast. It's filling when the deck floods and then spilling out at the base. We haven't been able to see it happening because of all the sails piled up. But it doesn't seem possible so much could get in that way.

We have other problems with the rig, though. The mast seems to be shaking itself to pieces and the gooseneck fittings look none too secure. What a bloody, bloody leg this has turned out to be. I keep wondering why on earth I ever got involved.

Tracy stands just five feet two inches and, depending on whether she is sailing the boat or out at some function, she can appear purposeful – even severe – or quite stunningly pretty. She looks younger than her 27 years, although the months of the Race have given her face a new perspective, a mixture of serenity and gravity. Before she dreamed, now she knows. But Tracy's force comes across more in the way she stands: solid, rock-like, able to command without fuss.

When she began this 'impossible' adventure she was much, much younger, and far less able to cope with stress. Although she does still suffer from having to be a public 'face', her ability to cope has developed enormously. But, like many physically small people, Tracy Edwards has always made up for her size in the force of her personality. She tells you what is going to happen: on the whole you believe her.

Yet she is not particularly aggressive and, although she can dominate a room full of people, on the whole she chooses not to. As her public fame has grown in many ways she has begun to retreat, valuing her privacy more and more, both in thought and deed.

Her temper is legendary, yet she keeps it hidden from all but those close to her: she releases her pent-up feelings in rare *tour de force* cathartic sessions like a great storm enacted in private. Confronted by reports of it, she seems puzzled, genuinely surprised.

When she turns to smile, when she relaxes, another woman emerges. For those who have lived with her during the past three years, that ability to let go has become more infrequent. The control she exercises, has had to exercise, has been one of the more difficult among many difficult lessons she has learned.

This is proof that I was once taller than my brother, Trevor.

She loves to dramatise, says her mother, Pat Edwards. And it is true, she does. But Tracy has managed what few achieve – to make her life a living drama, working out her dreams, or at least this one, on a world scale – and with an audience to match.

Tracy was born 27 years ago into a fairly conventional home: her father, Tony, ran a hi-fi business, her mother, Pat, was an actress, and a dancer. Tracy was joined by her brother, Trevor, when she was a little over two. They inhabited an old coach house, near Reading in Berkshire, set in a small courtyard with other houses. Life for the children was a mad scramble of adventures.

Pat remembers they all had a lovely time. It was a middle-class, not overly indulgent lifestyle. The children helped both mother and father in the business from time to time. Life was easy.

Then, suddenly, Tony died. It was an appallingly traumatic time for Tracy, not quite ten years old. The night of his death is engraved on her memory, almost minute by minute. For Pat it was a total shock; a younger Trevor was spared a little, but not much. As it turned out that single event changed everything.

Tracy was a wilful child; looking back she'd agree she'd been spoiled, but no more than many other children in her circumstances. She had, however, two elements in her character that now came to the fore. First, she demonstrated early on an astonishing ability to organise: children's games in the Edwards' domain were put together like military campaigns. And, along with that, she had a wild imagination.

With her family life torn asunder, Tracy ran wilder still, in a dance with her own future which would last for nearly ten years. While her mother struggled to rebuild her life, Tracy demanded – and got – her way over her schooling. She was sent to a boarding school specialising in drama. Tracy had decided to be an actress.

Meanwhile, Pat had found a man with whom she believed she could remake her life. Tracy, needless to say, hated him. The family moved to Wales, Tracy switched schools to the local comprehensive and began a career teetering on the edge of delinquency. A frantic, unhappy bundle of suppressed fury, she acted out the uncertainty, the anguish.

It ended when Tracy ran away – when she finished at school – with few prospects. She escaped, by way of various interim stopping points, to one of the most conventional of resting places for all incurable romantics – Greece. There she found, if not yet herself, then peace, of a kind.

She also fell in with the sailing world, more or less by accident. Within two seasons she had also discovered off-shore sailing on the world's super luxury yachts, crewed by a young and drifting set, much like herself. In a deliberate form of self-denigration they called themselves (and still do) boat niggers: the underclass who sweat and toil and keep it all together. Tracy instantly identified herself as one of their number.

It would not be exaggerating too much to say that since the Whitbread Race began this secret – and secretive – army of boat niggers has worked to take the Race over and make it their own four-yearly worldwide regatta. However, they have never quite succeeded – until now. The Whitbread is the pinnacle of yacht racing. It is also a huge, rolling caravan of boat niggers, and their families and friends, junketing around the world.

By 1985, Tracy, bored with the routines of conventional charter yachting and regatta racing, wanted to explore a little further. Against the advice of good friends, who perhaps saw a glint in her eyes they could neither fully understand nor cope with, she signed on with one of the Whitbread contenders, *Norsk Data GB*.

When she discovered it was not going to be a serious entry in the Race, she walked away from it in Cape Town, and approached the yacht with the very worst reputation for male chauvinism and general skulduggery – *Atlantic Privateer*. Tracy, once again, was trying to test her own harsh judgement of herself.

What, instead, she succeeded in doing was to set herself the ultimate exam. She would, she announced on her return to England with the Race in the spring of 1986, be the first woman to put an all-woman challenge into the next Whitbread.

She had no idea what that easily spoken promise would mean. In the next three years she gathered a crew of 11 women, a shore team varying from six to eight, Royal Jordanian airlines as the main sponsor, and a number of smaller ones. By then, well over a million pounds had been spent. Her life was transformed – not always for the better.

The struggle to get as far as the start line, though, had made her stronger, more resourceful, more capable of dealing with anything the world could throw at her. She was to need all that strength and more as the Race progressed.

Paul Standbridge at the wheel of *Atlantic Privateer*.

There were people – some of them well-accredited journalists and 'experts' – who, when the *Maiden* left on the first leg of the Race were still saying 'let's hope they just get round'. It was a monumental misreading of Tracy's own purpose. She never entered the Race to just get round: she meant to win.

When *Maiden* came into Fremantle, leading its class in division D, on December 3rd, 1989, and the immediate welcomes were over, she looked at me and said: 'For the first time I can remember, I believe I have done the best I can. I am not blaming myself for anything, we did it all right.'

The most fascinating aspect of all this is the struggle of Tracy Edwards to realise her own vision. It does not end with the astonishing achievement of getting *Maiden* into the Whitbread. Tracy has struggled with herself all the way round the world – and won.

Tenacity and gutsy courage are Tracy's outstanding characteristics. She has had to fight with everybody in the established yachting world and with reluctant half-believers outside, and she has had to accept rejection after rejection from possible sponsors. All of this for a woman who craves love and affection to an almost obsessive degree.

It was in recognition of that – if belatedly – that the British yachting journalists elected her Yachtsman of the Year for 1989, a trophy never before won by a woman. When she was presented with it in Auckland it was, for most of the *Maiden* team, the pinnacle of the Race. For Tracy it was the accolade she had craved above all else.

The overcoming of her own doubts, which continued in one form or another right to the end, is the heart of this story.

Everyone has dreams; few of us realise half of them. Tracy had a dream so vast it was beyond all but a few to appreciate what it was, what it could be. The force that made the dream come true was Tracy; it was her obsession and she has managed over the past four years to forge it into a world-scale production involving dozens of people in hundreds of roles, whilst capturing the hearts of hundreds of thousands more.

And, while she never intended that *Maiden* would self-consciously wave the flag for women that, inevitably, has happened. More importantly, though, she has shown that with faith, with honour and with courage, anything is possible.

CHAPTER 2

Maiden
and the Maidens

For her crew Tracy knew she needed both sailors and specialists. A modern racing yacht has masses of complicated engineering, navigation, electronic and even rigging, all of which requires someone on board able to effect running repairs. As one of the other Whitbread shore managers said, 'what people don't understand is that this Race is a world-scale exercise in survival.'

And the yacht itself? The problem is that yachts, like so much else, have become much more specialised, much more high tech. Even sailors as recent as Clare Francis or Naomi James would be lost amid the mass of electronic and other gear that a more modern racing yacht carries. Tracy's first thoughts were to build a yacht especially for the Race – as the rich syndicates also intended.

When the money she had hoped to raise from sponsors failed to come early enough, her thoughts turned to second-hand yachts. She lighted upon one, previously *Disque D'Or III*, languishing in a Cape Town marina, as the possible answer. When she flew down to see it all thoughts of a reasoned appraisal disappeared. 'I fell in love with her,' she says simply.

Disque D'Or III was shipped back to Southampton in the late spring of 1988, in a terrible state (she would have sunk if she'd been sailed). But she had the characteristic shape of a down-wind yacht and Tracy believed, from her study of the charts and the route, that the fifth Whitbread would be overwhelmingly down-wind. She and her crew, along with various boat-builders and shore-side helpers set to work to get what was to become *Maiden* ready for her new role.

The work put in by the crew, assembling in ones and twos as the months ticked by, was to prove critical. They each had their specialities. Now they were fitting out the yacht working on those areas. Each crew member would know exactly what to do should anything go wrong: the builders would principally be themselves.

Poor old *Maiden*! I bet she didn't think she'd get to the start line.

There are plenty of women sailors; far fewer women sailors have specialisms in yachting. Part of the problem in the beginning was knowing whether it would be easier to find the specialists and train them to sail; or to assemble the world's best women sailors and put them through individual crash courses.

Tracy never had to advertise for crew. The word spread like wildfire among professional and semi-professional women sailors that she was intending to put an all woman team into the Whitbread. The applications began to come in – from all over the world.

There were inevitable hiccups. The most potentially damaging came early. Tracy had decided she would be project leader – and therefore skipper of the yacht. In addition, and because she knew she was very good at it, she would be the yacht's navigator. On many yachts in the Whitbread these two jobs are quite separate. Much later, Tracy realised why. It was the navigator everyone tended to blame for any poor performance the yacht might put in. The skipper could stand aloof from these disputes, if necessary sacking the hapless navigator and placating the crew.

But, if she were to take the overall management of the boat in hand – as skipper – as well as plot where it must go – as navigator – she decided she had to have a strong deck 'manager', a role traditionally held by the first mate. Her choice was to go for a French woman with a formidable reputation – Marie-Claude Kieffer. Kieffer brought with her another Frenchwoman, Michèle Paret, one of the world's top helmswomen, and a young Englishwoman, Jeni Mundy, a specialist in electronics.

Almost from the start Marie-Claude clashed with Tracy; and then in turn with just about everyone else. Among the more damaging of those other clashes was the running battle *Maiden*'s boat-builder, Duncan Walker, had with the fiery, opinionated Frenchwoman. It delayed the various re-fits the yacht had to undergo and it exhausted Tracy who found she had to mediate constantly.

In the end, it was obvious to everyone that either Tracy would give up any pretence at running *Maiden*, or she would have to sack Marie-Claude. Tracy's agonising over that move over nearly eight months in 1989, almost up to the start, finally came to a head in an accident to the yacht's cook, Jo Gooding, during the Fastnet Race in August.

Marie-Claude had told Claire Russell, the yacht's doctor not to bother with a full medical kit for the Fastnet Race, only the first-aid box. Consequently, when Jo broke her wrist, Claire could only give her aspirins. *Maiden* had to abandon the race and Jo had to endure 17 hours of agony before they arrived in Plymouth. Tracy had had enough. She asked Marie-Claude to go.

As a result, just three weeks before the start of the Whitbread, the remaining crew had to re-assess their attitude towards Marie-Claude's leaving. Many had come to believe that Tracy lacked the experience to race the yacht flat out. In many respects Marie-Claude had come to play a kind of surrogate male: now the younger crew of *Maiden* were, frankly, frightened at sharing the responsibility for running the yacht.

It meant, too, a last-minute re-shuffle of the management of the yacht. Tracy did not replace Marie-Claude. Instead, she created two watch captains, Michèle Paret and Dawn Riley, the latter the sole American on board. Already short of one crew member, she then invited an Irishwoman, Angela Farrell, who had sailed with *Maiden* in the Fastnet, along with a Finn, Mikaela von Koskull, who had phoned Tracy at the last minute, knowing she might be short. In both women Tracy found much-needed strengths; with her crew, as with so many other things, Tracy has had much luck.

She was lucky, too, in finding a last-minute replacement for Jo Gooding who, with a broken wrist from the Fastnet accident, was unable to sail the first leg. Kristin Harris, from New Zealand, was the professional yacht's cook aboard *Nirvana*, the super-yacht *Maiden*'s sponsors were to use as their entertainment boat on the day of the start. When she heard of Jo's injury she rushed to ask Tracy if she could do the first leg as the substitute and Tracy was delighted to have her.

To race a modern yacht like *Maiden* takes enormous skill and physical strength. Although smaller than the male crews, all the *Maidens* more than made up for the difference by putting themselves through a punishing schedule in the local gym. They gained in both confidence and strength, while honing their specialist sailing skills. The sailing controls alone are very complex and mistakes can cost the entire rig. The running of the deck demands more than strength and immense stamina over long periods. The rigging has to be checked and repaired, the winches, which enable the sails to be set, the hydraulics which determine the rigging tensions, and the sails themselves, all have to have regular and expert attention.

Down below there is a mass of electronic gear to maintain, and some fairly heavy engineering, for power, light and water. Even the cook on a trans-ocean race has to come from a very special breed – as Tracy has proved.

In picking her crew Tracy had to bear all this in mind. There was, as well, the need to pick people with a good sense of humour, people who would work well as a team and who would be able to keep their cool under great pressure – or in very dangerous circumstances. She also faced one problem no other yacht had. Although there were women sailors, few had ever done the Whitbread. If her first choice as crew were to leave *Maiden* at any stop-over she would face an almost impossible task in replacing them.

While the male yachts knew they could find replacements fairly easily, either shore crew, or from other yachts, or even off the dock, Tracy could not. Her immediate fail-safe plan was Sarah Davies as the reserve; after that, she had to rely on the crew she had. Making sure they would all get on for the duration of the race was doubly important to her. What at times had seemed a very picky attitude was her greatest strength. Not one of the final crew left.

Tracy decided, conventionally, that she must have a rigger, a sailmaker, an engineer and a diver. She was lucky in finding the first two quite easily; the latter caused some anguish. In the end Dawn Riley learned them by taking courses.

The yacht these 12 women had agreed to make their home for nine strenuous months, *Maiden*, is a 58-foot boat designed by Bruce Farr, a highly successful yacht designer with both the New Zealand ketches in this Race to his name and a long pedigree in ocean racing. Tracy's original plan to have a yacht built would have cost up to a million, and the money was never available. She had to choose a tried boat and for £115,000 the yacht was secured and brought back to Southampton on a container ship.

When *Maiden* arrived she was a mess. In fact, unknown to her new owners at that time, there was a hole in her hull where the aluminium had worn. To prepare her for any future as a racing yacht, she had to be re-fitted, almost re-built. The boat builders on *Maiden*'s shore team – first Duncan Walker, later Ian (Poodle) Bruce and Jonny LeBon – with an army of yard helpers, as well as those of the girls who had already been appointed to the crew, got to work.

The result, after two major and several minor re-fits, was an almost new yacht, still built to go fastest down-wind in heavy conditions – the very ones expected in most of the Whitbread course. Fractionally rigged, with a high-tech hydraulically-tensioned mast and boom, *Maiden* carried a massive suit of sails into the Race. She was a dry boat but, below decks, little had been allowed for anything other than the most spartan comfort.

Starting from the bow, down below, *Maiden*'s first dozen feet or so are taken up with two watertight bulkheads. The first is designed to protect the yacht should she hit something head on – a whale, a 'growler' (small iceberg), even a half-sunk container, washed overboard. The second space, although sealed from the main compartment, can be opened; the girls stow non-degradable inorganic 'gash' (rubbish) there while on passage.

Aft of that, under the forehatch (which is normally sealed), is a rack for drying seaboots on the starboard side; opposite on the port side is stowage for spare sheets and other gear. Behind that to starboard is the engine; it is boxed in and the surface is used as a workbench. The tools are stored aft (for weight reasons).

Just aft of that are the day fuel tanks (fuel is stored in the bilge to keep the centre of gravity well down). Fuel is pumped up when needed. This is Dawn's domain. Appointed as one of the two watch captains she is in charge of half the crew. But her specialism is engineering. It is her task to ensure that power (first among equals), light and heat are always available. Power is needed most to ensure the yacht's water-maker provides daily supplies of fresh drinkable water.

On the port side, alongside the engine are the water-maker and generator, with their associated control boxes. Working through the deck on the centreline is the mast, with its heel planted on the keel.

Maiden is then divided by a partition with a doorway, leading aft, On the aft side of the partition on the starboard side is the only personal stowage for the girls: tiny lockers, sealed by Ziplocs. On the port side is the on-board video control system and monitor.

Then come the bunks: 12 (a Whitbread requirement is that each

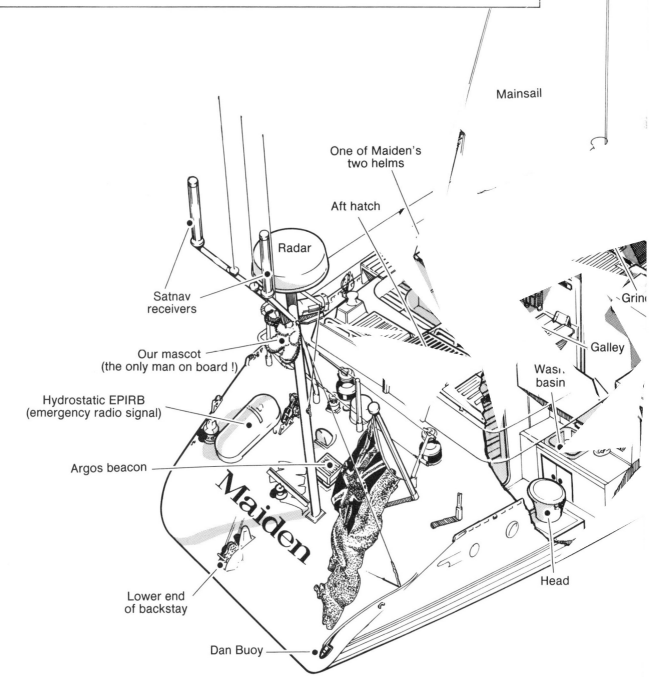

MAIDEN: SPECIFICATION

FLAG	UNITED KINGDOM	L.O.A.	58ft 17.71m
SAIL NO	K1418	LWL	50ft 15.24m
DESIGNER	BRUCE FARR	BEAM	16ft 5.02m
RATING	45.92ft.	DRAUGHT	10.5ft 3.20m
RACING DIVISION	DIVISION D	MAST HEIGHT	75.5ft 23.01m
RIG	SPARCRAFT FRACTIONAL	DISPLACEMENT	21,773 kgs

Mainsail

One of Maiden's
two helms

Aft hatch

Radar

Satnav
receivers

Our mascot
(the only man on board !)

Hydrostatic EPIRB
(emergency radio signal)

Argos beacon

Lower end
of backstay

Dan Buoy

Grin

Galley

Wasi
basin

Head

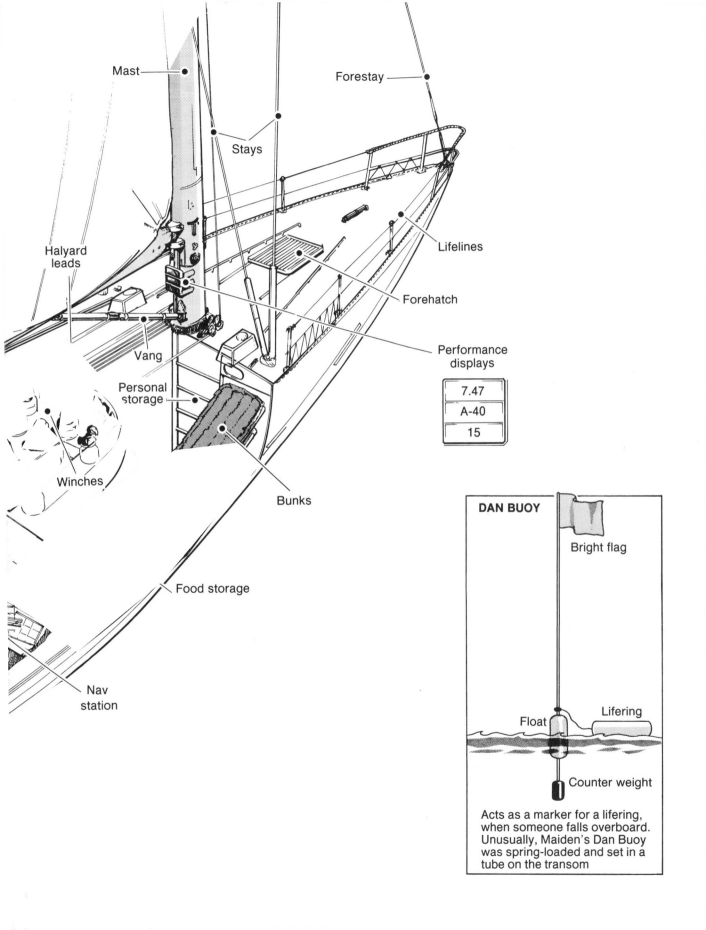

Mast

Forestay

Stays

Halyard
leads

Lifelines

Vang

Forehatch

Personal
storage

Performance
displays

| 7.47 |
| A-40 |
| 15 |

Winches

Bunks

Food storage

Nav
station

DAN BUOY

Bright flag

Lifering

Float

Counter weight

Acts as a marker for a lifering,
when someone falls overboard.
Unusually, Maiden's Dan Buoy
was spring-loaded and set in a
tube on the transom

crew member must have their own bunk, even if not used). In four ranks of three, two to each side, they're spartan in the extreme, lowered or raised by a pulley system so that when the yacht is heeled the bunks stay level. Each has its own light, a very small nod to comfort.

In the centre of the forward bunk space is the frame for holding the sails. These take up an enormous amount of the room below. The crew have to scramble across them to get aft or forward. When they come off watch or get dressed they constantly intrude. One small positive point is that they do cushion the unwary against a bad fall. Tanya, the sailmaker, sews her sails by clamping her sewing machine to the frame. It is an unimaginably awful place in which to have to repair anything, least of all something as immense as a yacht's sail.

Past this centre line space, on the port and starboard sides are Ziploc bags stuffed with freeze-dried food on trays, running from the floor to the deckhead, Behind that is the galley on the port side – possibly one of the best galleys for a Whitbread yacht. (But, then Jo Gooding had one great advantage: her skipper had been a Whitbread cook.) The crew, however, eat on the floor, as best they may.

Jo Gooding, the cook, oversees all of this, making up her daily menus to provide the maximum variety from what must be the world's least visually appealing food. For example, freeze-dried cabbage looks uncannily like grass cuttings.

Opposite the galley is the navigation station, Tracy's domain. The computer lives here, as do the two satellite navigation systems and a number of radios – two single sidebands (SSBs) for long-range, a VHF for short, and emergency beacons. There is a Brooks and Gatehouse 390 Hercules system for all kinds of data on wind and weather, along with a weather fax and a routeing system.

Jeni Mundy is the electronics specialist. With a degree in mathematics and philosophy, she took on the vital task of providing Tracy with her eyes and ears, her means of navigation, her communications with the outside world.

Finally, towards the aft hatch there is stowage for tools on the port side, the yacht's sole washbasin and head (toilet) on the starboard side and then, under the ladder and to each side, stowage for wet weather gear, safety harnesses and more sails.

Safety on board came under the watchful eyes of Sally Creaser, from Scotland. She had to ensure that the girls each had safety harnesses that fitted, emergency and electronic flares, should they go in the water. She had, too, to ensure that fire extinguishers below worked (fire is the most likely cause of hazard at sea), and to check that life-buoys, life-lines and the life-raft were instantly available for use in emergencies.

Some of the heaviest work on the yacht is sail shifting. Over the course of the racing the yacht did, the girls got faster and faster at moving these about the deck, but they always found the heaviest foresails, especially when soaked with sea-water, were a nightmare to handle.

Sails are normally handed onto the deck or back down below through the centre hatch. That leads directly into the cockpit area, with the life-raft underneath. *Maiden* carries detailed instructions, pinned by the navigation station, on how to react to any emergency, especially the extreme one of abandoning ship. Each crew has a duty which she is enjoined to memorise.

The cockpit is well-endowed with winches – and two 'grinders' to ease the work of raising sails, tensioning halyards or sheets. Overall, the deck is cluttered with lines, sheets, controls of all kinds. For anyone used to a cruising yacht, or even an average racing boat, *Maiden* is a nightmare of high technological yachting, at the edge of sailing knowledge. Her skipper and crew sail her like a dream, in all the conditions the world's weather can throw at them.

Nancy Hill is in charge of all the winches and their operation. It means that at each of the five stops she has had to dismantle each one to check the gears are all in order, re-grease and re-assemble them all. When the yacht is racing she helps trim sails for maximum power. In this she is helped by Angela Farrell from Eire, who was one of the last of the crew to join. Angela is in charge of the cockpit, the centre area of *Maiden* to where most of the deck lines are fed, so they may be sheeted in or eased off on the winches. In all this she is backed up by Mikaela von Koskull, from Finland, who, like Angela, joined *Maiden* late on, only just before the 1989 start. Mikaela also helps helm.

The principal helm – the steerswoman – is Michèle Paret from France, who is also the other watch-captain. Steering a racing yacht is an art, in which the 'feel' of the yacht under any condition of wind and water is vital. The ability to squeeze just half a knot of extra speed at all times means the difference between winning and losing. Michèle and Mikaela are joined by Dawn in making up the helming team, although most of the girls helmed from time to time over the immense distances *Maiden* travelled in the Race. The running and standing rigging is looked after by Mandi Swan, one of the youngest

CLAIRE RUSSELL
Doctor
English, 27, the least
experienced sailor

MICHELE PARET
Watch leader
French, 35, many
2-handed atlantic races

MIKAELA VON KOSKULL
Helm
Finnish, 31, already
circumnavigated the globe.

JO GOODING
Cook
Welsh, 26, sailed
since childhood

JENI MUNDY
Electronics
English, 24, sailed the
Caribbean for 2 years

DAWN RILEY
Watch leader
American, 25,
professional skipper

TRACY EDWARDS
Skipper/navigator
English, 27, professional
sailor and on last Whitbread

MANDI SWAN
Rigger
Kiwi, 25, has
sailed the Pacific

ANGELA FARRELL
Sail trimmer
Irish, 26, years
of local racing

NANCY HILL
Sail trimmer
English, 27, sailed over 35,000
miles delivering yachts

SALLY CREASER
Mast
Scottish, 28, has
raced dinghies all her life

TANJA VISSER
Foredeck
Dutch, 27, sailed
since she was four

crew from Auckland, New Zealand. Her daily tasks have involved her being winched to the top of the mast to check lines are not fraying and standing rigging not loosening (as it often did in the extreme conditions the yacht faced).

Finally, there was Claire Russell – the ship's doctor and least experienced sailor. Like most of the other serious contenders, Tracy had decided from the start that she had to include a fully trained medic in her crew. Claire turned out to be a lucky find. Her medical knowledge proved a life-saver; her quick mind meant she rapidly came to be an invaluable member of the sailing team. The dentist on board was Tanja (who had just passed her finals before the Race). Tanja was also the stills photographer, just as Jo Gooding was the video cameraman when occasion demanded.

Everyone had at least two roles, some three or more. All were able to adapt and help out when occasion demanded for this, the world's longest survival course: as they all found out, more than once, it was a case of 'now get out of that!'

CHAPTER 3

On the Start Line

The start of the fifth of the world's longest and toughest yacht race on September 2nd, 1989, was a mad scramble. The 23 yachts taking part fought for the best position immediately before the start. Around them a thousand or so spectator boats were crowded into a few hundred square yards off the bows of the frigate, *HMS Ambuscade*, from whose decks the Duke of York was to fire the starting gun.

The day had begun with a sparkle: there was high cloud, a slowly strengthening northerly wind; it was still warm.

Well before 8.00am on that Saturday, the first of *Maiden*'s crew had dragged the brand new Kevlar mainsail along the dock at Southampton's Town Quay, down onto the pontoon and craned it, using the winches, onto the yacht. They bent it on to the boom, as the sun rose higher and higher, just three hours before the start.

The yacht was still the recipient of massive press interest. Almost at the last moment, Tracy was still engaged in an interview for Soviet television. The first Soviet entry into the Whitbread, *Fazisi*, lay alongside the same pontoon. 'We feel very close to the Russians,' explained Tracy, 'Like us they are a first-time entry.' She might have added, but did not, that like *Maiden* the Russians felt outsiders, making their first and vital contact with this most strenuous of international sports.

Like the girls of *Maiden* the Russians had struggled for credibility – and for money. Their efforts, at first derided, had slowly gained respect, even awe. There were many parallels between the two yachts and their crews.

Maiden made an awkward departure from the pontoon. Big ocean yachts are not built to manoeuvre easily in the confined spaces of modern marinas. In the tense moments leading toward the start line it was perhaps not surprising that things did not go as smoothly as they might.

Out on Southampton Water, moving down to the start, the crew gasped: as far as the eye could see were small boats, big boats, and every size in between. The eye could not grasp the number of people making their way to The Solent to watch the Race round the world begin.

In The Solent proper, as *Maiden* made her way to the group of ships marking the southern line of the start 'grid', they witnessed one of those rare days when weather conspires to provide an unforgettable spectacle; an inspiring testimony to those who go down to the sea in ships of all sizes.

The entry was the biggest the Whitbread had seen. Thirteen nations were represented by yachts: Britain, France, Germany, Holland, Belgium, Italy, Spain, Switzerland, Finland, Sweden, Ireland, the USSR and New Zealand. Great Britain had the largest entry, and the widest spread. Her main chance in the open (maxi) class (A and B) was *Rothmans*, which also happened to be the biggest spending project (at a total cost of about £6 million). *British Defender*, the British-crewed combined services entry, financed by an Austrian businessman, was another hope in this division. Then came *Maiden*, the sole British entry in division D. Finally, there were the only two entries in the cruising division, both British, *Creightons Naturally* and *With Integrity*. But Finland had managed in the end to have three entries – the *Union Bank of Finland*, *Martela OF* and *Belmont*, all maxis. The latter was a 'cigarette boat' sponsored by a tobacco company. Tobacco corporations, denied many chances to advertise their wares in Europe especially, had turned to the Whitbread in larger and larger numbers. Of the 23 entries four were sponsored by tobacco companies.

The range of sponsors was wide enough, though. *Maiden* had Royal Jordanian airlines as chief backer; there was a bank (the Union Bank of Finland) for *UBF* and a finance house for *NCBI* (NB); two soft drinks manufacturers (*Pepsi Fazisi* and *Gatorade* (from Italy); two lager companies – *Steinlager II* and *Schlussel von Bremen*; a sports company (*Rucanor*), a furniture design group (*Martela OF*), a white goods maker (*Fisher and Paykel*). *British Defender* had their finance from Satquote, stock market information service, *Equity and Law II* from the eponymous insurance group. The Swedish-registered *The Card* were backed by Mastercharge, the credit group which includes Access, while *Liverpool Enterprise* had gained support from that city's redoubtable desire to re-generate its economy and not to appear too fusty in outlook. *Charles Jourdan*, from France, advertised those ultra chic goods for its parent company, while *Creightons* espoused cos-

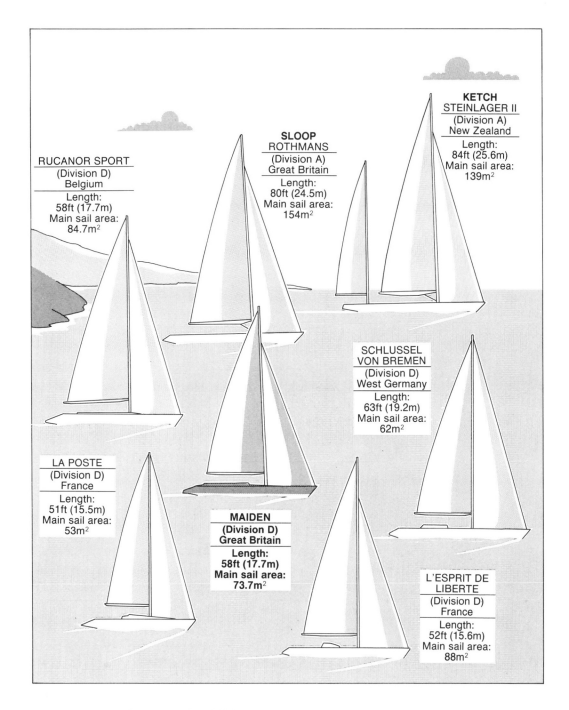

RUCANOR SPORT
(Division D)
Belgium
Length:
58ft (17.7m)
Main sail area:
84.7m²

SLOOP
ROTHMANS
(Division A)
Great Britain
Length:
80ft (24.5m)
Main sail area:
154m²

KETCH
STEINLAGER II
(Division A)
New Zealand
Length:
84ft (25.6m)
Main sail area:
139m²

SCHLUSSEL
VON BREMEN
(Division D)
West Germany
Length:
63ft (19.2m)
Main sail area:
62m²

LA POSTE
(Division D)
France
Length:
51ft (15.5m)
Main sail area:
53m²

MAIDEN
(Division D)
Great Britain
Length:
58ft (17.7m)
Main sail area:
73.7m²

L'ESPRIT DE
LIBERTE
(Division D)
France
Length:
52ft (15.6m)
Main sail area:
88m²

metics not tested on animals. *With Integrity* advertised another insurance group.

Finally, *La Poste*, a yacht destined by her waterline length always to come last, was backed by the French Post Office, leading inevitably to the standing joke about arriving by second class mail.

The breadth of sponsors and of national entry was exceeded by the range of nationalities of the crews. Apart from the largely nationally-crewed yachts – the Finnish, the Italian, the Spanish, Belgian and French yachts, crew came for other yachts from all points: America, Uruguay and Australia among them. *Maiden* had one of the most cosmopolitan crews, though, with six nationalities on board.

There was no entry from the United States. The Whitbread organisers had done their best and several well-known American sailors had promised they would be in. The addition of a stop in Fort Lauderdale, lengthening the Race both in time and distance, had been added to attract more American interest. It all came to naught, although there was, right on the start line, one drama which directly affected *Maiden*.

Early on in the *Maiden* project, Tracy had come across an American woman sailor, Nance (pronounced Nancy) Frank. After some time together, and with the original French mate, Marie-Claude Kieffer, it became clear that neither Tracy nor Marie-Claude could sail with Nance. Their whole approach was totally different. Nance left. But, back in the States she then announced she was going to put together a US Women's Challenge (although her final crew had some British included).

Right up to the start it was not clear whether the Nance Frank yacht was in or out of the Race. In an extraordinary decision which rankled until well past Uruguay with Tracy, the Whitbread organisers allowed Nance Frank to cross the start line before turning back to Southampton (with the owners' representative on board to repossess the yacht). Nance went home.

The Whitbread Round the World Race is yachting's longest race. It emerged as an idea out of the great pioneering voyages of lone offshore sailors in the 1960s – Sir Francis Chichester and Sir Alec Rose chief among them. After they had sailed single-handed round the world, Robin Knox-Johnston succeeded in being the winner (and sole finisher) of *The Sunday Times* Golden Globe Challenge for the first sailor to make a non-stop circumnavigation.

But that Race was a turning point. The stresses and strains of this kind of race appeared to be too much. But the interest remained and out of the sense of adventure generated by these achievements the agenda was (rather more slowly) set for a race which involved fully crewed yachts, roughly following the old clipper sailing ship route to Australasia and back round Cape Horn, the latter the *ne plus ultra* in the old sailing log of seamanship.

It took some time, but eventually the Royal Naval Sailing Association and Whitbread the brewers (who had backed Chichester in a very modest way), acting as financial backers, got the first Race started in 1973.

The cannon was fired by Sir Alec Rose from Southsea Castle in The Solent. The former single-handed round the world sailor knew exactly what lay ahead for the 14 yachts taking part. But, whereas Rose and sailors like him could heave-to when the weather became bad, for the Whitbread yachts this was a luxury they could not afford.

The first Whitbread was eventually won by a Mexican-owned ketch, *Sayula II*, although the first yacht home on uncorrected time was the British yacht *Great Britain II*, skippered by Chay Blyth with a crew from the parachute regiment. Three men died in the first Race, including one from *Great Britain II*.

Yachts in the Whitbread raced then and have done ever since for two kinds of prize: line honours, which the biggest yachts, barring accidents, will always win; and the handicap prizes which are awarded after allowances are made for the different sizes of the competing yachts, set against their 'ratings' and the distances run within the times taken. It is a complex subject that few of those racing fully understand. Suffice it to say that, at least until the fifth Whitbread, a time on distance system meant that the smaller yachts could – and did – win handicap prizes.

Technically, the first Race suggested that yachts taking part in a Whitbread would have to be built much more strongly: gear failure had plagued the first Race. But, against a sturdier built yacht, a higher rating would be set – and thus a worse handicap. This dilemma would not be resolved.

The second Whitbread, in 1977–8 attracted 15 entries; again *Great Britain II* won on the line overall. *Flyer* won the handicap prize. This was the Race in which a young Englishwoman, Clare Francis, competed, aboard *ADC Accutrac*. She had already become famous as the first woman to sail the Atlantic single-handed in the *Observer* Single-Handed Transatlantic Race (OSTAR). Women in yacht races of this kind were a rarity – even as cooks. It was, 13 years ago, thought to be too dangerous a venture.

By the third Race – in 1981–82 – 20 yachts were competing, including the first New Zealand entry, *Ceramco*, skippered by Peter Blake. It was the first Race for a smaller yacht than *Ceramco*, a Bruce Farr designed 58-footer called *Disque D'Or III*. Two Whitbreads later she would achieve lasting glory – as *Maiden*.

Simon LeBon at the start of the 1989 Race.

By 1982, though, the stakes were being raised all over the yachting world. What had started as an adventure had become a very serious world-scale race. Big money was now beginning to make its mark. Although sponsors had been involved from the start, the cost of putting a serious project into a Whitbread was soaring and any sponsor likely to be involved was insisting that there was an identifiable return on the invested capital. That, at base, meant winning.

The fourth Whitbread, run between September 1985 and May 1986, demonstrated these changes. Although there were only 14 entries, the competition in both the handicap and line honour stakes was at white-heat. There were two New Zealand maxi yachts, along with a largely South African entry and a Swiss, *Union Bank of Switzerland* (UBS), skippered by Pierre Fehlmann, who was eventually to win the line honours. There was, too, *Drum*, Simon LeBon's entry. And there was Tracy Edwards, cook on *Privateer*.

This time the drama mainly revolved around the notorious failure of *Drum*'s keel in the Fastnet Race, only weeks before the Whitbread start. *Drum* continued to have structural problems all the way round the world. It was not the only yacht: *Atlantic Privateer* on the first leg lost its mast, as did *NZI* on the third. *Privateer* managed to limp into Cape Town; *NZI* had to abandon the Race altogether.

Fehlmann romped home at the end; the handicap prize went to the French yacht, *L'Esprit d'Equipe* – which was to re-emerge in the 1989–90 race as *L'Esprit de Liberte*, a close rival of *Maiden*'s.

It was quite clear in 1986 that there would be a fifth Whitbread: almost as soon as the Race was over various syndicates, skippers and crew announced their willingness to take part. It was clear, too, even in 1986, that the 1989 Whitbread was likely to attract many more entries – people were talking of 40, even 50, yachts.

Sixteen years and four Whitbreads on, the Race had grown to Olympic size, with huge sums of sponsors' money being poured into ever larger and more technologically sophisticated yachts. Whitbread alone would eventually put millions into the fifth Race.

Apart from the money, other things were going to change for the fifth Race – one in particular was to prove very controversial. The nature of the entries has determined that they have to be divided into a number of classes, the largest entry this time being for the huge super-racers, the 'maxis', of anything up to 80 feet in length. There were five maxis in the fifth Race, from ten countries (two ketches from New Zealand, one from Sweden, three sloops each from England and Finland, a first Soviet entry, and yachts from France, Italy, Spain, Switzerland and Ireland).

Each yacht in each division (and there turned out, in the end, to be none in division B) could be said to have won the Whitbread – hence there would be three winners. But in division C there was one entry, the Dutch *Equity and Law*. As a result, an additional prize was arranged by the Race Committee for a combined division C and D entry of corrected time. Everyone knew that only *Equity and Law* could win it.

Herein lay the rub: previously small yachts had been able to win the Race on corrected time after the handicap system had been applied. It was on this system that *L'Esprit d'Equipe* won the 1985–86 Race. But a rule change to the handicap system made late in 1988 meant that no smaller yacht could hope to win that prize. As it had traditionally been thought of as *the* Whitbread trophy to take – and it now lay beyond the capacity of either division C or division D yachts – it was a cause of resentment amongst them throughout the race.

For Dirk Nauta on *Equity and Law* the handicap rule change was devastating. He had argued to his sponsor that with a slightly larger (division C) yacht he could win the Whitbread overall – and that meant beating the maxis on handicap. *Maiden* had similarly believed they could take the whole race in that way.

By Fremantle, the Race Committee decided that they would re-instate the old handicap system for the following Race. But it was too late. The prize that Tracy had originally entered the Race to win had been denied by the fumbling of the Race Committee. And the charge of amateurism, made by many of the entries over a number of issues, including this one, would stick like glue.

The prize that Tracy had to re-direct her sights to win, therefore, became the overall prize on uncorrected time for the combined six legs. She was also after leg prizes – the Beefeater Trophies. And she chased incidental prizes for the Best Communicator of a Leg and overall (British Telecom): while her crew looked for Best Seamanship, Best Camerawork (video) and Best Photographs (stills). Everyone on the yacht could hope to win something.

Amongst the division D yachts, *Maiden*'s chief rivals were *Rucanor Sport*, from Belgium, *L'Esprit de Liberte* from France and *Schlussel von Bremen* from Germany. The remaining yacht in this class was the tiny *La Poste*, the French Post Office entry. Although division D was much smaller than the division A and B combined maxi class, competition was fierce. Bruno Dubois with *Rucanor* had a highly experienced crew. That was even more true of skipper Patrick Tabarly and his crew on *L'Esprit de Liberte*. Tracy knew that this yacht was likely to be the one to watch not least because the yacht had won the previous Whitbread; *Maiden* had already beaten *Rucanor* in a friendly race in The Solent during the summer. *Schlussel von Bremen*, although really almost a division C yacht in size, and *La Poste*, the tiny French Post Office entry, completed the field.

Two cruising division entries – *Creightons Naturally* and *With Integrity*. Both older and heavier yachts, they were racing each other. They provided a training ground for amateur crews – and were to create their own controversy in the Race for doing just that.

As for the Race itself, at six legs and 33,000 miles, it was the longest ever run. And because of the extra leg it meant the yachts entered the Southern Ocean during the second leg earlier in the southern hemisphere year than ever before. Because the Race could not go to Cape Town, it also made the second leg of this Race the longest leg of any Whitbread.

In all, the fifth Whitbread was the most competitive and the toughest physically of all the Races to date. It was this Race that Tracy Edwards chose for her challenge of an all-woman crewed yacht. She could hardly have set out to break a convention – and all the associated prejudices – more starkly, more daringly.

This was the task lying ahead for Tracy Edwards and the *Maiden* crew, about to start on the adventure of the coming nine months. Single-handed women sailors had sailed around the world; never a fully crewed racing yacht, in direct and equal competition with men. A bastion of male-domination was about to be washed, like the tide-swept fleet, away down the channel, into the past.

The mêlée grew: just before the start it was difficult at times to see the water for the press of wood, metal and fibre-glass hulls upon it. The fleet attending the Whitbread yachts was so great that their engines threw up an entirely artificial chop, enough to make that part of The Solent temporary look like mid-Channel in a blow.

Hard though it was to see at times, the watching hordes heard the ten-minute, then the five-minute gun, fired from the Royal Naval frigate anchored on the start line. They saw the mass of Kevlar sail – that strangely coloured and shaped patchwork of brown and yellow space-age material which racing yachts use to go faster – suddenly intensify into a dense pack, charging the line.

Then a mighty BANG!, and a mightier cheer, which seemed to echo off the sky above and roll across this most famous of English waters. At 12.15pm precisely the fifth Whitbread Round the World Race had begun.

Tracy's own diary for the day reflects breathless disbelief that, finally, it was all going to happen . . .

September 2nd

I've just written the date and realised that I never thought it would come. What a mixture of emotions we all went through today. And the crazy thing is that I wasn't nervous once. Today not a doubt in sight. I was so sure of myself. When I have to be in charge I can do it. I think I was the calmest person.

When I woke up this morning I thought 'Right, get up and go and do the Whitbread.' I had a bath and finished packing. Simon was really upset last night but made a big effort today; I loved him for that.

Got down to the Pink House (where the crew lived in Hamble) on time after a sad farewell to the dogs. I'll really miss them and the house. It was a quiet still and cold morning with a mist on the river. The Pink House was dead when we got there but Pam and Linda were cooking. Good as gold eh?

People started arriving (Janie who employed me on my first boat). Then everyone was having breakfast – the girls slightly giggly. Sometimes I am so proud of them. Jeni was quiet, Nancy was in tears cuddling Pam. The shore crew have been absolutely brilliant, we could not have done any of this without them. There was a great feeling in the house. I left with Janie and Simon – still not nervous.

The quay was empty when we got there. The boats looked like racehorses straining at their halters. What a romantic sight as we looked down on them. I felt the first catch of my breath, a lump in my throat and my stomach jumped. My eyes stung: 'Don't cry'. So I put my head down and marched off along the dock to the boat not looking to left or right. Simon was very quiet.

When we arrived, Hugh Myers was there putting on the main – they had finished it! People began to arrive. I put my things away. Then we put the main up and looked at it – beautiful. More people and the pontoon getting lower. My family looked so proud – mum so small. Still no butterflies, just a million emotions fighting each other – happiness winning.

Then Howard arrived – we just held each other close – I still can't believe it. Howard got emotional; the hour dragged on with the girls fine but wanting to go.

I saw the love shining in mum's eyes: I love her so much. I said

Howard Gibbons.

goodbye to Simon: I'm really going to miss him.

I started the engine; other boats were leaving. 'Right,' I said, 'let's go.' Let's go eh? Who would have thought even a year ago, who would have thought . . .

We hung off waiting for *Rothmans* and *NCBI* and followed them out. The dock and quay above erupted with cheering and clapping. Gulp! The Solent had started to fill with yachts and boats of all sizes. It was a magic sight. Our support boats came up behind us, everyone looking ecstatic. By this time I was feeling very emotional. No sign of *Nirvana* with the Royal Jordanians and the shore team on board. We motored to the start line – God knows how there weren't any collisions. I have never seen so many boats.

As we motored around, the Duchess (of York) called us up. How fantastic! She wished us good luck and told us to win. We chatted away and the girls cheered into the radio. Then we went over to the ship they were on and cheered and waved. She waved back and shouted; the Duke waved as well.

Then we put the main up, still loads of boats getting in the way. Headsail up; misjudged the start badly. Whoops!

Can you believe that the only thing I was thinking of as we crossed the start was 'damn it, what a lousy start'. Not exactly what I had in mind. *Nirvana* closed in and our other boats found us. The Jordanians were ecstatic and so was everyone else.

Nirvana at the start. John, the skipper, watches his girlfriend, Kristin, sail away on *Maiden*.

Maiden ploughs her way through the spectator fleet.

Howard and Tim and I kept locking gazes and we knew what we were saying without words. We trailed after the maxis and *Rucanor*, ahead for once. Going down The Solent was bloody amazing. People waving and cheering. Michèle took over the steering for a while and, finally, I cried. It all came in a big rush. Great, in front of all those people and live on television.

Then the crew all cheered me and said thank you. The camera rolling away. *Nirvana* all waving, mum looking fit to burst. What a wonderful world. The girls were all beaming; Nancy and I exchanged a couple of glances. Even Jeni seemed really happy.

We reached all the way down The Solent ploughing past spectator boats. I wanted this to last forever. It suddenly seemed impossible to remember how impossible an all-female crew on the start line of the Whitbread was.

I steered again. God, my love for sailing has come back. I love the boat, I love the crew, I have my pride and confidence back.

As we headed past the Needles and out of The Solent boats dropped back. *Schlussel von Bremen* went on the Shingles bank – I felt really sorry for them. *Nirvana* went aground and had to go back. Didn't have time to say goodbye.

Then mum's boat blew its horn and turned; sad but happy. A few other boats came up and cheered us and then they were gone, too. And, quite suddenly we were alone.

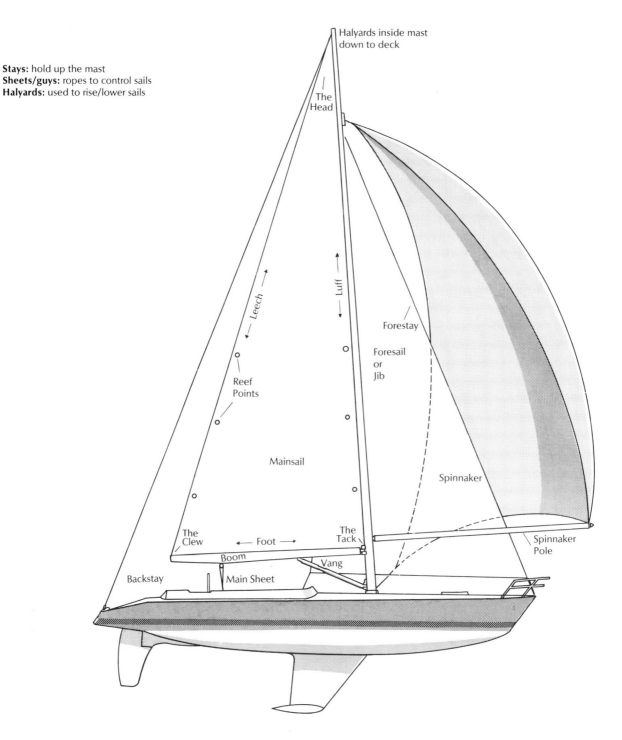

Stays: hold up the mast
Sheets/guys: ropes to control sails
Halyards: used to rise/lower sails

Halyards inside mast
down to deck

The
Head

Leech

Luff

Forestay

Foresail
or
Jib

Reef
Points

Mainsail

Spinnaker

The
Clew

Foot

The
Tack

Spinnaker
Pole

Backstay

Boom

Vang

Main Sheet

Maiden's full suit of sails numbers 42 but on any one leg she would usually carry 24. There are two mainsails, including one spare. Maiden carries five headsails and three 'reachers' (high cut for reaching).

There are up to nine spinnakers, of different weights for different conditions, ranging from the 0.5 floater for light winds to the 2.2 'Chicken Chute' for heavy weather. There is a storm jib and a storm trysail (tiny sails for the worst gales and hurricanes.)

CHAPTER 4

Shaking Down, Shaping Up

Getting *Maiden* and her crew to that start line had cost three and a half years of solid effort, a slogging away at a sceptical world that had left Tracy frequently exhausted, occasionally in despair. Once, just once, she had walked out of *Maiden*'s office saying she would not go back. She did, though.

Now, in a way, she was in shock. This was the moment, the waking-up, the knowing that despite all those trials, all the black moments of the past, they had found sponsors, raised enough money, brought the yacht and themselves to pass – almost casually into the record books.

Bob Fisher, doyen of British yachting journalists, and initially a sceptic, as he was later to admit, was giving the commentary for television on that sparkling September day. Even he, though, missed the immediate historic significance of *Maiden*'s crossing the start.

Later, in Auckland, he was to coin a phrase Tracy and the girls relished: 'not just smart tarts,' he would say, 'but smart *fast* tarts.'

As *Maiden* sailed away down the Channel on that warm September day she could not stop exulting. She sat, silent, in her favourite place on *Maiden*, just ahead of the helmswoman, on the cockpit coaming, hugging these thoughts to her.

'We did it. We bloody did it!'

Then, imperceptibly at first, the Race began to take over. For the next five weeks she was never again to think about the achievement of getting to that start line. From now on the Race, and winning it, were going to dominate her thoughts, and her actions, in the claustrophobic way that only long-distance racing sailors fully appreciate. As her personal log relates, she lived the Race without cease, often foregoing sleep to push *Maiden* and its crew to the limit.

LEG ONE

FROM THE SOLENT TO

PUNTA DEL ESTE, URUGUAY,

6,281 NAUTICAL MILES,

SEPTEMBER 2ND, 1989–

OCTOBER 7TH, 1989

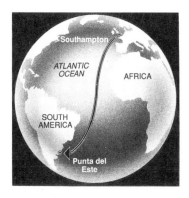

September 3rd   French Coast, South of L'Ouessant (Ushant)

The girls have slipped into the watches very well – Kristin is a star. I also can't believe how much I like Dawn. She's great.

When it got light we were about 15 miles from the French shore and about 40 miles from L'Ouessant. *Rucanor* and *L'Esprit* were way ahead. We crawled along the coast all morning. I had forgotten we were the duty boat until *La Poste* called me. Michèle had to speak to them as their English isn't brilliant. *Rucanor* called along with *Equity and Law* and *L'Esprit*. Couldn't get hold of *Schlussel*, *Creightons* or *With Integrity*. Never mind.

We got to L'Ouessant about 2.00pm but did not go on the inside (an inner channel between the offshore islands) as both *Rucanor* and *L'Esprit* had screamed along outside. We followed, although the wind was still poor. I finally got some weather faxes through this afternoon. There is a huge high over the north east Atlantic moving very slowly. At least the other boats will be in it as well.

I slept from 2.30pm to 6.00pm. a wonderful deep sleep, the first for ages. When I got up we were still coasting along, course not too bad, so I decided to stay inshore as there was no wind further out. After dinner I steered; ugly wind but we are doing OK in the circumstances, about 30' above course at 4-5 knots. The floater was up – a nice sail. The foot of the main is too long and the shackles fell off the slides this morning so Tanja had to go up and replace them.

Evening has now closed in, a new moon hanging in the sky, gentle music on deck, Radio Four on down here. I love evenings on the boat. *La Poste* controlled the evening schedule; it is so funny listening to French and Germans talking in English to each other. They are so serious. They gave their positions – not good for us.

I spent the evening up and down – eventually I slept on deck.

September 4th   47'43"N   06'23"W

There was a beautiful sunrise this morning; Tanja filmed it. The wind was down, but at least we were on course. I listened to the Argos positions at 10.00am. The maxis were 80 miles ahead; *Rucanor* and *L'Esprit* 30 miles. *La Poste* and *Schlussel* were ten miles behind. What a disgusting position! Dawn and I tried to figure out how we are doing so badly. I told Michèle to steer for speed.

The wind picked up during the day; but it was all the time up

Michèle at the wheel.

48

and down. The speed of the boat is bad – poor baby. But everyone is getting on so well which makes up a bit for our slowness.

I called in at the 11.00am schedule to *La Poste*. *Rucanor* was even further ahead. I don't think people are racing the boat enough; it is difficult. Got some weather charts – ugh. The high is moving very slowly.

I slept from 3.00pm to 6.00pm. Dawn woke me up and asked if we should gybe as the wind was pushing us up and up. I said yes. When I got up I went through the weather charts – not much to see. I wish I could get better ones. Kristin was busy making dinner.

The navigation position on *Maiden* is exactly opposite the galley. Tracy enjoyed having someone to talk to; occasionally Kristin's constant chatter annoyed her. She missed Jo, her old school friend and *Maiden*'s permanent cook. But Jo was many miles away, still nursing her broken wrist.

The wind was coming up all the time and although our course is not good (at 240') at least we are doing 8 knots. The sea is quite calm and the current is pushing us forwards and out. There was a great atmosphere on the boat. I feel more a part of it than before; the girls talk and laugh with me and treat me like a friend. Everyone is so happy. I don't know about Michèle though; I wonder if she is missing Marie-Claude?

There are good wind clouds on the horizon; we will keep going out as we have wind. Dinner at 7.00pm was – yum – chilli with cucumber and yoghurt. Everyone was sitting around, listening to music and eating. Domestic bliss. There was a lovely sunset and we have a really good speed. I feel close to God – what a lovely feeling, I am so happy I could explode. No press, no people, no noise, no hassle. Here we are, having a hell of a time.

Mandi has really come out of herself – great to see. Everyone shines in their own special way. Rock on! A great evening's sailing. I am so comfortable on the boat now I can't believe how unhappy I was before. I feel like I am back in my own skin and I am wearing it, well, like a glove. There is peace and comfort in my soul.

The wind has been coming up all evening. We have now changed to the 0.75 spinnaker; so even the boat speed is up. At 11.00pm I called *Equity and Law*. They are close to Finisterre and

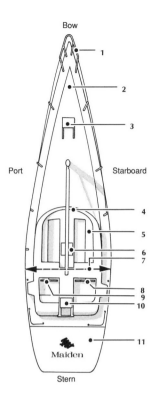

1. Pulpit
2. Foredeck
3. Forehatch
4. Coaming
5. Cockpit
6. Centre Hatch
7. Beam (widest point)
8. Port Helm
9. Starboard Helm
10. Aft Hatch
11. Transom

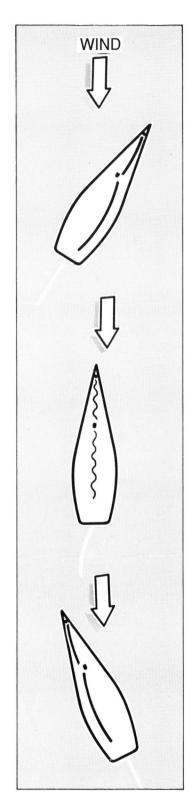

WIND

Tacking: much safer than gybing, as the bow of the boat goes through the wind and not the stern as in a gybe.

they have 30 knots of wind; *Rucanor* has 25 knots. But *Equity* are 140 miles ahead, *Rucanor* 90 miles. Unbelievable! We should be next to them. I have decided I ought to stay up tonight.

The two people on a racing yacht who normally do not stand watches are the cook and the skipper (and, if there is a separate person, the navigator.) But they are available if needed to help with running the boat. The skipper, of course, is never technically off watch on a passage, being the first person any watch will call to ask advice or for assistance when the going gets rough.

September 5th   45'49"N   08'23"W

My birthday! (Tracy was 27 on this day.)

I slept from 1.00am to 3.00am in the end. We peeled to the 1.5 spinnaker when I got up; smoothly done. Then Tanja went up the mast to take the halyard over. She worries me sometimes; she doesn't have any fear and she doesn't say what she is doing a lot of the time. I napped on and off from 5.00am to 7.00am. It was a great morning when I woke up – a really vital day. Strong seas, a dark, dark blue, with stormy skies and lots of wind and the boat doing what she does best – sailing fast in heavy conditions.

A wave flopped over the deck this morning and everyone looked like drowned rats, all laughing. I think we all feel released, being here. What a wonderful birthday. But at 10.00am we got the Argos positions: we have lost ten miles to *Rucanor*, gained ten on *L'Esprit*, 30 on *Schlussel*, 20 on *La Poste*. *Equity and Law* are now 80 miles ahead and the maxis 180 miles. Hell. So much for winning on handicap. But *Equity* have run out of wind; good, I hope *Rucanor* have too.

I called mum and the office; they all wished me 'Happy Birthday'. I got a bad cough today – it seems as if everyone is getting Mikki's cold. Everyone is sleeping a lot. I slept from 12.00 to 2.00pm. Changed to the 2.2 heavy runner. Nancy and Jeni are getting on well – lots of giggling fits.

We are having great sailing today, as we approach the Spanish coast (we were 60 miles off at 3.00pm). Dawn got 14 knots out of the boat at one point today.

Kristin has spent the evening trying to cook and hide my birthday cake. Jeni sorted out the telex and I read all the bumph to try and use it. Dinner was freeze-dried curry, not too bad at all.

The wind was strengthening all this time. Then Michèle came down for her supper; that's when it all started. . .

We did a spectacular broach with Tanja at the wheel. Michèle and I rushed up on deck; let the sheet out. Tanja steered down and finally got control. I decided to take a reef. That went very smoothly. The wind kept coming up; the waves were the real problem – the current and the tide fighting each other with us caught in the midde.

It's funny how when you are on land you forget the fury of the sea. Well, it all came back with a rush. We were surfing at 14 knots all the time, the boat shaking, vibrating. A mountain of spray and foam cascading outwards. The noise of the seas and the wind were deafening: it was as if God had switched off all the lights and turned the wind on.

I decided to change the spinnaker (bare-headed). I got everyone back on deck, but then no-one was getting any sleep anyway. We took it down – not too much trouble. I thought we should take another reef before we put the other spinnaker up. Tanja had to go out along the boom, way out over this boiling sea, to put the reef-line through. She was really scared. I have never seen Tanja scared of anything. Dawn and I shoved her up. She did it fine and came down smiling; another hurdle cleared.

I made sure everyone had harnesses and was clipped on, and I put the radar on. Three ships were near us although we could not see them over the mountainous waves. Even with just the main up we were doing 11–12 knots and we were being laid right over regularly.

'Yea, though I walk through the valley of the shadow of death' came into my mind. Oh well, it certainly shook the cobwebs off! We put the second reef in; it was so difficult to move or do anything – there were 35 knots of wind at this point. Then we hoisted the 2.2 chicken chute. I noticed the running backstay block making a weird noise so Michèle looked at it and decided the sheer pin was going.

As the sea was also getting worse and we were going all over the place we decided to take the spinnaker down. So I got everyone up again. Tanja stayed at the wheel, while Michèle shouted instructions. I did the guy. Wonder of wonders the sock (to 'snuff' the spinnaker and make it controllable) didn't work: it got a quarter of the way down and then the sheet shackle broke. The spinnaker went everywhere.

It was an absolute horror show. People were shouting, I was

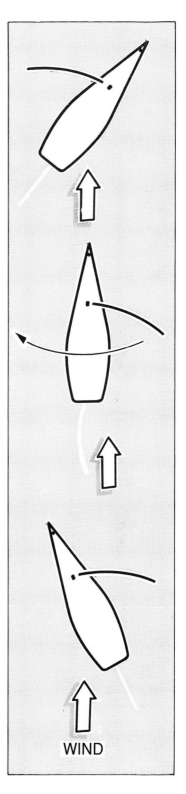

WIND

Gybing: often a violent manoeuvre as sails and boom sweep across deck rapidly. Accidental gybes can result in broken masts and injured crew.

All hands on deck.

worrying because I couldn't see further than the deck with all the lights on while I knew there were ships all around.

Eventually we got the guy onto the pole and clew, tripped it and pulled in the spinnaker. We had torn it in two places. God, what a hairy five minutes. Everyone calmed down; we put the spinnaker below and tidied up the deck. Some people went to bed. There was slightly hysterical laughter scattered around the deck. Curiously we felt exhilarated; this dance with danger.

We fixed the sheer pin on the running block; got the reacher on deck, and poled it out. We were still doing 10–11 knots; Nancy was steering by now. I slept on the sails for two hours at midnight. Missed the chat show altogether, while my birthday cake with its candles sat, dejected, on the stove. Goodnight!

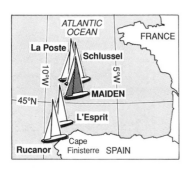

L'Esprit and Rucanor stay in; Maiden and Schussel head out.

The yacht's log entry for this day reads:

22.00, 35 knots apparent (45 knots true). Rounding Cape Finisterre. 'Horror Show'. 2 reefs, chicken chute, then blast reacher.

That's all.

I got up at 2.00am and checked our position. The wind was down a bit, although it was still screaming in the rigging. I got undressed and got into bed. Arrhh, how lovely and warm and cosy; sleep, sleep. I was up at 4.00am to check the position; everything was fine; the reefs were out.

Everything seemed better in daylight – the sea and the wind were right down although we were still trucking along with the reacher at 8–9 knots. It was, though, a lovely day. We put the 1.8 reacher spinnaker up, doing 9 knots all the way down the coast of Portugal.

It is strange how everyone feels the morning after a fight with the elements: total exhilaration; sheer joy at being alive and well, pleasure in everything around, love for everyone on board. We have moulded together as a team who have challenged and fought the elements and won.

I finally had my birthday cake for breakfast. Dawn gave me a present and a card from everyone; great. But I have caught a cold from Mikki and I spent the day coughing my guts up and sniffing.

I got the reports in at 10.00am. We have overtaken *L'Esprit*; but *Rucanor* is still ahead. The maxis are now 300 miles ahead. We are doing really badly at the moment, steering all over the place. I am not making the right decisions quick enough. Ah well, we are all learning – fast, I hope.

We gybed to follow *Rucanor* although the wind direction was awful. I felt lousy and slept down below from 3.30pm to 7.00pm. When I got up we were going in the right direction at last at 8 knots. Our course on the chart looks awful; I think Michèle, Tanja, Dawn and Jeni are unsure of me.

Dawn tactfully said Jeni perhaps ought to try the weather fax; well, what would I know anyway! I couldn't eat dinner, felt awful, really low. I'm really feeling the pressure of doing badly and everyone thinking it was because Marie-Claude isn't on board. Yet they are my mistakes and I would have made them with her here or not.

Mandi spent all day leathering; Tanja repaired the chicken chute. After dinner I waited for the chat show. Spent a couple of hours mucking around with the computer – Einstein would have had problems with it. Chat show at 23.00hrs didn't sound good for us; oh well, cheer up, at least we're here. I slept from midnight–5.00am – or tried to when I wasn't coughing. A miserable night.

Protecting wire from chafe by sewing leather round it was a full-time job for Mandi.

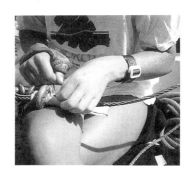

September 7th   39'46"N   15'17"W

I called the office and spoke to Poodle (Ian Bruce) about the problems with the runner blocks and the vang seal and the deck compasses (both of which had been reading wrong). At 10.00am I got our position. When I plotted the positions of the others it didn't look too bad on the chart.

But all was not doom and gloom: we had a good course and a good wind today. We are also going in the right direction. I did some stuff on the computer; difficult. I felt really ill by lunchtime, coughing my guts up, my nose running, headache, bodyache. I went to bed and slept on and off.

There was lots of joviality on deck. Sally is so funny. I felt even worse this afternoon; oh, for a nice warm bed and someone to look after me – and give me a cuddle. I am feeling lonely and depressed today – on top of which the log started reading backwards. The wind was constant all day – it came round a bit. We were doing 8–9 knots most of the time.

It is a bit of a problem, people learning to steer, but better now than on the next leg. There was a beautiful starry night, tonight, a quarter moon hanging in the sky in front of us, making a silver sea for us to sail on. A huge, huge sky. I lay on deck for hours with Clannad playing.

There has to be a God: how could anything as beautiful as tonight just happen, just be random, with no mind behind it?

September 8th   36'34"N   15'11"W

I went to bed at midnight and got up at 5.00am, the best night's sleep I have had; felt a lot better. Plotted our position; did the log. Then I watched a fantastic sunrise: gorgeous pink sky. It is going to be a beautiful day.

There was lots of silliness on deck today. Claire washed the boat down. I read and glanced at the computer with loathing every so often – but I got a good weather map this morning. Ploughed through the computer again; bloody thing. I hate it. Lovely day today, though. My cough is much worse, nose running all the time. I feel like a phlegm factory.

I called Howard after the positions report; the poor thing has the 'flu. God, it's a tough life. The position report was OK; we are definitely holding our own. I feel really unsure sometimes of what I'm doing; I just pray it's right.

The many faces of sailing.

The girls are all blossoming forth into real people; they are good sailors; they think so much more about what has got to be done now that Marie-Claude has gone. They ask loads of questions and take real pleasure in learning about the boat. They help each other so much more; there are no 'sides' any more, either.

I am really pleased that I worked out the watches as they are one old girl and one new as partners; no competition among them, just helpfulness. The only competition is with Dawn and Michèle, which makes the boat go faster

September 9th   34'00"N   18'32"W

A lovely day again: sunny. The wind dropped during the day. We gybed at 9.00am because the wind has swung so far. I plotted a new course of 210' which puts us following *Merit*, which has to be good. Not only that, we were able to steer the course during the day. It is a real test of concentration for the girls to go between speed and course. Everyone waits for 11.00 like Doomsday.

Beating: when the boat sails as close to the wind as possible.

Reaching: when the wind is coming from abeam.

11.00am in the morning and 11.00pm at night were the times for the 'chat show', when all the yachts in Tracy's group call each other to give positions and information. Although she was getting Argos satellite positions as well, it was the detail that was missing, apart from the human contact. The chat shows could be listened into by yachts in other groups (like the maxis) and often were. In all, the system was a valuable safety channel, and a time when the Whitbread crews felt they were perhaps not so alone. But, it was double-edged. As Tracy relates, if you felt you were not doing so well, this was the time you really found out.

I have started writing down where everyone is and how far they have to go, then comparing them with us. It is a good way to keep everyone racing. We have done really well, gained on everyone in our class and overtaken *With Integrity*. Hurrah! Everyone cheered and clapped. Plotted some of their positions on the chart; we are just passing Madeira.

Steinlager is way out in front; we were right to hold on as long as possible before gybing; phew!, it is great when something goes right because you make a correct decision.

Lots of sunbathing went on today; not a lot of clothes worn. Everyone is comfortable with everyone else, even the new girls. A bit of a frustrating day for sailing, though. We were trying to alternate between speed and course; everyone is improving in leaps and bounds. I still haven't had the guts to steer yet. Maybe tomorrow; I really want to.

I caught the sun today; my backside is killing me; we are all a bit red. I spoke to Simon on the radio; he's fine. I slept in the afternoon. There was another amusing evening on deck. The wind had dropped before sunset and then came back again after dark; it was very pleasant sailing.

September 10th   31'03"N   19'54"W

I got up at 7.00am: the wind was on the beam, we were on course and doing 9 knots. Whoopee! I read for a while and had another fight with the weather fax; then we put the generator on. Dawn and Angela did the water-maker. I got the latest positions – bloody hell only five miles behind *L'Esprit*. Overtook *Creightons*. I posted the plots for the girls to read: 'things to do today: overtake *L'Esprit*.

It was another scorcher; really hot. Everyone is bright red. The wind dropped slowly but surely, heading us in the morning. By the afternoon we couldn't make the course with the spinnaker up.

Then, just after sunset, the wind dropped to nothing and we glided silently slowly forwards with Clannad playing, surrounded by an angry blue and black sky filled with clouds and the moon's silver rays sprinkling over us. How do you explain this feeling to anyone? It is here and now and even after being here I won't remember it exactly as it is. How do you capture it? It is one of the moments that everyone in the world deserves at least once. And I have had so many! I must be the luckiest person in the entire world. What did I ever do to deserve this wonderful, wonderful feeling?

Everyone is alone with their own thoughts tonight: we all feel it. Another of the pleasures of sailing with women, we know when to give each other space for thought. For the first time since I started sailing I feel as if I am on the inside looking out, instead of the outside looking in. It is a very comfortable and happy feeling; I like it. I'm glad, so glad I've lived through this.

We were duty boat tonight; talked to everyone in Group Three except *Equity* and *Creightons'*. The usual amusing banter was exchanged. We've caught up again. They are also doing Argos positions at 21.00 as well, now. Good. Bed at midnight.

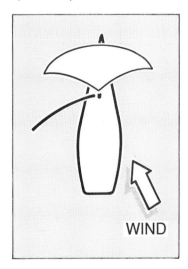

Running: when the boat sails with the wind at the back of the boat, filling the spinnaker.

On this same day the log records that *Maiden* had gained 46 miles on *L'Esprit*, 17 on *Rucanor*, 16 on *Equity and Law*, although she had lost 29 miles to *Schlussel* and seven miles to *La Poste*.

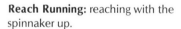

Reach Running: reaching with the spinnaker up.

September 11th   28'26"N   21'18"W.   4,257 miles to go

Claire started me on antibiotics, my cough is really bad. The wind started dropping through the morning. The generator went on at 9.00am; tried the telex again but it just kept saying that the printer was off line.

I was in a weepy mood today; I thought of daddy for the first time since we left The Solent. I wish he could have seen this. Anything sets me off at the moment; I am missing Simon and our little house as well. That's good. It is weird when all your emotions become heightened like this.

I spotted *Rucanor* on the horizon this morning - whoopee! We lost the wind completely as we saw them but later I called the

Race Office and told them we could see someone on the horizon. It made their day. But we are 16th out of 23 and *Steinlager* is 583 miles ahead, for God's sake.

I slept for an hour after lunch. We put the spinnaker up – only doing 4 knots most of the time with short bursts of 6 knots. The wind dropped completely during the afternoon. By sunset we were down to 1.5 knots.

It was another beautiful sunset; a huge orange globe sinking into the sea. We all watched for the green flash as usual – but there was nothing. There was some good talking on deck this afternoon and this evening. There is more opening up, learning about each other. Dawn, being American, finds frank discussion about nasty things most unattractive.

I listened to the Argos positions at 21.00. The maxis have now shot away, leaving all the small boats sitting in this hole. None of us have moved. The chat show at 23.00 was a comedy hour. *La Poste* on fine form. No one has any wind.

September 12th   26'59"N   21'51"W.   4,167 miles to go

I got up and, guess what? There was wind – just a bit. We are doing 5 knots – but in the direction of Africa! We'll have to see what happens during the day. I did the log and plotted our position. I actually got a weather map through, although it was unreadable. Tried to call Dakar again today; no luck.

I got the fleet positions at 10.00am; the maxis are gone – unbelievable. The small boats just sit here doing nothing; but at least it is all of us. I spent a frustrating day trying to keep course and speed; we did an average of 5 knots which is not bad. Everyone was sunbathing naked – that's a turn-up for the books. It was hot with little or no breeze. Kristin was sorting out the food and panicking if she had enough. I said 26 days were left at most.

September 13th   25'05"N   22'09"W.   4,069 miles to go

When I got up we were going in the wrong direction at 4 knots; wonderful. Why the devil didn't they wake me? Then, we put a hole in the 0.75 with the pole; put up the Hoods 0.75; Tanja got sewing. Meanwhile we gybed. The course isn't brilliant but at least we are going in the right direction. The wind is a bit more steady. I bet *Rucanor* were not arsing around in the wrong direction for two hours.

When we got the positions, sure enough, *Rucanor* are ahead by a long way; *L'Esprit* too. We gybed back at midday onto a perfect course with a good speed. The day was cloudy though it was still hot. We had a fast day although it could have been faster. The wind was pretty constant; the odd wave a problem.

Kristin made lovely bread at lunchtime. In the evening, listened to the positions: *Rucanor* is 54 miles ahead; *L'Esprit* 16. The maxis have stopped though. They must have reached the doldrums.

September 14th   20'05"N   24'47"W.   3,726 miles to go

When I got the Argos positions at 11.00 this morning, I found that *Rucanor* is 87 miles ahead; that really got to me. We have been doing the same course with the same wind. I got Dawn and Michèle down for a chat. I said about people sunbathing on watch; doing exercises on watch; hot drinks every five seconds, trying to grind and smoke a cigarette; that the music was too loud and that no-one really was racing. They agreed and said they'd try and get everyone back into racing mood.

The wind was up and down all day. Possibly for that reason I have been in a bad mood. The course we made good was OK but the speed was lousy. The results at 21.00 were not too bad; positions at 23.00 were disgusting. *Rucanor* are still 100 miles ahead.

September 15th   19'31"N   25'02"W.   3,689 miles to go

I woke up in a really bad mood which is unlike me. I miss having doors to slam when I feel like this. Michèle had woken me at 4.00am to ask if we should gybe. Every time the wind dropped we gybed west. There is always wind out there although the course is not brilliant. All the girls are on deck discoursing about the pros and cons of this course and that . . .

I'd have to say at this moment more or less all of them are getting on my nerves. I suppose they are thinking the same of me. I felt very detached today; so many things are annoying me. I made a big effort not to lose my temper.

I had a nap this afternoon; Dawn woke me and we gybed again. The reports at 21.00 were difficult to hear but we have gained 21 miles on *Rucanor*. The wind dropped so we gybed out amidst complaints from Angela that we would be going in the wrong direction. I have given up trying to explain the great circle route . I just said 'do it' and went to bed.

59

September 16th   15'28"N   27'11"W.   3,417 miles to go

I woke at 4.00 to the sound of laughter on deck because a flying fish had landed on the cockpit. I felt much better. We were doing 8.7 knots more or less in the right direction. I could have wept for joy. I made a good decision and we gybed at the right time in the right direction. There is something so satisfying about making a decision that makes the boat go fast. I had to suppress the urge to say 'I told you so' as pride comes before a fall.

The position report at 10.00am yielded more good news: we had gained 22 miles on *Rucanor* and 26 miles on *L'Esprit*. We had gained on most of the boats. I posted the positions and then plotted the important ones on the chart. *L'Esprit* and *Schlussel* are a long way east; *Rucanor*, as ever, is to the west.

It was a real scorcher today and as we ran the generator all day below decks was like an oven. I have worked out a good system with Portishead Radio, calling on 16Mhz and receiving on 12Mhz; it worked really well.

I talked to Admiral Charles Williams (chairman of the Race Committee) at the Southampton Boat Show (where British Telecom had a stand). It was incongruous, me sitting there stark naked and sweaty, talking to the Admiral and half the boat show.

I had a fun time on deck with the girls at sunset. All the talk was of men; it must be time to get there! God knows what the guys would say if they could hear how we talk about them. Dinner was OK but how I am looking forward to a nice meal with a bottle of wine (or two or three). I listened to the Argos positions and guess what!!! We had taken 16 miles out of *L'Esprit*, 16 out of *Schlussel*, 29 out of *Equity*. Things are looking good. It looks like *Steinlager* is out of the doldrums; they could be in Punta in 12 days.

Then we had the chat show at 23.00 and, joy of joy, we had overtaken *L'Esprit*. We have also caught up another 22 miles on *Rucanor* and 36 on *Schlussel* who are now only one mile ahead. Everyone is ecstatic. And so to bed with sweet dreams.

September 17th   14'58"N   27'32"W.   3,372 miles to go

I had a rude awakening at 4.00am, listening to the main flogging itself to pieces. The boat was going round in circles and Tanja, in her usual subtle quiet gentle way, was flinging sails around the boat looking for the wind seeker. I got up and gave a hand; couldn't find it anywhere. Some bright spark had put it on a bunk.

With much cursing we flung it on deck only to find that the wind had come up and we were doing 7 knots. I got up; then the wind dropped again, came up, dropped. The course was non-existent. Back to bed, pillow over my head. We put the No.1 light up, but we were only doing between 1.3 and 4 knots. I think we have hit the doldrums earlier than we expected. It is so hot you can't move; we had the engine on for the generator; it made below impossibly hot. Couldn't sleep, couldn't eat. Everyone is naked and cooking alive.

We spent most of the day just ghosting along with the light No.1 or the windseeker up. People tried to sleep and failed. There was a little bit more wind this evening; strange sky with clouds all jumbled up; stars hidden, moon trying to get through. The position reports at 21.00 were brilliant – they have moved us up: *With Integrity*, *L'Esprit*, *Schlussel* and *La Poste* are behind. *Rucanor* is only 33 miles in front. At 23.00 she was only 15 miles in front with no wind. I acted as duty boat as *With Integrity* has problems with her radio. *La Poste* has wind at last.

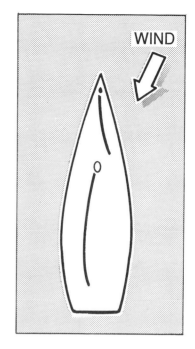

Heaving To: using the sails as brakes.

September 18th   11'45"N   28'17"W.   3,195 miles to go

No-one woke me this morning so consequently I got up late. It was hot already. I put our position on the chart, filled in the log. There was a little bit of wind; we were doing about 3 knots in the right direction. The position report at 10.00am was good: we had again taken miles out of most people and were only 20 miles behind *Rucanor*. But some of the maxis are through the doldrums. For us, just coming in, that means 600 miles of no wind, say six days.

Today it was so hot it was unbearable; everyone is sweating pints, trying to escape the sun. The decks are so hot you can't walk or stand on them for a second. The sun is relentless; The girls on watch take it in turn to hide under a small bit of shade under the main. We did quite well today – I think about 100 miles. Gybed twice for a better course as the wind is swinging constantly.

I had a wash today – the first for two weeks. It felt wonderful. Macaroni cheese for lunch but there was not enough. I must ask Jo to get lots of pasta whether Mandi likes it or not. I tried to sleep this afternoon but it was very difficult. Still, we are pottering along. We gybed twice in the evening; it took ages for it to cool down, down below. Everyone ate on deck. I couldn't get to sleep for ages; in the end I slept on the sails.

September 19th   09'47"N   28'08"W

I got up to find we were doing 6 knots in the right direction at last. Changed course anyway during the day to 234' as the equatorial current is pushing us east. We are making good progress. It was boiling hot at 7.00am again but we averaged about 5 knots all day. It was hard to get positions today as the reception was so bad, but when I did we had caught up another five miles on *Rucanor*.

I had a chat with *Schlussel*; he has such a nice voice; all the girls think so to and they crowd round and listen. We are fantasising about peoples' voices now! By the evening we were 21 miles from the half-way mark although the wind was beginning to head us.

September 20th   08'20"N   28'59"W.   2,989 miles to go

What a horrible day: squall after squall. There was wind just before the rain and then no wind; it rained on and off all day. The course varied from 300 to 180'. It was difficult to know which was the best tack as the current is still pushing us. One minute we had the windseeker up, the next the No.1 heavy. Then the Genoa down, No.3 up; wind down so No.1 up again: all day. What a nightmare. We found that the galley has a leak through the port compass housing; the nav station ditto through the starboard. Electronics wet, charts wet. I took the panel off and stuffed kitchen roll in; Michèle's bunk was soaked through due to a cockpit leak. We had to put a wire through the drain to clear it. Then the wind at one point, went from nothing to over 35 knots in a few seconds. We needed all hands on deck quite a few times.

Everyone was wrecked; wet clothing everywhere and it was hot and damp below as then hatches had to be shut. But the crew are learning about why you keep your clothes dry: valuable lessons for the Southern Ocean. There were a couple of horror shows on deck: they had tacked without moving the sail they had just changed off the deck. It got swept to the rail and nearly off the boat. It took eight of us nearly an hour to get it back, whilst taking a reef and putting the No. 3 up. What a night. Finally got to bed at midnight – knackered.

September 21st   05'41"N   29'35"W.   2,832 miles to go

When I got up it was grey and drizzling but we were doing 8 knots in the right direction. A good steady breeze but there was no smile amongst the crew: welcome to reality. I phoned Howard who said

we had, finally, overtaken *Rucanor*. I told the girls, they were
ecstatic. I can't believe it, we are leading our class. We spent the
morning tacking back and forth. The wind died and we crashed
about in huge seas. It is very wearing on the nerves.

September 22nd   03'45"N   30'27"W.   2,705 miles to go

The Argos positions at 10.00 still put us in front of *Rucanor* but
Steinlager is 1,569 miles in front: good grief! *Equity* are also
steaming ahead. Then, at the chat show at 11.00, I found we are
still in the lead – six miles now. What a match race! I finally got
outside on deck at 11.30.

I slept really well for four hours in the afternoon. We put a reef
in then took it out when I got up. With the No.3 up we were
overpowered, going sideways. It is so difficult living at an angle; it
makes everyone so grouchy and bad tempered.

When we were changing sails I asked Jeni and Michèle and
Tanja to put on safety harnesses. They said 'it's only 21 knots of
wind, Tracy'. I went berserk: the first time I really lost my temper.

Anyway we changed sails with harnesses on; I sat on deck
chatting with Sally and Nancy; those two are great, so stable. At
the chat show we found we were only 0.7 miles in front of
Rucanor. Stayed up to 3.00am watching the course.

September 23rd   03'01"N   31'03"W.   2,649 miles to go

Just before noon I saw *Rucanor* on the horizon, about five miles
ahead. We have some catching up to do. I thought today how
much the girls have begun to realise that they each know a good
deal about the boat and about sailing; they seem to have grasped
that it is not just one person that makes the boat go faster, it is all
of them. That's good. Everyone is a lot more active on the boat,
thinking for themselves.

Tonight we are about 20 miles from the Equator. Squalls have
started during the evening – at some points we had nearly 30
knots. The chat show at 23.00 put *Rucanor* 7 miles ahead. They
were having a party for the Equator. We crossed it at 23.45; no
celebration.

September 24th   00'21"N   32'17"W.   2,467 miles to go

I had just got into bed at 2.45am when a squall came through. Up
on deck changed down to No.3 from No.1. Then the wind

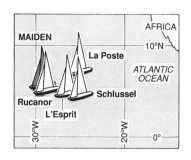

L'Esprit did well by staying east.
Maiden and *Rucanor* go west.

dropped and we changed again to high clew reacher. We could see *Rucanor*'s nav lights on the horizon; in the morning we had changed again to the blast reacher. I got up, finally, at 8.00 – I just could not wake up.

The Argos report put us six miles behind *Rucanor. L'Esprit* is catching up. *Rucanor* is on the horizon dead ahead now. It has been a rainy and squally day but the wind has started to back. It is getting to be a real hassle living on our ears all the time.

By now *Maiden* had settled into a daily routine. But the wind conditions – with the wind coming from ahead, or varying from hardly any to sudden squalls, do not suit the boat at all. Or its skipper and crew. And the constant strain of trying to hold a course and keep ahead of all the other division D boats was beginning to tell. The yacht was now over the equator heading down the coast of Brazil.

What an unbelievable day. Everything that could go wrong did. Tanja had a drink of water when she came off watch and it was salty. I did the chat show quickly. We switched over to another water tank; then I stayed up a couple more hours as we were passing through Rocas and Fernando Islands just off Natal. I finally got to sleep at 1.30am. Then, I got up at 2.30am to do positions and lo and behold the other water tank was salty.

Dawn came down off watch and we talked about why it had happened. We reckoned there had to be salt water leaking into one tank and then into the other. Switched to another tank; got the generator going and the water-maker. More problems as the electronics in the control box have been ruined by salt water. Meanwhile we're over on our ear ploughing through squall after squall.

We finally got the water-maker going. Dawn slept next to it. The next thing I know I have water spraying on my face. I leap out of bed; it turns out to be shooting out of the tank manifold. Dawn switched tanks and we went back to sleep. Then, at 7.00am, Angela woke me: there is salt water coming out of this tank, also.

We switched to another one; just the same. Oh God. Dawn got up and we all put our heads together to try and figure it out. I called the office at 8.00am and told Dee to tell Duncan (the yacht manager) that the water tanks were leaking.

Meanwhile we have the chat show; *Rucanor* are still six miles in front. But *L'Esprit* are only 14 miles behind.

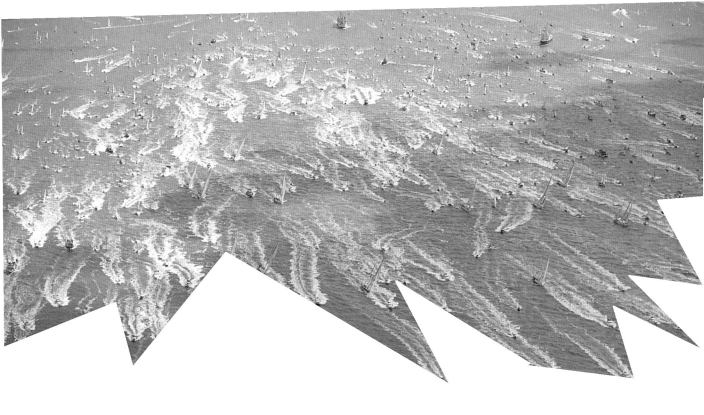

A dream come true: *Maiden* starts the 1989-90 Whitbread amid thousands of celebrating craft on The Solent.

Left (above):   The *Maiden* shore team. *Front (left to right)* Dee Ingles, Sarah-Jane Ingram, Linda Trumble, Pam Hale. *Back (left to right)*   Jonny Le Bon, Ian (Poodle) Bruce, Duncan Walker.

Left (below):   Howard, Poodle and Tim (Madge) follow us out to the start line.

Right (above):   The one and only: *Maiden*'s complete crew captured for a unique picture in Auckland, including the reserve Sarah Davies. *Front (left to right)*: Tanja, Tracy, Jo, Mandi, Dawn, Claire, Michèle. *Back (left to right)*: Angela, Jeni, Sally, Nancy, Sarah, Mikki.

Right (below):   Tracy in the nav station.

No skipper or crew in sight as *Maiden* sails herself. A brilliant design. So where were we?
It's 4.00 p.m. – tea time!

Hugging her thoughts to herself, Tracy dreams of victories yet to come.

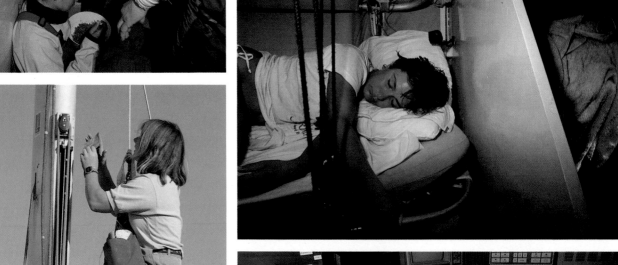

Life on board: whatever the weather, wherever we were, we had to cook, eat, sleep, maintain our home – and keep on heading in the right direction.

Above: Michèle (on the helm) shuts her eyes against the wind and spray whilst behind her Sally (left) and Angela (right) brace themselves on *Maiden*'s heaving deck.

Below: Jeni manages a smile as she trims *Maiden*'s mainsail. The angle on the radar on the mast behind her shows how far the boat is heeled over.

Left (above): We arrive in Uruguay – docking the boat was always nerve-racking for me.

Left (below): At our press conference in Punta del Este.

Right: The entire Whitbread fleet ready to go.

(Inset): It was an honour to know Alexei, the skipper of the Russian boat *Fazisi*, in the tragically short time before his death in Uruguay.

L'Esprit de Liberte and *Schlussel Von Bremen* were our chief rivals: both bigger than us and very hard to beat.

Opposite: *Rucanor*: out of the eight times we raced them, we won five times.

Below: *La Poste*: the smallest yacht in the entire Race. These guys really deserve medals.

Left: Squally weather: whenever one hit *Maiden* it was always a fight to get the sails down and to keep the boat under control.

Right: Getting the spinnaker down in lots of wind calls for strength to get it on deck and courage not to let go as it tries to pull you overboard.

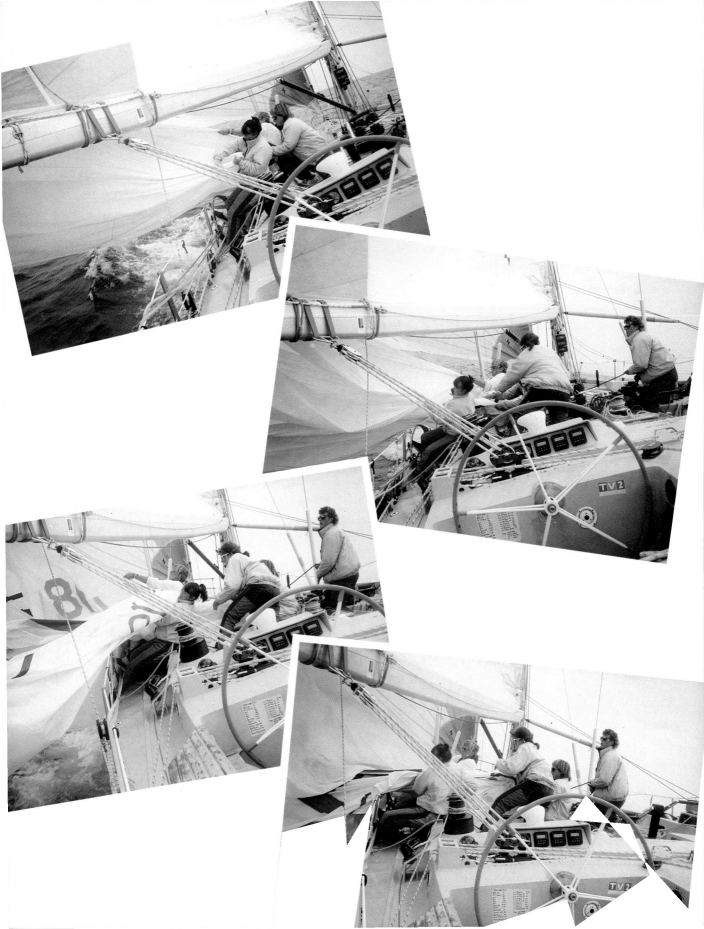

Left (above):   All smiles as we approach Fremantle. We have arrived in Australia and we've won!
Left (below):   Sweet victory: David Pritchard-Barrett from Whitbread presents me with our first Beefeater trophy.
Right: An action-packed start to Leg Three from Fremantle to Auckland; squalls, rain and rough seas.

We're in there somewhere...

I went back to the water-maker. I pumped out all the bilges; loads of water. While I was doing that we hit a really powerful squall – 36 knots in about 30 seconds. We all raced up on deck with only t-shirts on. The boat was on its side, Sal battling with the wheel, Michèle and Tanja trying to take the headsail down.

I let the vang and the main sheet off. Blinding sheets of rain; I couldn't see or breathe. It was truly terrifying: the sea almost flattened by the wind; spray everywhere, visibility nil. It was freezing cold. We went through that one; we put the No.3 up and then got hit by another squall just as we were reefing.

Then it was back to the water-maker: by now we had decided to put the water from the water-maker straight into containers. Jeni now joined in, trying to work out why the fuse box had shorted out. Meanwhile lots of bilge pumping. We thought that by this time it must be the water-maker itself putting salt water into the tanks. Great.

The water-maker: Dawn hated it but she never let it beat her.

The girls started collecting rainwater. We worked out that we could all pump our own drinking water with the hand held water pumps (thank God I got them) and live on crackers and chocolate as we wouldn't be able to make enough for the food. Nancy pumped the water tanks dry by using the bilge pump connected to the water tank manifold. Jeni was still battling away with the water-maker.

Dawn, meanwhile, was running up on deck to look after the watch when another squall ripped through. In the middle of all this someone stood on my bunk and broke it. That upset me more than the prospect of dying. Then Tanja complained that she and Michèle never had enough chocolates at night because the watch before stole them . . .

Jeni and Dawn had a breather while I worked out a watch system for the hand pump. I broke into my coconut and we all had some. It was lovely to be able to actually chew something.

A few more squalls zipped through and then we tried the water-maker: it worked! Dawn had to watch it for two hours to make sure it didn't start pumping salt water again. We filled up every plastic container we could find. Of course the tanks are now salty. Maybe we can flush them through tomorrow.

The dinner time (curry and butterscotch) squall appeared without fail. I only got some of the positions at 21.00: *L'Esprit* has overtaken us. We gained two miles on *Rucanor* – they are now only four miles ahead. The weather has been growing constantly worse during the evening – staying at 21 knots at 40′ apparent most of the time. You really feel you are living on the edge. It is so tiring and it wears you down. Sometimes you wish you could just stop and stand still for two seconds.

Maiden were never to regain their lead position on this leg and, indeed, the relative distances between the first three yachts would remain more or less as they were from that night. That was nine days ahead, though. In the Atlantic all three yachts were well aware of each other and the threat they posed. The crews of both *Rucanor* and *L'Esprit* never lost sight of the challenge *Maiden* was presenting just over the horizon.

September 27th   10′17″S   35′11″W.   1,836 miles to go

Today was Sally's birthday. I was up early. I called Simon – I really miss him when I talk to him. I miss our little house and the dogs – our home. He was not very forthcoming, as usual, so I did most of the talking.

It is very hard to say 'I love you' when you know there are hundreds of people listening; not to mention half the Whitbread fleet. I called mum – she's OK.

Up on deck the day looked different – more settled. We were trucking along but the wind still won't come back and stay. Sally got up at 8.00am; we called the office and they all sang 'Happy Birthday' down the radio. I had a hell of a time getting through to Portishead; we go up and down the frequencies until we find one that works. Sal did her interview with Scottish TV; then she went back to bed.

I was duty boat for the chat show; I really enjoy doing it; the guys are all so sweet (when they are in front, of course).

When Sally got up for her evening watch we all gathered outside the galley, Tanja camera in hand. Kristin lit the candles on the cake and we got Sally down and sang 'Happy Birthday' to her. She was really pleased. We gave her her present (a Batman T-shirt) and her card and the poem Claire had written. Things got raucous and the party moved on deck. We all had a great time (largely talking about men).

It is funny sitting in the nav station and watching the comings and goings. It is at times like these that I feel really fond of them all and totally in love with life. Even if we are third from last it doesn't matter.

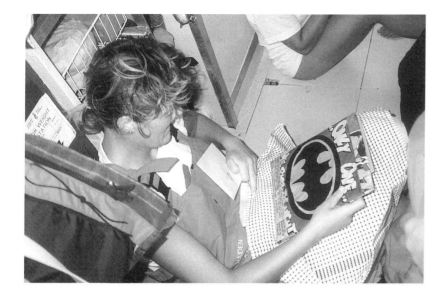

We were sure that Sally would want a Batman T-shirt for her birthday . . .

Between September 27th and October 1st, Tracy and the girls, although well behind the leaders in division D, went through a magical set of sea changes. It was, she later recorded, a very private few days when the talk was intimate. On the 28th, at sunset, after they had covered over 200 miles, those thoughts gelled.

> There was a beautiful sunset and it was then that I was overcome by this absolute togetherness, something which had been coming but which had not quite arrived. Now we were a team.

The next seven days were to prove the most frustrating of all. Knowing they could not win, nevertheless they wanted to get in. The wind seemed determined to keep them delayed from that simple ambition as long as possible.

October 1st   980 miles to go

> Last night was a horror show. It has been up and down all night. The wind eased gradually; one reef out then the No.3 and second reef out. No.1 up finally. There was still a good atmosphere on the boat. But by lunchtime the wind was down again. It was a strange day with everyone lost in their own thoughts; gone before you knew it. But a beautiful evening.
>   When you are out here you are lucky enough to be somewhere man hasn't destroyed; there is no evidence of him anywhere.

* At sea, distant lights can be
seen glowing over the
horizon.

Columbus or Drake would have seen exactly the same in every detail. Being out here makes you want to join Greenpeace and save the world. (The girls saw a whale two days ago; I haven't called on the radio since then which makes me feel a lot better.)

Rucanor now looks in a good position: we don't. I hate telling the girls – everyone goes so quiet. We passed Rio in the night; we could see the loom – very bright.*

October 2nd   24'41"S   42'46"W.   885 miles to go

Beautiful sunrise: I really enjoy the early morning watch. The positions at 11.00 were not good, but there is nothing we can do. Meanwhile, the wind built up; green sea, blue sky, puffy clouds. The course is not good, but the crew's work is improving all the time. In the afternoon we were creaming along at 9–10 knots with bursts of 14 knots. The sea was very good for surfing. Jeni and I finally got a map out of the weather fax! But it was wrong!

Everyone is in a great mood because the end is in sight. The position report at 23.00 was suicidally bad; I must keep morale up.

I was a bit worried about going to bed as the wind was still up and Dawn's watches are the least experienced. I lay down fully clothed. It was just as well because at 2.00am all hell broke loose. The wind was up to 32 knots and the boat was going in the wrong direction, broaching merrily away. I had to get everyone up to put a reef in and to gybe. We put the 2.2 flanker up; then everyone went back down below. Then it happened again. Finally we got the spinnaker down and I said we'd pole out the blast reacher. That was a horror show too, but we got it sorted out finally.

The result though was us creaming along at 10–11 knots with bursts of 15 knots – quite safely and happily. The atmosphere changed from on-the-edge terror to relieved laughter. It is amazing what a little common sense can do; I stayed up after that.

October 3rd   27'47"S   45'46"W.   641 miles to go

We spent the morning doing a good speed through grey skies and seas. The wind came forward again. The temperature has really dropped. It was a horrible day: the mood on the boat not good. Then the wind rose violently during dinner again from around 4 to 34 knots.

It is so miserable beating our brains out and not doing the course. *Equity and Law* got in this afternoon; Punta del

Este yacht club called to say. *Rucanor* is now 60 miles ahead,
L'Esprit 100; our *ETA* (estimated time of arrival) is Friday.
    I had to do the bilges later, they were so full. Kristin helped me.
I got into the most foul mood I have had on this trip.

After this date Tracy's personal log entries dry up. She knew they
had lost this first leg; she felt she had let everyone down, however
much they might have felt she had not.

The ship's log (the formal document for *Maiden*'s passage
making) is much more laconic, reflecting the real mood on board. In
the last few days it reads:

October 5th

At 13.00hrs: – 283 miles to go; course 197 (T). Remarks: no wind,
no speed, no course, no weekend!
    21.00 hours. Incredible, good course, good speed, Saturday am?

On Saturday morning, October 7th, *Maiden* formally entered the
record books when she became the first all-women entry in the
Whitbread Round the World Race to cross the finishing line of any
leg. She had an enormous welcome from the crews of the other
yachts and from the thousands of Uruguayans who crowded onto
the dock. *Maiden* had come third in division D, a creditable performance and one which, as soon as she had landed, Tracy announced
she would better in Leg Two.
    So she did. But that was quite a story in itself.

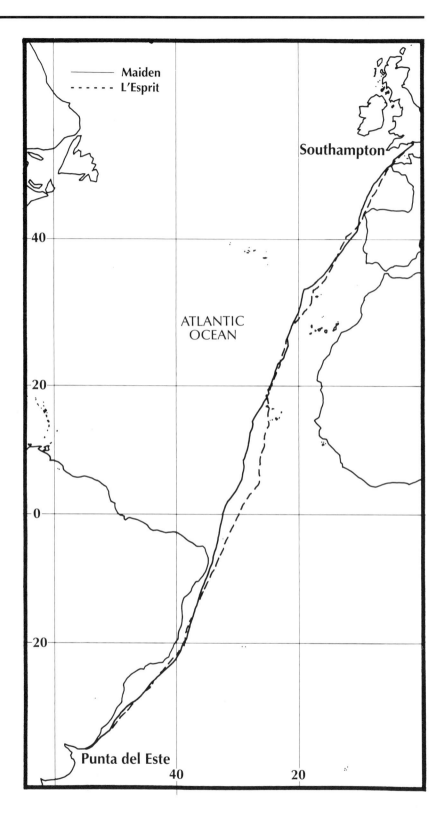

A Summary of Leg One: Port Fevers

Steinlager won the first leg for the maxis; Peter Blake had at last found the yacht and the crew he needed to fulfil his 20-year obsession with the Race. But his first clash with rival Kiwi ketch, *Fisher and Paykel* had ended when her mizen mast snapped.

This needle match between the two Kiwi ketches was to continue all round the world. But Grant Dalton, although he tried, could not catch Blake in these first few thousand miles. When his mast snapped off the Brazilian coast it was all *Fisher and Paykel* could do to keep her hard-earned third place.

Second place had gone to *Merit*, the Swiss yacht skippered by Pierre Fehlmann, who had won line honours in the previous race in UBS. Fehlmann was a canny sailor and the only real challenge to the ketches in the early stages. Britain's best maxi hope, *Rothmans*, skippered by Lawrie Smith, made a bad decision early in the leg. Off Cape Finisterre in a gale, she went too far east and slipped inexorably into fourth place.

The Card, the Swedish ketch, managed fifth place, which put ketch rigs in first, third and fifth, seemingly demonstrating their superiority in this race.

The first leg saw considerable damage to yachts, and in conditions which were not that strenuous. Part of the commotion in Punta that October was to constantly revolve around the possibility that in designing the maxis for speed at the cost of weight, technology had over-reached itself. The yachts were too light, too vulnerable. Whilst *Fisher and Paykel* had lost a mast, *Rothmans* had developed a bad deck crack. *British Defender* had lost her spinnaker 'crane', *Martela*'s and *L'Esprit*'s keels were hanging off.

Among the maxis, the Russians had done well to arrive in seventh place, while *British Defender*, its crew unhappy with the skipper (who resigned in Punta), crawled in in ninth place. All the maxis reported phenomenal daily runs, with *Rothmans* claiming that on one stretch they had been out of control for 150 miles. Exaggeration or bravado apart, it was clear that the leg had not been quite what anyone had expected.

All the yachts arrived much quicker than predicted, so much so that the Whitbread officials only just made it to the port for *Steinlager*'s arrival. *Maiden* came in on the day the first maxi had been predicted to arrive.

The smaller yachts, in division D had fought long and hard to establish their final positions. They too had experienced bad weather early on. Tracy berated herself for failing to make the decision to fight on the start line; and a little later not to get across the French side quickly enough. That and a decision in the doldrums not to cover *Rucanor* when the latter gybed, she believed had cost her the leg.

But *Maiden* had held the lead – if narrowly – for a day or so and it showed the girls they had the ability and the tenacity to do it. Meanwhile the eventual fight was between *Rucanor* and *L'Esprit* which the French yacht narrowly won, by just 90 minutes.

For everyone this first leg was experimental: the Race had never gone to Uruguay first before, and the courses and the weather encountered were new to everyone. It was, in truth, a shake-down leg, where yachts and crews tried and tested themselves and their equipment for the first time under the hazards of this Race. It was generally thought, in Punta, to have proved very little about the long-term chances of any of the yachts. In one way, at least, and outside the handicap controversy, in Punta everyone was level rating everyone else.

That first leg, however, did dispel one myth, which had persisted right up until the start. It was the old chestnut that women could not live together in a confined space, like a yacht, be bossed by a woman and not fall out. If anything, *Maiden*'s progress round the world was characterised by good humour and laughter, to the point where the television producer editing the on-board footage asked if he could have a bit more grim-faced action, if only to convince viewers it wasn't such a holiday.

Ports rot ships and men, so the saying goes. The truth of that came home rapidly for the Whitbread yachts at their first stop-over in Punta del Este.

The stop-overs have become an important part of each race. They enable crews to recover and yachts to be repaired. As the pressures of racing have increased, so these opportunities for both have been welcomed. There is, though, an optimum time and in this Whitbread the length of the stops was a problem.

There are two reasons why skippers dread these lengthy stays. The first is cost: at around £10,000 a week a yacht only the shore sharks gain. The crews, too, get disaffected, bored, then potentially dangerous. They no longer have the drive for the Race and, when the next leg does finally start, all that teamwork may have been dissipated.

Of course, time in port can count in favour of longer, rather than shorter stays when it is necessary to get the yachts back into condition. In Punta, many of the yachts needed major repairs. The 'shake-down cruise' of leg one had shown up many hasty and ill-constructed features – particularly on some of the maxis. *Maiden*, by contrast, apart from a few minor equipment problems, faced nothing serious on the repair front.

Yachts in port mean shore teams and *Maiden* had gathered one of the biggest: Howard Gibbons, the project manager and Sarah-Jane Ingram as the deputy were to go all the way round the world. In Punta, Duncan Walker, the first boat-builder and Ian (Poodle) Bruce, who took over in Fremantle, were present. Meanwhile back home in Hamble, Dee Ingles had the vital job of keeping Tracy and the crew in touch with base. Although a professional sailor Dee had elected to run the shore office for the duration of the Race, thus largely missing out on the stop-overs.

Pam Hale – 'I'm just a housewife from Netley' – was in charge of parties, although this somewhat joking title disguised how important Pam was shore side, in organising everything – and raising morale. As the Race developed she proved to be a tower of strength: when things looked grim it was usually Pam who raised a smile. But Pam also dealt with seeing to the *Maiden* crew's every wish on shore.

Tracy, in imagining the project, had determined it would be a first class ticket to ride: her girls were to be as pampered as possible in each stop-over. In Punta they got half a dozen apartments between them, food in the fridges and a shore allowance. There were many parties.

Meanwhile, *British Defender* changed skipper. The story of Frank Essen's resignation was as rumour-laden as are all yachting tales. The crew had rebelled; rumour control said they were going to be tried for mutiny. Anyway, Essen went and a new skipper was appointed.

The project manager of *L'Esprit de Liberte*, Patrick Dubourg, had not turned up, generating yet more rumours. For a while the crew slept on friendly floors while skipper Patrick Tabarly rushed home to try to bring the errant manager to book.

It was the Russians, though, who were having the worst time. Their main sponsor, the West German subsidiary of Pepsi Cola, dropped them. It was a complicated story, with as many twists as a Dostoevsky plot. The Russians had recruited Skip Novak, an American sailor of immense experience, as a consultant. As time passed it became clear he was in fact going to have to be the *de facto* skipper of the yacht. Novak had skippered the Simon LeBon part-owned *Drum* in the last Whitbread, and was a world-class sailor. No Russians could match his experience; a pre-glasnost few, if any, had been allowed to roam the world's oceans unsupervised.

But there was a Russian skipper – Alexei Grishenko – nominally the man in charge. On that first leg it had quickly become obvious that Grishenko was a poor off-shore sailor. Skip ran the yacht and got its creditable seventh place. But Grishenko, who was among the few on board *Fazisi* who spoke no English, felt more and more isolated. In despair, as only perhaps a Russian can be, he hanged himself.

The crew of *Maiden*, who had adopted the Russians when they first came to the Hamble to fit out their yacht, were shattered. Tracy, who reacts emotionally to tragedy, hardly knew what to say or do. In the end all the *Maiden* team went, in silence, to a memorial service at the Palace Hotel, where the Russians were staying. It was a moving, dramatic half hour: for the Russians it cleared the air. For the rest of the fleet nothing but leaving port could do that.

Then came another death: this time it was a motorcycle accident involving a crew member on *Equity and Law* and Janne Gustavsson, a crew member on *The Card*. Both were on motorbikes which collided. Janne, in a freak fall, fractured his skull and never regained consciousness. Tracy, who counted him a close friend, was totally prostrate with grief for several days. For the Whitbread as a whole, both deaths seemed a portent of their worst fears about the second leg. Now, they wanted to get going, to exorcise the ghosts.

The first stop in Punta was not all tragedy. There was the prize-giving (the first of six) where the Duchess of York presided. Later she came to visit a few of the yachts, in particular *Maiden*, which she had christened in the autumn of 1988. Later still, the girls were invited to lunch at the Polo Club owned by the Duchess's step-father, Hector Barrantes. Fergie gave Tracy an engraved porcelain pin box; there was the growth of a warmer, relaxed friendship. Fergie's parting shot to Tracy was 'win next time; my street cred is suffering.'

The month passed and, apart from the work on the yachts, all the crews enjoyed parties by and for themselves, with horse-riding and golf, tourist trips up country, shopping sprees in Buenos Aires and Montevideo. Uruguay turned out to have the best beef in the world; and plenty of alcohol. *Maiden*, for the first time, had a taste of the public welcomes to come. The Uruguayans gave everyone an excellent reception.

As suddenly as they had come to Punta del Este, the Whitbread yachts left, on October 28th; the locals now had to wait four months before they would see their fast-made friends on these ocean greyhounds again.

CHAPTER 5

Coming Adrift

Tracy Edwards was born at 2.00am, on the 5th September, 1962 in Reading Battle Hospital. Her first entry was typical of later enthusiasms. She arrived feet first, after giving Pat Edwards six hours of hell.

Pat and Tony Edwards, her parents, were prosperous middle-class folk. They lived in a converted coach-house in Purley (now Purley-on-Thames) near Reading, where Tony had a business making the cabinets for hi-fi speakers. 'I didn't want to move away from Reading, where I was born,' remembers Pat, 'but Tony and I wanted something a little bit more adventurous, so we found this derelict coach-house. It was just at the time when people started to convert places.'

Tony and Pat lived in a caravan while work on the house began, and continued for five years. When they had finished it, the living spaces were upstairs while Tony had his workshops on the ground floor. 'It was an upside-down house,' Tracy recalls. 'Dad had his factory downstairs and then you walked up to this massive sitting room.' In that sitting room Tony had built the ultimate stereo system: 'If a mouse ran across the floor, the stylus would jump, it was so sensitive,' says Tracy.

The garden was at first floor level at the back of the coach-house. It was a big garden and it formed part of the adventure playground Tracy and her brother, Trevor, were to share with their cousins, Gregor and Graeme Bint, who lived next door. For the coach-house was part of a much larger group of buildings, all attached to the big house at the end of the drive. The whole was a community, and the children of the various families were able to run riot in and around the grounds.

Trevor, Tracy's brother, had been born two and a half years later than her, in 1965. It had been a brave decision by Pat to go ahead with another pregnancy: ten months after Tracy was born she found she had multiple sclerosis. For an active young woman, whose career had principally been as a ballet dancer, it was a shattering blow. Undeterred, she switched to acting where she could concentrate on the words rather than the actions. Her way of putting it is that she only really got into acting when she started to fall over when working as a ballerina.

Their early childhood was very happy. Tracy says, simply, that she had lovely parents, a beautiful home. Her father's business was successful: the hi-fi craze of the sixties was taking off. When he had a very big order Tracy and Trevor would go down to the workshop and help him pack – putting labels on and so on. Pat also worked for Tony overseeing the paperwork, whilst she kept up her theatrical career.

Tracy says of her father: 'He was a wonderful man – very quiet and shy. As mum is five foot three I never stood a chance!' Tony was a member of MENSA, the society for the super intelligent. He and Pat used to go rallying when they found time. He also loved sailing.

However, he did not like family holidays much. As the family were less than overjoyed at the prospect of sailing, Tony would go off with his friend, David Merry, who kept a yacht on the south coast, while Pat would take the kids to Majorca.

Tony had taken the family sailing – once. Trevor remembers it mostly for being as sick as a dog. His condition was not helped by lunch, a large part of which, he recalls, was a tin of Tyne Brand steak and kidney pie. For years afterwards he couldn't eat one. Food apart, Tracy didn't like the sailing either. In fact, Tracy was afraid of deep water and hated swimming, after an incident in which she had been pulled under.

Back at home Tony had decided to build his own boat. A massive 80 feet in length he worked on it for months and months, until Pat one day asked him which wall of the house he thought he would demolish to get it out. Tony had fondly imagined it would be possible to somehow manhandle it round the corners and out through the doors. He took it apart and re-built it outside; in the end it was a project destined for abandonment.

Tracy went to the local primary school, Highlands. She was 'quite good' says Pat, but adds that she was a character. Tracy's real interests were outside: ballet for years dominated her thought, as acting was to later. Her mother believed she had a budding superstar on her hands. Tracy, determined as she was in the things she wanted, was not willing to put in the practice needed to sustain her early prize-winning. The blunt truth was, she says now, that 'I was into anything I thought was easy: that's why I switched from ballet to acting when I realised how much hard work was involved in ballet.' And, she adds, 'I never used to stick at anything.'

She had no real need to. Secure in her home life she was able to construct a child's imaginary world. So much so that a neighbour once reproached Pat for letting Tracy frighten her daughter. 'She told my daughter there were tigers in all the bushes,' the outraged parent berated Pat, 'and she believes it.'

But Pat did not let that, or many other incidents, inhibit Tracy's free-flung thoughts. Like any mum, of course, she was very proud of her daughter's ability to create, even when the result was havoc. That came fairly frequently. Tracy's early organisational ability came graphically to view when she arranged various 'entertainments' back at the house. Villagers would greet Pat in the street with 'Thank you so much for the invitation, we'd love to come.'

Pat, hurrying home and quizzing her daughter, would discover that Tracy, Trevor, Gregor and Graeme would have devised, scripted, costumed, rehearsed and then sold tickets for various pageants, of which one, the mediaeval jousting contest, still sticks in her mind. 'I would have minded less,' she says, 'if the tickets hadn't specified refreshments and food.'

On one occasion they decided to re-enact the Great Escape. In the garden shed they began to hack away at the floor. The plan was to dig a tunnel from there right under the garden wall, some considerable distance away. Fortunately for themselves and the family, the plan faded away as the magnitude of the task became apparent. One plan, though, that did get carried out, much to the fury of Tracy's Aunt Edna, was the burying of 'treasure' for a future generation to dig up.

The treasure was real enough: it consisted of Pat's and Aunt Edna's jewellery. The conspirators thoughtfully provided a note for posterity and then dug the hole. The trouble started when it became horribly clear that they could not remember where the 'treasure' had been buried. The jewels were eventually recovered – but not until years later.

Pat worried rather less about this kind of childish prank. Her view, born out of her own very happy childhood, was that if the sun was shining then the day should revolve around that, not whether there was washing up to be done. One day, a neighbour had arrived with a child, having been told by Tracy that the Edwardses would take her out with them. 'Oh,' she said, eyeing the chaos of the kitchen, 'Tracy said you were going out.' 'We are,' said Pat, to the woman's horror, 'that mess will still be here later, but the sun might not.' They went to the zoo.

'I wanted a family, but a united one,' says Pat, 'one that worked together towards each other's aims. I used to encourage the children to talk. I think it is a problem with humanity that they don't talk to each other enough. Quite early on I used to encourage them to have moans in front of dad and me; it doesn't hurt to hear. I also tried to get the children to appreciate each other. I used to say you can bash the living daylights out of each other – and they would – but then they would calm down and they would end up laughing. I think they grew closer that way.'

On Tony's birthday in 1972 he decided to take the family for an outing on the Thames on a boat. Tracy remembers it well.

> We went down to the river and I took one look at the boats and started screaming and said that nothing on God's earth was going to get me on the water in a boat. The water terrified the life out of me – and swimming still does. By the end of the day there I was steering the boat . . .

That outing was to be among the last she remembers having with her father. When she was ten years old, on January 11th, 1973, Tony died.

> He died in bed with my mum; it was very very sad – I heard it all going on and that affected me quite deeply. I can remember the whole night. I can remember mum screaming, calling up Aunty Edna, and saying, 'Get an ambulance, Tony's having a heart attack.'
>
> I stayed in my bed but I knew something really bad was happening and I knew that everything was going to change. I sat in bed and waited. I eventually couldn't stand it any longer so I went out into the corridor. There was all this coming and going; the ambulance came. Then mum came in and sat on the bed and I knew. I knew.
>
> She said 'Dad's had a heart attack and the ambulance didn't get here in time and he's died.' I said everything is going to be all right, I'll look after you.
>
> Mum took me into her room to say goodbye to dad, which I'm really glad she did because otherwise it would have been so horrific for me; he looked calm and peaceful. I kissed him goodbye. Then, apparently, I offered to make everyone an

Top left: My father.
Top right: Pat, my mother.
Bottom: Tracy with her
grandmother – spot the round
the world sailor.

Opposite page. *Top right*:   My
first boat. This was when it was
fun to have water on the
inside...
Top left: Me as a budding
ballerina.
Bottom: My father's sailing
companions – Uncle Arthur
(*left*) and David Merry (*right*).

omelette. It didn't really hit me until a lot later, but it did change me, because, from that night, I thought, well, I can't handle it if he's dead and going to be buried in a box in the ground, but I can handle it if I think God's taken him somewhere. I think that's when I started believing in God.

'The funeral was dreadful because I couldn't stop laughing – release of emotion. I couldn't cry. Trevor couldn't take it in – for about two years after he used to say every day 'When's daddy coming back?' In the end mum had to shake him and make him see.

Life really changed from that day; all the happiness evaporated. My mum kept on running the business with my dad's secretary, Ann Guy, who was a fabulous woman. They were both running families as well. But the two men who worked for Dad left because they didn't think women could run a business.

Mum started losing orders from people who didn't think a woman could run a company. She kept fighting. I went off to boarding school; it was quite sad because I got the letter from the Arts Education School saying I had a place, about two weeks after he died.

Tracy had decided that she was not going to make it as a ballet dancer. Instead she had bullied her parents into being allowed to go to a boarding theatre school – if she could get in. Trevor was already at boarding school, partly because he had suffered from a speech impediment and it was thought a change of environment would help. Tracy had, in the meantime, gone on attending Highlands Primary School.

Despite her father's death she convinced her mother that she still wanted to board, and she left for her new school at the beginning of September, 1973. Pat, meanwhile, was getting ready to work in a new play in which she had the leading part. She was sitting at home in Purley reading through her lines on the evening the play opened when the telephone rang. 'It's me,' said a voice, 'I hate it here, you'll have to come and get me.'

Tracy had been at the Arts Education School for one day. 'I woke up on the first morning feeling sick: it was loneliness, something I had never felt before,' she says. 'All the other new girls were clinging to each other, but I didn't want to be a part of that.' Instead she fled later on down to the village pub, the Rose and Crown, where she phoned her mother. 'You can imagine how I felt,' says Pat now. 'All I really wanted to do was to rush off and fetch her, to gather this little bundle in my arms.'

But on the telephone she said none of this, telling Tracy she had to go straight back to the school where everyone would be getting worried. Tracy, much to her own surprise at the time, found herself obeying her mother. Within a couple of days she was over her initial fears and she began to see just what the school had to offer.

Most of that revolved around the theatre. Really, she says, we sacrificed lessons for the theatre – drama. All morning they would act, or dance or do mime. In the afternoon conventional schooling took over with English, French, Maths, Biology and sometimes Geography and History.

And the school was sited in a big old house, reputedly built by Charles II for Nell Gwynne. It had plenty of its own history, bags of atmosphere and numerous stories attached to it; there were hints of secret passages. It was bound to suit an adolescent girl with a big imagination and a yearning for drama. Tracy stayed there until she was thirteen.

* * *

Back home other dramas were unfolding. Pat, who had fought and fought to build Tony's business, finally sold it. By now she was suffering from her own acute loneliness. Both her children were at boarding school. Even when they were home there were strains. The old Edwards family mantra of getting the children to talk out their gripes to mum and dad wouldn't work when only one parent was there to listen.

'The difficulty was that they couldn't work off one parent on the other,' recalls Pat. 'That's quite a natural process. It became very hard to give them this. I would shout at them to go to bed and then I couldn't say to them "I am now taking off that hat and I am now going to be a person you can have a moan at." I used to say "I've got my other hat on." I don't know if they understood.'

Pat was finding it difficult to meet bills and the pressure was growing on her – a young widow with two children – to do the conventional thing and remarry. She owned the house which helped her be independent but in the inflationary seventies standing still in income terms meant sliding backwards, faster and faster. The cost of sending Tracy and Trevor to boarding school was met by the Masons, but Tracy has never worked out, nor sought to discover, how her mother managed to pay for things in general. She knows what a struggle it must have been.

The children, like children everywhere, kept on making demands. One – Tracy's – was to prove more fateful than any other.

81

Looking back it is possible to say that without this single innocent request Tracy's whole life ahead might have been different. It all began when she said to Pat that she and Trevor would like to go pony trekking in Wales.

> 'Mum said "Great, two weeks rest"; she drove us down. It was during this holiday that Pat met Peter. She just needed someone, she had had enough. The past two years since dad's death had been awful. Mum was terribly lonely, especially with everyone going on at her, telling her she couldn't run the business, couldn't bring up her children on her own.
>   Trevor needed a father – that was true – and he thought Peter was brilliant. He was only ten at the time, and he missed his father.

Tracy, who was usually polite to her mother's friends, mistrusted Peter from the start, but she concedes that he was 'incredibly' talented, and appeared to be able to turn his hand to anything he wanted. But, whatever she felt, Pat and he were eventually to marry. Tracy had acquired a step-father.

Tracy, swinging between one possible future and another, unsettled by the events at home, had decided she no longer wished to act; she wanted, now, to be a vet.

In part, this had been precipitated by plans Peter and Pat were making to sell up in Berkshire and move down to the Gower peninsula in Wales. Peter had a plan to set up a wildlife park. If he had been trying to win Tracy's heart he could not have picked a better project. She was enchanted by the idea.

They sold their coach-house, making a good sale as the mid-1970s property boom was inflating prices, and moved to the Gower near Swansea, one of the most beautiful landscapes in South Wales. It was the summer of 1976; Tracy was close to fourteen. As she recalls it, although Peter had made some effort to try to win her affection before they moved, afterwards he made little or no attempt. To be fair, Tracy was making no effort either. What had been simmering now boiled over into permanent and growing hatred. In Wales Tracy declared war on Peter.

Tracy had many adjustments to make. She was a young adolescent wrenched, by her own decision, from the closed but comfortable world of her boarding school, failing to come to terms with her mother's marriage, plunged into a very different culture and, as it turned out, a very different school.

I went to the local comprehensive, Gowerton. The first day I walked in someone nearly blew the doors off the chemistry lab. I had often been in trouble at my boarding school but there was nothing to get my teeth into. Here, I thought, I can cause havoc. I became an utter tyke. I rebelled against everything: mum because she loved Peter; Peter because I had decided he was an idiot; even Trevor, although I didn't see him much, largely because he avoided me whenever he could. I was very aggressive, very violent. I was always having fights at school; I got suspended frequently, although I was hardly ever there.

Looking back she finds it hard to understand why she felt the way she did. Causes of human behaviour are complex, but it is not too difficult to see the mechanisms which were driving her to extremes. Part of the problem was that she simply stopped talking to her mother, the resentment of Pat's love for Peter intervening whenever she might have requested one of the cherished family chats of the past.

Tracy felt she had been usurped by Peter. Her brave words of the night her father died, that she would take care of everything, were now shattered by adult – and therefore unattainable – passions. Her rebellion was a natural process of growing into a young woman; and it was magnified a thousand-fold by the circumstances – and her brutally strong personality. Tracy, in truth, at the time relished being as ghastly as possible.

The house they had intended to buy fell through and they eventually bought a derelict cottage on a hillside with seven acres of land. There were gaps between the walls and the ceilings. Of course, the kids thought it was heaven.

This had much to do with the kind of friends Tracy had picked. Her boyfriends were, by her own recollection, dreadful. When she arrived at the house with the newest beau her mother would tear her hair out. With such a satisfying result from the one person Tracy was subconsciously trying to impress, Tracy would repeat the performance, but with an even more extreme version each time.

While all this was taking place, Peter was putting into action his plans for a small wildlife park. The master-stroke, he believed, was to invite local authorities to send deprived children down to experience a farm environment with rather more exotic attractions than normal. There was a fashion in the seventies for these experiences, preferably out in the sticks, and at that time the money was still, in theory at least, available.

To effect the plan animals had to be bought. 'We collected this weird selection', says Tracy, 'a wild pig called Honky, pigmy goats, a wallaby, a llama, rabbits, ferrets. Peter built a miniature farm where all the animals were small.' Over the horizon, though, trouble was brewing. Among other concerns in Llanmadoc was the herd of red deer Peter had by now imported, and the chances of them breaking out and doing serious damage to local fields and crops.

Tracy and her friends, though, could not believe their luck. Surrounded by animals, growing up on a farm, was a dream. The arguments with Peter went on, but at least they were modified by the setting.

At last the day for opening came. 'Five minutes after we had opened, Swansea Council served a writ forbidding the whole enterprise.' The immediate cause was the failure by Peter, in realising his dreams, to provide sufficient car parking or lavatories; there was, said the order, no appeal.

Peter took the news badly. Perhaps as a result, or merely as a logical extension of the tension between him and Tracy, the battle intensified. The family now started to fall apart.

'One day Peter had said we could have a barbecue. All my friends came round and he said they could all stay until 10pm. He came out at 9.30 and said "What the hell are you lot doing here?" I could never keep my mouth shut. Everyone just scarpered and he started on me. He really started laying into me and I was going back with fists and kicking. It was now open warfare with my mother caught in the middle.'

For Tracy the choices were narrowing fast: 'In the end I couldn't handle the unhappiness I was bringing to mum. It all seemed to be such a waste of time. I thought: I am never going to amount to anything, nothing is ever going to work; really this is the pits. So I ran away.'

CHAPTER 6

Dead Reckoning

In Punta del Este the *Maiden* team had stayed in the Lafayette apartments. From the windows of the flats it was possible to see the Whitbread yachts, lined up on the main breakwater. Punta was a compact stop-over; everything felt as if it were within reach; you would walk ten yards and see someone you knew.

The world's press tended not to be there, so the crews liked it enormously. On top of that, the Uruguayans and the numerous Argentines were extremely welcoming. The night the Race left, at a party given by the Whitbread organisers to the locals for all the help received, there came a moment when the largely British group sang *Auld Lang Syne* with the Argentines: it was a magical night, an emotional moment.

But by October 28th, some of the fleet were beginning to believe there was a jinx on the race. Sailors are more than averagely superstitious and they all breathed a sigh of relief when, after the two tragedies, the doctor on *Creightons Naturally*, broke an arm just before the re-start.

Here, they all said, was the third and final accident. But fate had cast only a first throw in what was to prove the Race's worst accident.

The re-start from Punta del Este was on a bright spring day. After the weeks in port, everyone was more than ready to go. General apprehension about the Southern Ocean leg had been growing; the general attitude was 'let's get it over with'. Because the Race had by-passed Cape Town (for political reasons) the second leg was the longest yet devised for the Whitbread. It was also the earliest in the year that the yachts had entered this treacherous and lonely ocean, and fears about the extent to which the Antarctic ice would have drifted northwards dominated conversations in the last days in Punta.

LEG TWO

PUNTA DEL ESTE, URUGUAY,

TO FREMANTLE,

WESTERN AUSTRALIA,

7,650 NAUTICAL MILES,

OCTOBER 28TH, 1989–

DECEMBER 3RD, 1989

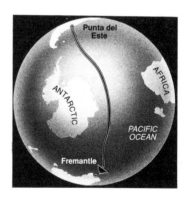

For *Maiden* there was a crew change. Jo Gooding, the cook, re-joined the yacht and Kristin Harris left – as it turned out to do the next leg on *Creightons*. Jo, although apprehensive that her first taste of the Race would be in the Southern Ocean, could hardly contain her excitement. The crew, too, now felt they were complete – ready to do battle to win what they had always believed could be their best leg of the Race.

Sunday October 29th   37'20"S   52'02"W   7,425 miles to go

I spent Friday night until 2.00am packing – and I still didn't get it all done. Sarah-Jane can do it, I hope. I didn't sleep very well; in the end I got up at 5.00am. I was very, very nervous – much much more than I was in Southampton. Actually, I was terrified.

But when I looked out of the window it was a nice clear day – although there was no wind. Howard came up; I phoned Trevor (her brother) and mum: tearful goodbyes. Howard and I talked about how much more money we need to keep the boat going. He went, I finished my sea bag, picked up my boots, took one last look round the room and then went down. Duncan took my bag to the boat – what an angel. I walked down with Howard.

It was really quite calm. I put my stuff on board and unpacked everything and put it away. Got the nav station ready: charts all sorted out; sat navs (satellite navigation systems) and instruments on. Here we go again, I thought.

Then it was 'let's go, engine on'. Poodle did the lines using the *Zodiac* (*Maiden*'s shore-based inflatable dinghy) – a nice manoeuvre to get us out. No problem. Everyone was on the dock cheering and clapping. We followed other yachts out round the island to the start line, staying close to *NCBI*, motoring up and down.

Then at 11.15am all the crews on the boats lined up on their aft decks for one minute's silence and to throw wreaths in the sea for Janne. It was an incredibly emotional moment to see everyone. I cried, I couldn't stop it for a while; Oh, Janne!

We got the main up and the headsail with just 20 minutes to go. It was a very close start – Michèle was steering. For us it was brilliant – we were right up with the maxis (at last!). *Fisher and Paykel* were over and had to go back – poor guys. Anyway onto the first mark where we made a perfect rounding behind *Rucanor*. Then up with the spinnaker – wrong one!

We nearly missed the second buoy and had a horror show.

Throwing the wreath over the side for Janne – goodbye to a friend.

But when we made a gybe to get back round it it was not half as bad as *L'Esprit* who lost loads to us. *Rucanor* had to beat back and go round it; took truck loads out of her. Unfortunately *Schlussel* and *La Poste* didn't miss it. So as we left the land it was *Schlussel*, *Maiden*, *L'Esprit*, *La Poste*, *Rucanor* all in a line.

We spent the rest of the day and night all within sight of each other. It was very close. We did the first duty boat round; there was a bit of confusion with the channels, but I finally sorted it out. I talked to *NCB Ireland* after that and then Grant (Dalton, skipper of *Fisher and Paykel*) came on and told Balls (*NCBI*'s radio man and a Kiwi) he was boring. I can see the chat show turning into a free for all.

I was really seasick that first night (the Saturday). I put the wrist bands on; they work.*

October 30th   38'36"S   49'36"W

I got up at 4.00am to do the weather charts and all hell broke loose. The wind went from nothing to 30 knots in ten minutes. Luckily we had just taken the spinnaker down to put up a headsail. I got dressed; we put up the No.4 with two reefs in the main. Incredible wind – I watched it change as it went to 40 knots. Ugh. I went up and steered. We took the No.4 down and just sailed with the main for a while.

There was water all over the place, the seas were horrible. Put a third reef in and the No.5 up. We were managing the course – sometimes. Then it got light – it was a dreadful grey day with very heavy seas and the wind finally steady at 30 knots.

* A band on each wrist which puts pressure on the pulse; many sailors swear by them; others say they're useless.

* Chinese gybe is an uncontrolled one – potentially highly dangerous as the forces on the mast can snap stays, and bring the whole rig crashing down.

The chat show at 11.00am showed that everyone has the same weather – *F and P* managed a Chinese gybe*. I spoke to Punta radio to ask for Duncan to be in the radio room tonight. Tried the telex and it went to reduced power. Talking seems OK though. We are getting weather maps from Buenos Aires.

Tracy's problems with the weather fax on the first leg had been solved: the machine had been replaced.

It is interesting to see the routes that everyone is taking. *British Defender*, *Gatorade*, *F and P*, *Rothmans* are all heading for the South Pole. *Steinlager* is staying north, while *Merit* is doing the same course as us – that's good enough for me. *Creightons* turned back today – their cap shrouds have gone. Poor things – we all gave them our condolences.

We passed *L'Esprit* today – they were sailing without a main until they saw us! The wind gradually became easier so we put the No.4 up. *Rucanor* is dead ahead and we caught up a lot during the storm. We *can* beat these guys with lots of wind. I slept a lot today – everyone did.

October 31st   39'30"S   46'00"W

We had the full main with a No.4 up. I got up at 4.00am for the weather chart: got a good one. I stayed up for a couple of hours mucking around in the nav station, listening to the girls on deck singing. Yes, singing! I must have the happiest crew in the Race. It's so good to be on our own again, away from everybody else. There's so much outside influence on the project now. We are back to what we should be doing, to what we enjoy the most, where we should be – out here clear of arguments, the bitching, the aggression, the snide remarks and people stirring things up. The only company we've got here is an albatross constantly wheeling behind and above us, which we have named Fred, and the voices of our friends on the other yachts. It is a secure feeling; knowing they are there, around us.

November 1st   41'19"S   41'26"W

What a day! Up at 4.00am again. There was no weather chart. The barometer was dropping, though slowly. One of the mast 'D' fittings is coming unscrewed again. I went back to bed.

When I got up at 9.00am I found the gas had failed as Jo was doing breakfast. Jeni tried to figure it out but couldn't, so she went to bed. Jo did cereal in the end.

I called *NCBI* after the chat show to ask if they knew what it was; Skip (Novak, skipper of the Russian yacht, *Fazisi*) called and said they were having the same trouble. It's dirty gas from Uruguay. He said to clear out the regulator and the hose. Then Balls called in from *NCBI* and when I told him about the rig he laughed and said – don't tack, don't gybe, go and make yourself a nice cup of tea; ha, ha.

When Dawn got up I told her about the gas. After she had thought about it for a while she came up with a brilliant solution and she rigged a filter from a cigarette tip. Meanwhile we were all figuring out if we could survive without cooking food. The conversation was hysterical. Sally was on the wheel and she turned round and said 'am I dreaming or are we talking about eating cold freeze-dried food?' Everyone is in exceptionally good spirits, as always in an emergency.

Mandi checks the rig yet again.

Mandi went up the mast and tried to fix the 'D' fittings that were loose so we can go downwind. We'll have to see how it is tomorrow. But Dawn did get the gas going; as she did so the water-maker broke down.

I was in the nav station all day, working the computer, running Dawn's watch. I tried to telex Cougar (their telex link in Hamble) and the electronics went mad; then nothing worked. Jeni and I sat cursing everyone until we realised Dawn had switched the batteries off. Scream! When she turned them on the water-maker started working as well.

Shortly after I got a weather map through. It is a joy when everything works. Now we have only to worry about the rig and steering. We had a great early evening session on deck. Today we have had sun and the seas are calm. We are heading further south now to keep with *Rucanor* and *L'Esprit*.

November 3rd 44'08"S 34'46"W 6,510 miles to go

Yesterday was a great day although there wasn't much wind. It turned into a lovely night sail, though. This morning we had the full main and No.1 up. There is a front moving towards us; I hope we are in the right place. It is difficult to tell as the lows are above and below us. The air is definitely getting colder. I plotted our position – we had a good night's run. I went back to bed but I couldn't sleep – too hyped up, thinking too much all the time. Everyone is still in good spirits, I think it is relief that the weather has stayed good. It was sunny, but cold.

We now have a beautiful huge albatross following us. I keep thinking of Janne when I see it. (Sailors believe their souls will inhabit an albatross when they die; hence the disaster that befell the ancient mariner when one was shot.)

We had a long talk on deck today: marriage, babies, returning to normal life. Everyone is terrified by the thought of the end of the Race. Even I get nervous. Sally reminded us that in ten days it will be a year since we sailed out of England to do the Ruta.

We have all been together so long now; eight of us for a year and a half, the others for six months – and more. It suddenly occurred to me how much I will miss them all some day. Sobering thoughts.

Then we got the 11.00am positions and found that we were ahead in the class, although everyone is in a good position. I gave a pep talk: let's race this boat type of thing. I got it right by going slowly south instead of diving like some of them. The homework paid off. I'm really, really pleased – and so are the girls.

Then, in the afternoon, the wind dropped and swung ahead. The night closed in and we all remembered where we were. It is very cold now, wet and grey like a cloak.

But, down below, the nav station and galley are becoming a hive of activity, especially around meal times. Now Jo is back with us we feel complete, invincible, strong, confident. We are a team, an army, a family and we would die for each other as we live for each other. I wonder how many skippers in this Race could write that?

We heard this morning that *Creightons* had restarted from Punta.

November 4th   46'24"S   33'48"W

It is extremely cold now, very foggy, wet and grey. Miserable. The girls are still cheerful, though. We put the heater on for the first time and shut the hatch. The boat was very cold this morning. The wind is almost letting us do the course. It is so frustrating the way it keeps heading us south, we have to hope we don't lose our average. There was a good weather map showing a high pressure system to the north, while we remain in the tail end of a front.

Tracy was trying to position *Maiden* sufficiently far south to catch the northern edge of the huge westerly air systems which sweep across the Southern Ocean and create the 'roaring forties'. Too far south and she would end up in much worse weather than the yacht could cope with, being forced further and further south into the ice. Too far north and she could be caught by the high pressure systems with no wind, squeezed between the next set of depressions. It was no easy task to work this out, but Tracy got it right.

At the chat show at 11.00am we found we had kept our lead. GREAT! The other yachts have come south too. There is a huge school of pilot whales following us. I told the *NCBI* guy today that we had changed out of pink shorts into thermals; he believed me, the daft bugger!

November 6th   48'41"S   22'18"W

This evening watch there were very sloppy seas and we had to gybe. It proved very difficult so we decided to take the spinnaker down, at which point the wind decided to come up. We put the No.3 headsail up, which Claire sheeted in. The other dropped the spinnaker and because Claire was by then trimming the No.3 she was behind the spinnaker when it came down. It was proving very hard to get in, so she reached forward to help. At that moment a huge gust of wind took the spinnaker and filled it and because Claire was off balance it picked her up and flicked her over the life-lines. Thank God she was clipped on; her own harness tautened and jerked her back. Tanja was able to grab her and pull her into the cockpit. It was very scary. We now call her the flying doctor.

November 7th   48'41"S   16'42"W   5,312 miles to go

We started an iceberg watch on Sunday. The maxis spotted a whole load around 17'10"W and at 49'S. I stay up now at night and watch the radar; I try to grab a couple of hours sleep in the day. It is difficult as there are the chat shows to do, calls to make, telexes to send and receive, weather faxes to get. Mandi saw penguins on Sunday; penguins, I ask you! The fog has receded today but has been plaguing us, making the girls constantly wet and cold.

Nancy at the wheel.

The wind patterns change all the time. We get on the right side of the lows, surf with the wind behind for a day, then it's on the nose again. I decided to stay north and go south gradually, which really has paid off because all the other boats in our class dived south and lost loads to us. We are still leading our class (*Maiden* never lost the lead from the time she gained it, a few days before).

Now they are all following us. They've been all over the place. The girls have been great, not complaining about being very cold and wet most of the time. There is a lot of laughing and joking. It is funny for me, to sit in the nav station and watch the procession of watches, getting dressed, getting undressed. Everyone has their own method of staying warm. The foot, hand and body warmers are very effective. I use them at night because the boat is so cold. The heater is useless, we should have made a curtain further aft to stop the heat getting out and brought more fuel as the batteries are always low.

The sat nav packed up for two days; it had happened to *NCBI* as well, apparently. But I haven't had any weather maps for two days and I really need to know what's coming. We passed a lot of icebergs tonight.

It is bitterly cold; the wind just bites through all the layers of clothing. Fingers are permanently unworkable. It is getting to be freezing down below as well, so you can't warm up. The heater is about as effective as a candle. It switches itself off as soon as the batteries go down, which is most of the time. You can't start it up without the generator. We should have put more fuel on and sod the weight.

I would not recommend this God-forsaken place. We have all decided that hell is not fire and brimstone; hell is here.

November 8th 49'50"S 10'57"W

The wind is still being a pain and not quite coming round, though it got better during today. I got really worried at the chat show as *Rucanor*, *Schlussel* and *L'Esprit* are still heading north. I thought I may have misunderstood where the low is from *UBF*'s (*Union Bank of Finland* – a maxi) info. I spent all day trying to work it out and what to do as we had tacked in the morning to do a better course East South East. There was no weather map at 14.45. We'll stay on this tack until I get one. The girls have every confidence in me, which makes me feel a lot better and gives me confidence in myself.

Then when I got a sat nav fix at midday I found that my DR (dead reckoning) was only five miles out. Finally, when we got the Argos positions I found we were 147 miles ahead of *Rucanor*, 170 in front of *Schlussel*. Both *Rucanor* and *L'Esprit* are coming south again so I must be right unless they think I know something they don't.

I telexed Sarah-Jane (in the *Maiden* shore team office in Hamble) to say it was great to hear what was going on in the real world. The *Neighbours* update was good to hear, but what we all really wanted news of was *Eastenders*. We have seen a huge school of pilot whales, more than I have ever seen. And we had an enormous sperm whale come straight for the boat; only at the last minute it swerved. Phew!

This leg is proving very tactical and very psychological. But I think that *Rucanor* and *L'Esprit* are making desperate and panicky decisions which is good for us. It has been bitterly cold today; there are loads of birds following us.

Jeni doing the worst job on the boat – packing the spinnaker.

November 9th   50'27"S   08'42"W

We are getting sick of beating*; we must be the only people in the world to beat through the Southern ocean. The maxis have caught the first low and are doing 350 miles a day surfing. We're doing 175 miles beating. Nerves are wearing thin. I have to control my temper when it's like this; the slightest thing sets me off – and its so cold. Even with the heater on the nav station is freezing; I have to wear a hat and coat in here now – I've got five layers on now. But I think everyone is about the same.

We saw two icebergs today. Nancy was on deck when we had a glint of sun. She started to say 'Over there that looks just like an ICEBERG!' We saw another one later. The bad news was that we couldn't pick either one up on the radar.

We spent the whole day going way off too far south but not being able to tack because *Rucanor* was catching up. Praying for the wind to come aft so we can do the course. No weather map again. It seems that the low above us is finally moving, though. Time to go north.

The wind came up early this evening and we tacked, after calculating that if we went north for five hours we would hit 50' at 23.00 and *Rucanor* would catch up 20–40 miles. But we had to go, we can't go any further south. When we did tack the waves were very bad, lots of freezing water on deck. We have stayed hard on

* Beating: when the boat is sailing as close to the wind as possible, it is crashing into waves whipped up by the same wind.

the wind for five hours.

We then tacked back at 50'S when the wind swung right on cue and let us do the course. But of course it dropped, too. Tanja had to talk to *Equity and Law* tonight – they had a tooth problem.

November 10th   50'04"S   04'54"W

I woke to the wonderful feeling of the spinnaker up and pulling. Whoopee! Only, there was no wind. But we are doing the course, so two out of three ain't bad. It was foggy, raining and well below freezing on deck. I spent all morning trying to get a weather map. I sat down with the one I got two days ago and the one from yesterday and I worked out what should happen. We should be on the right side of the next low. Unfortunately, so should *Rucanor*.

The wind came up in the early morning; the fog cleared as well. Which was just as well, because if we'd seen any icebergs dead ahead we would have had no time to miss them. But by the evening we had the wind again and we were doing 10 knots. *Rucanor* benefit from this too. They had taken four more miles from us today.

November 11th   50'15"S   01'44"E   4,731 miles to go

Today I made a stupid decision. I can't believe how I go on sometimes. I decided we could edge up north to meet the next low. We did really good boat speeds all day and had a brilliant run, only to lose miles to *Rucanor*.

The wind was up and down; something strange is happening to the compasses; they are maybe sticking. (They were: *Maiden* had been supplied with the wrong ones for the Southern Ocean legs.) It was much warmer and the fog lifted as did our spirits. I stayed up all day and got some very good weather maps; another low is coming. I'm getting the best faxes from the Russian station in Antarctica. We have now been a fortnight at sea, without washing or changing. I had a quick flannel wipe. It was very cold. No-one seems that bothered; we must all stink though.

When I got on the chat show I found out that *With Integrity* had lost a man overboard – but recovered him. I said I'd call the Race Committee for them. All the time this is going on I'm trying to work out where *Rucanor* is. Then I heard that *Creightons* had had an injury. I spoke to Claire about it. Later I talked to *NCBI* –they were very down as they had broken their boom.

Rucanor is now 57 miles behind; this is all so nerve-wracking. The conditions are perfect for them and bad for us. What we need is a hurricane. The Southern Ocean is behaving like the Atlantic.

Ahead but feeling the pressure of both *Rucanor* and *L'Esprit* close behind, sailing in freezing conditions in which she was daily hearing of broken equipment or men swept overboard on the maxis, way out ahead, Tracy was now to face the biggest crisis of her leg.

Creightons Naturally, having put back into Punta del Este to repair its mast, had been struggling to stay in touch with the rest of the Race. The delay in having to return had undoubtedly annoyed them and they were pushing the boat, as it turned out, too hard for the conditions. Nearly a thousand miles ahead *Maiden* knew little of this until the 12th.

Dawn concentrates on getting one last knot out of the boat.

November 12th   50'24"S   07'33"E   4,544 miles to go

A strange day. This problem with the course and the magnetics of the compasses dominated most of it. The wind came up and went down again. It was quite foggy and then it cleared, and came back again. There was a quick chat show in the morning – no dramas. *Rucanor* still 70 miles behind.

Everyone was a bit depressed last night with the positions we got, but they perked up today. I spent the day trying to work out which course to steer to go east. There has to be a magnetic anomaly around here – or is it the compasses? I sent a telex off for Tanja tonight and then I saw Janne's name in it and I started to cry. It all came out, I couldn't stop. I kept seeing his face so clearly. It sank in that I'll never see him again. I telexed the Race Office and then I called Simon. He sounded fine. I miss him so much, can't wait to see him. I realise how much my best friend he is, which I'd never thought of before. I've got so much to tell him.

I've been thinking a lot today about after the Race. How do you just stop? Discovering that I can skipper my own boat has had a profound effect on me. I wish now that I had had another ten years to go before thinking of getting married. I want to settle down but I just wish there were ten years between 27 and 28. There is so much I want to do all at the same time. I feel as if I had been caged somehow when I was sailing on other peoples' boats, and now I have been let loose. I want to do the Pacific and also Tierra del Fuego – cruising. I want to do a single-handed trans-

Atlantic, the Paris to Dakar (road rally), learn to fly a helicopter and have three kids all at the same instant. All I can do is to try my damnedest. They said this was impossible, too.

I've never been so happy at sea before. I feel totally and utterly free as if the last strings had gone. A strange way to feel when, after travelling for ten years, marriage is only nine months away. But maybe that's part of it, because I have an anchor now and I feel safe to lift it and sail away, knowing what I have when I get back. I wonder how the girls feel about this? I know most of them appreciate what all this means. Jo certainly feels it. It is as if we have both been looking for this all our lives and now finally, found it – along with many other things along the way. I am totally in love with life at the moment; I think that's why I cried when I thought of Janne. I do feel under a lot of pressure as well. Sometimes it is like a time-bomb waiting to go off. I have never wanted to win anything as much in my life as I want to win this leg (and the Race).

But now I feel a lot more capable than I did on the first. The girls help. If I was on shore now this would be one of my most dangerous moods when I start shocking people, getting loud and aggressive. The sea channels this feeling and gives it direction.

I haven't read one book this leg. I find so much more to do – constructive things. Everyone should feel like this once in their lives: complete.

Dinner tonight was lamb and peas. I am eating like a pig; I wonder if I'm fat under all these layers. It'll be a novelty to see my body again. The wind died away during this evening and came aft. Should we go north or south? The low to the south would be a better bet but would we get there in time. I'll wait for the chat show to find out what everyone else is doing. . . .

The chat show: Jesus! *Creightons* called us to tell *Liverpool* they have a problem; they wouldn't give details but they said they'd call us after. I relayed all this plus the rest. Then I tried to raise *Creightons* again. When I got through I had missed the first part. What I got was 'a man fell overboard today. He was in the water for 25 minutes; he had been resuscitated but has suffered from hypothermia and now looks as if he has pneumonia'. We changed frequencies to six megaherz which was better. Claire spoke to them and advised them. John Chittenden (skipper of *Creightons*) asked Claire whether they'd know about him tomorrow. I said we'd keep radio watch constantly for them.

I hope the guy is OK. Four men overboard so far. God almighty.

Claire and I stayed up for the 1.00am call. Meanwhile, I worked out the positions: *Rucanor* are 90 behind, *L'Esprit* 141 miles and *Schlussel* 213 miles! Better go north now to catch that low, but gently, slowly, so as not to lose any more miles and to keep the speed up. The wind remains all over the place but visibility is much better.

What Tracy did not know at that time was that one man – Anthony Phillips – had already died on *Creightons*. The concern was for the other, Bart van den Dwey, who was seriously ill. The tragedy everyone had feared, the third death, had happened.

November 13th   49'58"S   12'41"E

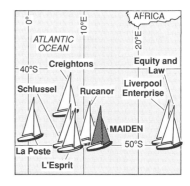

Maiden heads down gradually, whilst *L'Esprit* dives further south.

I will remember this day as long as I live. I kept watch on the radio all night. At 1.00am Claire spoke to them again and the guy seemed to be stable. Claire took over from me at 4.00am. I slept until 7.45 – the first sleep in 17 hours. I was completely knackered. When I got up there was an iceberg on the horizon and I got it on the radar which was a relief to us all.

We put the generator on; it went on and off all day, using up our emergency ration. Anyway, John Chittenden, skipper of *Creightons'*, called us and gave us a telex to try and send to Race HQ as they couldn't get through.

This telex read: 'At 03.32 on Sunday 12th November the yacht gybed heavily running before a westerly gale. The weather runner broke and the yacht gybed again breaking two of the grinder pedestals. The main was taken down and the lee runner was rapidly being set up when we were hit by large seas – at 03.45. The yacht broached on the second sea and our poled out yankee was set aback breaking the spinnaker pole. Two men, Bart van den Dwey and Tony Phillips, were swept overboard. Both men were equipped with life-jackets, flares and personal EPIRBs. Two life-rings and a Dan Buoy were sent in after them.

The headsails were dropped and the yacht motored back on a VHF/DF bearing. The first man was located with the aid of parachute flares at 04.15. Bart van den Dwey was successfully recovered and resuscitated.

At 04.32 Tony was recovered and resuscitation begun and continued until 07.17 without success. Bart's life-jacket was inflated when he was recovered, Tony Phillips' was not. We think Tony hit a stanchion as he went overboard and it is thought unlikely he was conscious once in the water.

The two EPIRBs were recovered but the two life-buoys were not. Two crew members went into the sea to assist with the recovery. Barry Mercer and Julian Morris went in three times. The sea temperature was 7°C and there were heavy seas running. Both actions were, in my mind, heroic, Julian's in particular. Twenty-four hours later Bart is recovering well from hypothermia and shock. From John Chittenden, skipper. Ends.'

Chittenden asked Tracy to pass on a message to Tony's parents asking permission to bury him at sea (although he knew, in truth, he would have to). He did not want the rest of the fleet to know the answer, so he asked Tracy, on receiving a reply to her telex, to signal affirmative or negative only.

But this was to come later. At the time she took down the radio message Tracy could hardly believe her ears.

As John read the message Claire took it down and as he was getting to the point Claire and I both realised what had happened. Nancy and Jo were in the passage listening. We just gaped at each other in silence as the voice on the radio told us they had in fact lost two people and that Tony Phillips had died. Claire just looked numb as she said 'I copy that loud and clear'. No one said a word. I went hot and cold and started to shiver. My God.

Claire got it all down and then I spoke to Andrew (on *Creightons*). Then he added, 'What do the parents want us to do with the body?' I felt the tears sting; I had this vision of asking someone the same question about one of us. I said we would do our best to get an answer. I sent the crew our deepest sympathy. Why do words seem so stupidly inadequate?

They told us they would be standing by on six megs and call if Bart got worse. At the chat show I told the other boats I didn't know anything, as that was what *Creightons* wanted. But the gossip started.

I spent all day trying to get the telex through. Tried Cape Town, Portishead, the lot. I thought I would go mad. I couldn't get any weather maps because of all this, and all the while we were having horrendous problems with the wind and where we were trying to go. The wind kept on coming up with a heavy sky and ominous seas. (They were beginning to get the gale which had passed

98

Miserable conditions on *Maiden* and a two-minute silence for Anthony Phillips.

Creightons with such devastating results.) The sun disappeared again. Finally, it looked like the Southern Ocean.

Creightons called a couple of times; Claire spoke to them. Bart seems to be a lot better. I finally got to sleep for a couple of hours. Jo kept radar and radio watch. I got up to find another iceberg really close, very impressive. I took the positions to get the girls' minds off the day's events. They are very subdued. It gives us something else to think about. We are all terrified of icebergs! It is something we feel between us rather than talk about. It is like driving through a minefield with a blindfold on, sailing at night. The ice is so far north.

Anyway, I finally got the telex through at 16.00hrs. I sent another one to Cougars to tell Howard to phone parents and assure them we were all right. They telexed back, they already knew. I am sure that *Creightons* don't realise that.

I finally got a message back from Race HQ. Tony's parents want him to be buried at sea. Meanwhile Jo was cooking, watches kept coming and going. Claire was on and off the radio to *Creightons* and the boat was bowling down 15 foot seas at 15 knots. *Creightons* called us later; they had managed to get through to Portishead. Andrew (their radio operator) sounded a lot better, more positive, a good sign. Bart now wants to eat and Claire had to explain how to inject him to stop him puking everything up.

We talked again later and *Creightons* asked us to relay a message about what had happened to the rest of the fleet. At the chat show I read it. Very sad. I then relayed it to *NCBI*. Balls just said, 'Yes, I copy'. He sounded shattered. *The Card* heard and as they were duty boat Roger (Nilson, the skipper and a doctor) relayed the message to the rest of the maxis. He sounded pretty distraught.

Tracy, exhausted, retired to bed. In her absence the boat's compasses, still acting up, had forced *Maiden* 20 miles further north than she had intended. For her actions, especially her hours of working the radio messages for *Creightons*, she was awarded the British Telecom Communicator of the Leg Award.

November 14th   49'24"N   19'05"E

I spent the whole day in a dreadful mood because we had gone too far north. When I finally thought I had sorted it all out, the sat navs packed up. I started praying my calculations had been right, but I have no way of checking them. Dawn, Jeni and I wracked our brains trying to work it all out. Why did this have to happen when we were first? Well, we won't be for much longer. *Rucanor* will have creamed past us last night.

I stood by for *Creightons* all day. Bart is getting better all the time. I had a message for them from *British Defender*.

At the chat show, sure enough *Rucanor* were only 39 miles behind with lots of wind. I had to fight my temper – difficult. I still couldn't get weather maps because of being on stand-by. It was too cloudy to take a sight (using a sextant). I am beginning to feel, too, that if we can't sort out these compasses in Freo then the girls can get themselves another navigator, I've had enough. I expect *Rucanor* can't believe their luck.

November 15th   49'40"S   25'17"E   3,960 miles to go

I kept getting up in the night to check on the sat nav. Nothing, bloody nothing. We had pancakes for breakfast but Jo was in a foul mood. I missed *Creightons* calling as I was trying to deal with a couple of our own problems. If anyone who didn't sail had been on the boat today it would have put them off sailing for life. It very nearly did it to me. What a nightmare. The wind, too, was up and down. No weather charts again – very bad reception.

It was very cold and damp and miserable – now there is

something wrong with the breakers (for electric power). I wonder if they are leaking into the hull and creating the compass problem? At one point everything went. I screamed for Jeni and we sat down and went round and round in circles trying to figure it all out.

We checked everything: the compasses again, the cables to the sat nav, the computer. Tempers were again a little short today. Then, at the chat show, things were not too bad. *Rucanor* and the others are still in the high as well as us. We'll try to head south again as they all are. *Rucanor* is still 40 miles behind (are they sailing backwards?). I really thought they would have overtaken us last night. *L'Esprit* is 100 miles behind, *Schlussel* 173. Good.

Everyone else is very fed up but trying to make the best of it. Good on 'em. I stayed up all day but did manage to grab two hours this afternoon. Finally, the sat nav took a fix in the early evening; then it immediately stopped again.

Dawn had worked out the fuel. Because of *Creightons* (not that I mind) we will probably run out during the last week. Thank the Lord for the emergency batteries. I have worked out that in five days we can finally head north. Jeni will be pleased – she has been suffering badly from her frozen feet.

We went today onto the chart which has Australia away in the corner. *Rucanor* are not on it yet. That makes things seem a lot better. But, while we were gybing Sally managed to slam the hatch shut on my hand. When Jo brought some water to soothe it she stumbled and spilled it all over the chart. If I hadn't been crying, I'd have laughed.

I heard via Portishead from S-J today that we now have huge money problems. Oh dear God I have had enough. I want to be at home curled up in front of the fire with Simon, watching *Coronation Street*, and stroking Punch (one of her dogs). I have never been as highly strung on a boat as I am now. I feel like punching walls (except my hand hurts too much). I am just hanging onto my temper; God help anyone who sets me off.

I have to make such an effort at the moment to stay calm; worrying about the money is not helping. I suppose I will find out in Freo soon enough. Finally, tonight we were doing 9 knots in the right direction and we had taken another 14 miles from *Rucanor*.

November 18th   51'30"S   42'53"E   3,286 miles to go

Things are looking up. The sat navs are now working and the compasses seem OK. We have had to take our main down to

Exhaustion takes over – me
sleeping in the nav station.

repair the battens and the maintrack slides which had pulled out.
We spent a couple of hours with no wind; it was cold and raining.
Then both the compasses and the sat navs packed up.

I can't begin to write how angry and frustrated I am. Everyone is
down in the dumps – and it is raining again. *Rucanor* is now only
23 miles behind; everyone has caught up. I still don't know where
exactly we are. I got my sleeping bag and snoozed off and on in
the nav station, waiting for a fix. I got one at midnight and then
worked out how much the compasses were out. I gave the watch
a course. Jo is now getting up to do breakfast. I have been up for
19 hours.

November 20th   51'05"S   57'22"E   2,746 miles to go

It is getting warmer; lots of birds now follow us. Meanwhile the
pressure is building on me to do the right thing. The compasses
seem OK; sat nav still on the blink from time to time. We spotted
another iceberg, a large one. The wind is yuk, so is the sea. I got
some weather charts and as a result I am heading north slowly.
Rucanor have given up to go above Kerguelen.

I can't make up my mind, it is one of the most difficult decisions
to make. I think *Equity and Law* are going north too. There is a
high pressure system over us and it is taking its toll. I am now
terrified to use the telex because it seems to screw up the B and
G. We have heard that *Fortuna* has two men injured and that
Schlussel have broken a pole.

Stress and strain all round. The position reports have become
the most important part of the day. We are all getting physically,
emotionally and mentally knackered.

November 21st   50'49"S   60'38"E

The big decision point: which way
round Kerguelen? All went south
of the islands.

I live, eat, breathe, sleep course, course, course. Which way to
go??? I can't believe how pressured I feel. Exploding point is not
far away. Even if *Rucanor* overtake us it will be a release –
something to let the steam off. My stomach is playing up and my
neck is stiff – all the classic symptoms. I just wish this leg was over.
I feel that if we lose we will have let so many people down.

Today started off badly with the wind directly behind us. We
gybed and still had a bad course. The wind kept going back and
forth. *L'Esprit* is still going our way – south of Kerguelen. What a
stupid place to put an island!

There was blue sky today and some sun, fluffy white clouds and a lovely rolling sea. We had a good wind speed – just the wrong direction. Still, everyone was cheered up by the day. The spinnaker tripped itself twice today – bloody dangerous – but the girls have got it down to a fine art in getting it back. The boat is now filthy: it looks like a pig pen.

We got some brilliant speeds today but at the chat show I found out that both *Rucanor* and *L'Esprit* had taken miles from us. I heard Fremantle Sailing Club talking to *Steinlager*. Yippee, there's life out there! During the chat show the reacher went up and we went over very badly. Horror show.

After this date, with the pressures building all the time, Tracy's log becomes more formal, laconic, with the occasional lengthier entry.

November 22   50'54"S   63'02"E

Difficult to steer course; squalls coming through. Large rollers off the quarter with awkward motion. Kerguelen is 76 miles off.

November 23   50'21"S   69'45"E   2,302 miles to go

38 miles south of Kerguelen. Wiped out totally at 03.30 doing 15 knots. Right over on our side, water pouring into the boat. We had a new record recorded speed (by Jeni) of 17.11 knots. The peak wind was 42 knots.

November 24th   47'56"S   82'53"E   1,739 miles to go

I have been like a cat on hot bricks going around Kerguelen, knowing that at any time we could lose the lead. The whole boat was like a time bomb. In the end it was me and Michèle. She told me this was not a race around the buoys. Well, after the last second Whitbread leg I did with *Atlantic Privateer*, when we finished seven minutes in front of *NZI Enterprise* I had to disagree. So we had a screaming match. Everyone agrees I get Bitch of the Leg award. But when we got round Kerguelen there we were still in front – now with a massive advantage. I got worse as I began to realise we really could win this leg.

For three nights now I have not slept. I just toss and turn, wondering if we are doing the course, what the wind is up to –

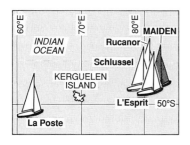

Maiden lengthens her lead as we head north.

even (still) am I doing the right thing? I am confident but my nerves are raw. The *Maiden* bravado is cracking up right now. It got a bit better when we found we had taken more miles out of the others, the weather was better and we did some great surfing with a poled out reacher.

It was perfect Southern Ocean stuff so it's a shame we are now coming out of it. Then the wind dropped again tonight, so I am gritting my teeth waiting for the chat show. *L'Esprit* is beginning to overtake *Rucanor*; in general I can feel them both willing us to make a mistake.

November 25th   48'06"S   82'09"E

Wind all over the place but the sun's out and it's a beautiful day. *L'Esprit* is gaining. Tanja managed over 17 knots today. We don't know exactly how fast as we all shut our eyes.

November 26th   46'44"N   89'55"E   1,523 miles to go

We put the clocks forward today to Australia time. The wind is steady though we are still getting the odd squall. We took miles out of all the others today.

November 27th   45'14"S   92'51"E

It is warm enough to open the hatches. Wind picked up, it was a grey day with rain. *L'Esprit* are 110 behind, *Rucanor* 179 and *Schlussel* 188.

November 28th   43'24"S   97'40"E   1,061 miles to go

We had 56 knots of wind today. We left the spinnaker up as long as we dared. We were hurtling down the waves at breakneck speeds, our hearts in our mouths. When we did take the flanker down, it was gusting as high as 65 knots. We broached twice whilst trying to trip the spinnaker. The mast went completely in the water; the keel was out of the water on the other side. It was terrifying. Water went everywhere, all over the place, all over us. We were gasping and choking in it. Finally, the spinnaker tripped, but by the time we got it down it was in shreds.

It is almost impossible to describe how angry the sea was, how violent the wind. When it had calmed down a little we poled out the blast reacher. By then everyone was soaked through and freezing cold. The compasses are out again.

November 29th 41'21"S 101'48"E 856 miles to go

'When you pass through deep waters, I will be with you. Your troubles will not overwhelm you.' (Isiah)

I haven't been able to write for days. We are now absolutely exhausted. I feel as if I have been walking on a cliff edge in a strong wind for weeks. My emotions are up and down. One minute I am as high as a kite, the next suicidal. The girls are so tired they have to concentrate on not falling asleep the whole time on deck. We eat, sleep, work, eat, sleep, work. As I write this there are 700 miles left. I don't think we could hold on for much longer. Everyone has pushed themselves to their limit; there is still not a whimper of complaint.

These are 11 very special women. We all feel about 20 years older – and look it. The trust we now share is immeasurable. You might know someone all you life and not trust them as much as we do each other. I have seen the most extraordinary acts of selfless caring, heroism, courage, will-power, kindness – and achievement.

If nothing else, we have to win just to vindicate all that. L'Esprit now has not let up for one minute; they wait for us to break the boat or just to break. I have been terrified, ecstatic, depressed, confident, unsure, brave and cowardly. I am ashamed I ever doubted we could do this, proud of myself for the first time in my life, not tearing myself apart for once, or looking for faults. I have finally found all the good bits I knew were there somewhere in me. I think the girls would say the same about themselves.

And, of them, I am so proud I could burst.

Just over three days later *Maiden* crossed the line off the North Mole in Fremantle, first in her division. The next yacht, *Rucanor* came in 30 hours later, giving *Maiden* an overall lead of 16 hours. She was followed closely by *Schlussel* and then *L'Esprit*.

Maiden had not just won this most difficult of legs: she had achieved the best result by a British yacht in the Whitbread for 12 years; and she had nailed her last critics to her mast, with nothing left to say.

For an early Christmas present it could not have been bettered.

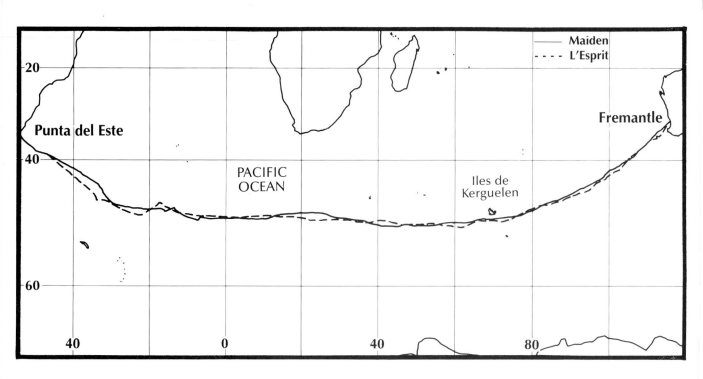

A Summary of Leg Two: The Final Toll

The second leg, said Tracy Edwards to a television reporter in Fremantle, was all we had feared, and all we had hoped it would be. It was as bad as we had expected and as good. Her summation was echoed by every other yachts' crew and skipper.

In Punta the loose talk had been arranged around fear: that the leg was going to prove the Race Committee were wrong in sending the yachts in early in the year; that the competition, especially among the maxis, would ensure those yachts dived south and ran straight into trouble.

In the event some of the maxis did dive south – and found little comfort but not the extreme dangers predicted. Others – including *Maiden* – exercised more caution in their route. They still found themselves in what had been rather melodramatically called the 'screaming fifties' which did not scream so much as the crews, faced with fickle headwinds and sloppy seas.

At the front of the race, among the maxis, the leg was dominated by a small group of leaders, who changed around a little but who had settled at the end into a very similar set of duels between the leading ketches and the leading sloops. Once again, *Steinlager II* eventually beat Grant Dalton's *Fisher and Paykel* into Fremantle.

Immediately behind *Steinlager*, though, came *Merit* and *Rothmans* who together indulged in a fantastic gybing duel up to the finishing line which left *Rothmans* just 28 seconds in front of Pierre Fehlmann's Swiss entry. Lawrie Smith basically tricked Fehlmann into the battle; *Merit* might well have won had she not started to 'cover' *Rothmans*.

Other maxis had at times held the lead, notably *Martela OF*, from Finland. *Fortuna* from Spain had had the fastest daily run at 394 miles. They actually did over 400 miles in this one 24-hour period, but did not break the century old daily distance record for a sailing vessel because the period did not cover the noon to noon traditional measurement period.

After the first four across the line in Fremantle came the ultra-light French maxi, *Charles Jourdan*, then *The Card*, *Martela OF*, *UBF* and *Fortuna*, hampered in the end by the number of injured on board. In 10th place was *Fazisi*, then *Gatorade*, the Italian entry. *British Defender* came a disappointing 12th (they had had more gear failure), then *NCB Ireland*, *Belmont* and the lone division C entry, *Equity and Law II*.

After *Liverpool Enterprise* came *Maiden*, leading division D, followed by *Rucanor Sport* and *Schlussel von Bremen*. Despite the weeks of chasing, *L'Esprit de Liberte* was pipped at the post by the other two division D boats. These three finished within twelve minutes of each other. *With Integrity* came in ahead of *Creightons*; *La Poste*, as ever, brought up the rear.

Altogether (including Claire Russell as a very near miss) six people ended up going overboard; one – Tony Phillips on *Creightons Naturally* – died as a result. Not since the first Whitbread, when three men died in the Southern Ocean, had there been so many injuries, or near deaths. The one fatality ensured that in Fremantle and thereafter this Whitbread would be dominated by concern over safety.

In addition, there was the problem of the cruising entries – *Creightons Naturally* and *With Integrity*. Both yachts suffered from injuries, men overboard, serious gear (including radio) failures which hazarded their crews. *With Integrity* lost several crew in Fremantle because they no longer felt safe on the yacht (and had lost a couple in Punta on the same grounds). The Race Committee ordered a safety check on the yacht – the oldest in the race – as a result.

But, underneath this official level, many other crew and skippers were pondering the wisdom of allowing what were basically amateur yachts to compete in what was now a professional race. In part it came back to the same argument: was this a Corinthian event – as the RNSA people kept insisting – or a world class professional event? If the former then the cruising class might have a place; if the latter then most certainly not.

The Race, then, had begun to fragment some more. It left a general feeling that the Race organisers were not on top of the Race as they ought to be. In fact, in Fremantle, the Race Committee were agreeing they had messed up the handicap system. But they did not intend to change anything for the current race.

Aside from those issues, the leg had been a highly successful one. It had generated a lot of publicity around the world; it had provided more than enough drama. It had, too, proved that the big New Zealand ketches were going to be very hard to beat; and, so it began to emerge, were the girls on *Maiden*.

Fremantle was determined to give the Whitbread fleet a superb reception. Host to the 1987 Americas Cup, the port city, adjunct to Perth, capital of Western Australia now saw itself as a sailing city *par excellence*. It could hardly have been a greater contrast to Uruguay. A modern Aussie city on the western edge of the vast wastes of central Australia; and very, very hot.

The main drawback, which became almost instantly obvious, was that in the scattered suburbs of Fremantle–Perth the 23 crews completely disappeared. Whereas in Punta, arguably, everyone was on top of everyone else, in Fremantle, unless you made a very big effort, you would see no one.

For Tracy, Fremantle ought to have been a triumph. Mostly it was, not least because after all her worries about money, the Royal Jordanian sponsors agreed to provide the further money required to continue through the Race. But there was an underlying unhappiness. Simon Lawrence, her fiancé, had arrived in Fremantle from London the same day as she and *Maiden*. Jet-lagged, he had not provided the welcome she had hoped. Both of them realised that her triumphs might not always quite coincide with his. Tracy, who had been unsure throughout about whether his being at any stop was a good idea, found the whole basis of their future on shakier ground than she had thought. For her, too, it was a recognition that, however much she loved him, he would come second while the Race was on. Simon understood that too, but it hurt. What was beginning to worry him was whether her previous denial that she would ever want to do another Whitbread might not now be changing, the result of the sweet taste of victory.

Fremantle did provide the first hint of what was to come in the way of rewards. The press coverage of *Maiden*'s win was immense, both locally and back home. Tracy found she had been awarded the Royal Ocean Racing Club's rarely given Dennis P. Miller Trophy, for the best performance in any year for a British yacht racing abroad.

At the prize-giving, in the Sailing Club, it turned out to be *Maiden* benefit night. Apart from getting the leg win in division D, *Maiden* was now winning on elapsed time for the two legs combined. Tracy also won Communicator of the Leg award for her radio assistance to *Creightons*; Jo Gooding and Tanja Visser won second prize for their video shots. For the first time in the Race, *Maiden* was being treated as an equal in all respects by other skippers and crews. The last vestiges of patronage had gone.

The yacht had suffered surprisingly little damage in the Southern Ocean. The compasses were checked and found to be the wrong kind; they were replaced. Much effort went into fixing the electronics, especially the sat nav systems. The boat was hauled out and her rudder looked at; as was the mast. The Whitbread insisted that yachts were hauled out, either in Fremantle or in Auckland for 'statutory safety checks'; *Maiden* elected to have hers done in Fremantle.

Mandi spent a lot of time re-splicing worn rigging and sheets. Nancy, as she was to do each time, stripped every one of her 17 winches and cleaned them thoroughly. Everyone else mucked in and did what was needed. There were some notable social events – like the *NCB Ireland/Maiden* party at which the girls first sang a song about the Race. This event was to become a feature as the Race progressed. In Auckland *Maiden* performed their version of *South Pacific* with the guys from *NCBI*.

Everyone in 'Freo' had basked in some of the hottest weather Western Australia had experienced in early summer for years. Yet, despite the shortness of the stay, fretfulness to get going again began to show. For *Maiden*, the pressure was on: they had won the second leg. But was it the only leg they would win? Could Tracy now take *Maiden* and, in a much shorter, more tactical leg, drive the crew and boat to a second victory? It looked unlikely but Tracy, as ever, had a plan.

More than that, she had gained an immeasurable amount of confidence; she knew her yacht, she knew her crew. She knew that, given one or two weather breaks, she could take *Maiden* further out in front.

CHAPTER 7

Runaway

Tracy was 16 in the summer of 1979 when she took off for the hills.

I ran away while my mum was up in Reading visiting relatives and my step-father didn't do anything about it. I went to live with my boyfriend, Chris, in a tent on a hillside about two miles away. It was quite hidden in a gully. I didn't have any money and I used to go and scrounge food off people – it was a ridiculous situation. My friends knew and they were loath to send me back. Trevor thought I was mad, and in the end I began to think so too. You know adults have to be right – I began to think I was quite evil so if I was not there everything would be all right.

When mum came back and said, 'Where's Tracy?' Peter just said, 'She's run away.' She went crazy with fear. She reported it to the police – but they had known where I was the whole time. She said, 'I don't necessarily want her to come back if she doesn't want to, but I want to find her.' This really neat guy, Tom Edwards, came down and said, 'Come on, Tracy, you've got to go home and see your mother, like, because she's really worried about you.'

I went home with him, I insisted he came with me. He said he would come with me, but when we got home mum wasn't there, which was really unfortunate. I walked in and Tom said to Peter, 'Tracy's willing to come back but you've got to stop being so nasty to her.' He said, 'Oh, I never am, she does all this to herself.'

I couldn't believe that this was an adult lying. I was thinking maybe I really am round the twist. Then Peter said, 'To tell you the truth, I don't want her back.' Tom said, 'Well, her mother wants her here.'

Anyway, Tom left and I had my sleeping bag with me and Peter said, 'This door gets shut at 11pm, and whether you're in or out makes no difference to me, but whatever you decide we are going to stick by it.' I looked in and thought – I don't think I can bear being locked up in there with this man – so I just took my things and went off again. I was gone another month. As far as Mum was concerned, she was happier knowing I was with Chris and safe rather than at home fighting Peter.

She and Chris had camped in the ruins of an old Welsh fort; the spot was heartbreakingly beautiful, but the atmosphere was sinister. Tracy recalls: 'There had been a great battle and thousands had been slaughtered. We used to think we could hear the sounds of people breathing in the night. What it was, of course, was sheep, but we never stopped to think about that.' Occasionally it got so frightening that they ran back to their friends' farmhouse, down in the valley.

On other occasions during what never ceased to be a stormy relationship, Tracy would stalk out of the tent alone; pride would keep her away longer than commonsense or her own fear of the dark secrets of the hill fort dictated. On the whole though it was a period more touched by farce than tragedy.

But, behind the summer's comings and goings lay important decisions. Tracy, in the end, had to go back and face living in the same house as Peter. Her solution was to leave her clothes there, and her belongings, but basically never inhabit the place. She drifted from house to house, taken in by sympathetic friends.

She had left school that summer, with a clutch of 'O' levels – no surprise to her but a source of wonderment among her teachers. Had they misjudged this wild and unruly girl?, they asked each other.

For a week, in the autumn, she tried secretarial college but it was no good. She simply could not settle to the idea of work being like this. After her adventures in the local hills, her horizons were beginning to expand. She and Chris made plans, worked in various jobs, mostly in bars, as the autumn gave way to winter. By early 1980 they knew what they were going to do.

'She came to me,' says Pat of this moment, 'and said, "I'm going to Greece." I had to swallow hard, give her a pat on the back, as she sallied forth with about £30 in her pocket. I had asked her "Have you got a job?" and she said, "No," She told me she'd find one when she got there, as a waitress. I think she got one the night she arrived and then she graduated to working in a bar.' For Pat this was one of the worst moments but she toughed it out, as Tracy had learned to do before and, to her triumph, in the future.

It was in February, 1980 that Tracy and Chris finally took off for

Athens and the unknown. Halfway through her 17th year she was young for her age, although beginning to get streetwise with a rapidity which startled her, as well as those around her.

She had arranged for a job as an au pair in Greece, as a sensible course of action; 'I made the mistake of telling the family that Chris was coming too,' she says ruefully, 'and they said, forget it.' Faced with no immediate job prospects, she and Chris went nonetheless, on February 29th, 1980.

It was to prove a suitable day. Tracy did not propose to Chris, as women traditionally do on that day, but she was to take charge both of him, and of her own life. They found a cheap hotel to stay in while they sorted out jobs and a more permanent place to live.

We arrived in Athens and we got a taxi to Plaka in the city. We each had about three suitcases, quite ridiculous, and I wasn't feeling at all well. We had no idea where we were going, we must have looked like a pair of idiots. I phoned home and I had to try hard not to cry; I just said everything was fine.

We spent the next few days spending far too much and we had to find a cheaper place to stay. I remember it was in Niki Street, and things had got so tight we ended up sleeping on the roof. But by then I had found a job working in a restaurant – it was called the Erato and it was an Italian restaurant run by Greeks. They were lovely, crazy people. The manager, Angelos, adopted me – he had children about my age. His family really took me under their wing. The cook there had worked on a sailing boat, years before and the mast had come down and hit him on the head. He used to get lapses of memory. His doctor had told them that whenever this happened he had to stand quite still until things started coming back; so he did, wherever he was – even in the middle of the road. I remember too, that he used to come into the kitchen and open the fridge door and talk to the food: 'Hello, chicken, how are you? Hello, spaghetti, how are you? and so on all through the shelves.'

She liked her job and she worked hard. Chris **used to** come and meet her at the end of the day and drink at the bar until she finished, usually around 2.00am. But one thing that began to worry Tracy was that Chris seemed unable to get or hold down a job.

I started to find that I was really in charge, more and more, and that I could handle it. I found us a flat to rent; I had a job so I paid

111

the rent. I came home, did the washing and the cooking; I took care of everything. I had believed for years that I was just wasted space, now I found out that maybe I wasn't.

They decided, after a while, to leave the city and go out to explore the islands. Like so many travellers in Greece before and since, the journey was a revelation. On their way south they met a true traveller, a man called Shacks, who taught them how to survive: where to look for work in the islands, where to sleep, what places and people to avoid. 'When he met us, he must have thought how stupid we were,' says Tracy.

They were learning fast. They meandered across to Crete, the southernmost Greek island to pick olives; they explored other tiny scattered jewels in the Greek crown. And then, at the end of the summer, they grew sick for home. They came back to Athens, sold all their surplus clothes in the flea market and flew home. Tracy went back to Wales where her step-father's greeting drove her more or less immediately away – to Reading and her aunt and uncle. It was around this time that Pat divorced Peter and also moved back to Reading.

Tracy began to wonder anew what it was she wanted to do. Her first thoughts were to revive her acting ambitions and through that winter she went to auditions – none of them successful. Meanwhile she worked in pubs around Pangbourne, living with a group of students for a while. Chris had moved to London.

By now she and Chris were at breaking point. When Tracy decided, in the spring of 1981, to return to Greece, it was fairly certain Chris would not go with her. She left on her own, this time very much in charge of herself. She went to see Chris's uncle, George Rees in Athens, who pointed her to a job in a marina – Zhea Marina hard by the port of Athens, Piraeus.

The marina was a bizarre mixture of ecstasy and agony. On the one hand it was packed with luxury yachts, motor and sailing, which Tracy used to fantasise about. On the other, the bar also filled with a curious mix of the dead rich and the dead beat, the latter largely expats with nowhere to go.

Tracy was earning 'truckloads' of money and she had a flat over the bar where she worked, as part of the deal. She shared it with a girl who was dating a crew member on one of those luxury yachts – *Blue Jacket* – and Tracy's growing interest in them was, in part, stimulated by what she overheard.

Three months passed happily. Tracy began to feel she could live there for the rest of her life. But she was canny enough to notice that, while she was having a good time, many others were not. One of her other friends, for instance, who had a Greek boyfriend, was regularly beaten up by him. The area around the marina was a dangerous place for women. Prostitution, and all the problems associated with it, lurked like a ghost at the feast.

One night, the skipper of one of the yachts she had noticed sliding in and out of the marina on various charters, came into her bar. He came straight up to her: 'Fancy a change?' he asked. His name was Mike Corns, he was the skipper of a 100ft luxury yacht, *Kovalam* built in Britain in the 1920s. Tracy hardly had to think before she said yes.

The yacht was leaving next day on its new charter. She packed her things and joined later that night. The most important decision she had made in her life had gone by, as so often happens, without a second to mark its passage.

She was taken on as a stewardess. Luxury yachts, of all shapes and sizes, exist all over the world. Many are the exclusive plaything of the rich and super-rich. The cost of maintenance, the cost of crews, the harbour dues – all can be crippling.

But, aside from the oil magnates, the shipping tycoons, the city slickers who want to impress (perhaps just themselves), there exist a huge number of luxury vessels whose main purpose is for charter. They may be owned by individuals, they may be owned by companies set up to be in this business. They provide an expensive but exclusive way for the not-quite-so-rich to see the coasts of the countries wherever they roam. They need skippers and engineers and crew, just like their private counterparts.

It was into this world that Tracy had now plunged, utterly unprepared for what she was about to find.

Tired after a long day's work aboard *Kovalam*.

> I'd give anything a go and went along on the trip just to see what it was like. Frankly, it was awful. Stewardess is the most thankless, revolting job in the world. You are waitress and chambermaid at the same time and still expected to do the sailing and watches like anyone else. I was sea-sick again. I thought I'd never get over it.

She was violently and repeatedly sick. So bad was this – and it kept on happening – that she seriously began to think she might not be able to continue. But Mike Corns liked her and she did her job well. He decided to step in.

Sea-sickness among sailors is so common that most conversations among them turn to it sooner or later. The main discussion centres around cures, and the dangers of that minority of sea-farers who dismiss sea-sickness as the complaint of the weak. Tracy was to learn this over the months that followed, but at first she believed its onset disqualified her from being part of this happy band, roaming the Mediterranean.

Mike would not let her take sea-sickness pills; he also made her eat with the rest of the crew, even though she often had to rush on deck after to throw it all up. By keeping food moving through her stomach he kept her from gagging on air; by making her drink he kept her from the most deadly of sea-sickness effects – dehydration. That, and Tracy's persistence, got her over it.

When she came round, so to speak, she could hardly believe her luck. They roamed the Greek islands – and beyond, to Italy, to Yugoslavia and Turkey. They took on board a wide variety of charter parties; all were fun to be with; many Tracy is in touch with still.

Tracy had found her medium.

> When I wasn't up to my elbows in water or feeling sick I enjoyed it. It gave me the idea for the first time that I wanted to be on boats – but not as a stewardess. For the time being there didn't seem to be any other option and I went from charter to charter all around the Med: Greece, Italy, all over the place. *Kovalam* was home for the rest of the summer and the next year I was back for another season.
>
> In 1982, I was dropped off in Palma, Majorca, and rented a flat. I was hooked and decided that if I was going to make a career of working on boats I was going to get to the top.

Tracy left *Kovalam* and started day work on any yacht that would have her; beginning with a replica galleon, *Dolphin*. She moved, meanwhile, into a flat onshore, where she met many other yachtsmen who were to become part of her life in the coming years, among them Neil Cheston and Mike Bastenie. Mike was to sail with her on *Atlantic Privateer*. Now she had moved to an entirely different part of the sea-faring world: the sailing yachts looked down on the motor yachts. It had long been so. Joseph Conrad, writing a hundred years ago, compared a steam tug pulling a sailing bark out of an Indian river to a black beetle, allowed to crawl in front of a supreme being.

Tracy had long been aware of this. Often when *Kovalam* had come into port they had had to endure the jibes of yachtsmen and women, laughing at the 'gin palace' moored alongside. Now she began, dimly, to see why. And she devised a project: she would 'cross the pond' – traverse the Atlantic on one of these magnificent boats.

Most people come to yachting through day-sailing, perhaps on the south coast, more likely in the nursery of British sailing, The Solent. Tracy, never the conventional, proposed to introduce herself to this universe by a rite of passage that would have startled Columbus: a mere 3,800 mile hike across one of the toughest oceans in the world.

Undaunted by any fore-knowledge, she set out to find how to get a berth. She was faced with hundreds of rivals, many with vast experience and equal determination. Many, too, knew skippers, and that counted a lot more than Tracy was, initially, prepared for.

One day, the skipper of the yacht she had been working on told her that another yacht, *Southern Star*, had a spare berth. Tracy rushed over to see. When she got there the skipper of *Southern Star*, John, and his girlfriend, Browne, agreed there was space but, they said, we're looking for a couple.

Tracy didn't pause for breath; 'I am a couple,' she said, 'wait here,' and she rushed back into Palma to the local yachties bar, Mams, found a Dutch guy, Marcel, whom she knew wanted to cross over, informed him he was the other half of the couple and took him, bemused but not protesting, back to *Southern Star* and its waiting skipper. 'They knew what I had done but they decided to take us. We started day-working on *Southern Star* to get her ready for the crossing.'

They left, in the company of a number of other yachts, in late October. Their first port of call was Gibraltar, where they were stormed in for nine days. While they waited they explored the rock, flew over to Morocco for a day in a light plane they had chartered, and bought a parrot they called Rocky.

Eventually they were able to leave. 'The delivery was the best thing I had done,' says Tracy now. 'We went straight across; I thought it was wonderful.' The yacht was an old one, a 76ft sloop. She was beautifully made, superbly fitted out. Although the motion of a sailing yacht gave Tracy another bout of sea- sickness, the thrill of the silent passage, spinnaker flying out ahead, made up for any discomfort.

Once she was over her illness she was able to join in the fun. There were fancy dress parties, songs to sing to a guitar accompaniment, fish to catch and eat. Rocky the parrot amused himself, she remembers, by steadily eating his way through the saloon down below. They stayed in company with the other yachts and she never felt alone, even in the vastness of the mid-Atlantic.

They arrived in Antigua the day of the agent's show at the turn of the year, 1982. Each year the yachts' crews entertain the agents who get the charters for them, with a variety show. As they anchored in English Harbour Tracy could hear the sounds of people having a good time. She already believed herself to be at the gates of paradise; now the trumpets were sounding for her to come on in.

She did not worry that she was now going to have to leave *Southern Star* which was to start chartering almost immediately. She had arrived in the Caribbean; she was at the start of a whole new life; she was among friends. Someone would provide.

Now a different kind of apprenticeship was to begin. She had learned to cope with the sea, and then the ocean. She was beginning to learn seamanship – the art of moving boats around. On her Atlantic crossing she had begun to learn the art of sailing – and had taken to it. Here, in Antigua, she was to become a member of that fraternity of professional yachtsmen and women, the boat niggers, who would provide the bedrock for her career: as fellow workers, as professionals willing to teach her their ways, and as friends, on whom she could, and would, call on one day for help.

The International Boat Nigger's uniform!

CHAPTER 8

Triumph

The re-start from Fremantle was on December 23rd, 1989. The day began with blustery winds. As the yachts set sail and prepared for the start, a series of heavy squalls began to blow through from the west. Rain fell and what might have been a brilliant regatta turned into a stormy summer's day. For *Maiden*, however, the conditions could not have been better.

LEG THREE

FROM FREMANTLE TO

AUCKLAND, NEW ZEALAND,

3,434 NAUTICAL MILES,

DECEMBER 23RD, 1989–

JANUARY 8TH, 1990

December 23rd   Fremantle

What a brilliant start. Most of the yachts came past us and cheered before we started. We were right up with the maxis, between *Steinlager* and *F and P*: I looked one way and could see Peter Blake looking down at me; then I looked the other way, and there was Grant (Dalton).

The weather was very squally and we were on a beat up to the first mark. *L'Esprit* and *Rucanor* were behind, *Schlussel* just in front. Just by tacking properly we managed to get ahead of the rest and led the division D boats down the coast.

December 24th   34′47″S   115′34″E

The electronic compass is ten degrees out. The radar was very iffy as we went round Cape Naturaliste. To tell the truth, I have hardly ever been more frightened than going round this Cape. I couldn't get a sat nav fix. Then I looked at the chart and there were these two reefs and they were right where we were. The wind then dropped and it eventually came aft.

We came round Cape Leeuwin at 8.00 in the morning – missed the chat show. *Schlussel* was to port and losing ground to us. They appeared to have stopped in the night; we actually wondered if they had hit the reefs. The weather was cloudy. In the evening I changed course to a more southerly one to get the wind and to cover *Rucanor* and *L'Esprit*.

This is such a weird leg; people are already asking me how long it is before we get into Auckland. It feels too much like a delivery – getting the boat there so we can get stuck into the next proper leg. Even I am thinking a bit like this. It is going to be very difficult to get everyone motivated and to keep boat speed up.

December 25th   34'03"S   119'54"E

I have picked what is really a great circle course to Tasmania; but I am also going to keep south. It is much cooler now at night. This morning it was a lovely day with sun, blue sky.

Christmas! Jo and I got up early and got the stockings filled and the champagne ready. We put them by their bunks: Tanja and Michèle didn't know what they were. Everyone had a great time opening them: it was like a kids' Christmas, with wrappers everywhere, and streamers – Nancy in her bunk drinking champagne. Everyone was really amazed. At the chat show at 11.00am everyone was chatting and having fun.

We had a lot of maxis calling us up – they did it all along on this leg – usually to ask about the weather.

December 26th   38'54"S   124'00"E

Today was grey and cold with a light wind. The barometer was steady, though. It is getting cold. It keeps shifting around too, so nothing has changed. We seem to find these conditions wherever we go: is there never going to be a steady wind for us on this Race? Trying to understand the weather pattern around here is difficult. There are just a succession of highs with fronts suddenly bursting across us; you can time them almost to the minute – then they are gone.

December 27th   40'03"S   128'58"E

We are doing our course but we have been sitting in the middle of a high pressure region. Then this evening I heard from La Poste that they had 45 knots of wind. We copped it later; the wind kept on coming up all through the night till it reached around 45 knots.

We had a third reef in; because the second reef line had broken, Michèle had to go to the end of the boom to fix it. The thing has been that although we found the wind, it chose to come from ahead, as usual.

But we are ahead – just – two miles from *Schlussel* and *L'Esprit*, and seven from *Rucanor*.

December 28th   41'25"S   131'54"E   2,353 miles to go

It was grey, misty and damp today but, very slowly, the wind started to go aft. All the division D boats are very close together now. It is getting to be a strain, sailing like this. Tanja mended the main reefing line. Dawn got the generator working. At last, this evening, we got the spinnaker up; about time. When in the evening the spinnaker tripped itself and while Tanja was trying to sort it out the clew of the sail flicked into her eye.

She was very lucky, it just missed, but she had a very deep gash. Claire had to stitch it while Jo held a torch on her face. Watching Claire do it was very gruesome. About this time I discovered that the log was beginning to go backwards. Boat speed is still up, tonight, and we have a good course. The sky is clear.

There has been a lot of moaning and whining; it is just a general feeling of discontent. I think having *Schlussel* and *L'Esprit* so close is getting to people. It's not true of Dawn – she just wants to win,

I pointed the camera but I had to look away.

119

the whole time. If someone has a suggestion she's happy to take it up and try it. We are sitting between fronts right now. The wind is all over the place. *Schlussel* were off our port bow.

December 30th   43'01"S   140'10"E   1,889 miles to go

I set the boat's clock forward to New Zealand time. We did OK today although the high pressure is nearly on us. We are still just holding the lead; although *Schlussel* is keeping up, both *L'Esprit* and *Rucanor* are behind. They are trying so hard, though.

December 31st   43'57"S   143'54"E   1,767 miles to go

We have the heavy No. 1 and a full main up, but then changed down to the No. 3 as the wind came right up. The barometer started to plummet and the wind kept shifting back and forth. It was a grey day; we were doing a lousy speed and I just can't shake the other yachts off. In the evening we had Tasmania to port; it got very cloudy.

At midnight we opened a bottle of champagne and celebrated the start of the new decade.

January 1st   43'28"S   149'18"E

What a day. There are two low pressures heading for us. We may miss the next high. In the morning we have a good speed with the wind coming aft. Later in the morning we gybed; we were doing a good course and speed. Then the spinnaker tripped; it took everyone to get it back together. I had gone up to help, not really thinking. The next thing I knew I was swept off the deck as the spinnaker re-filled. No harness, no life-jacket: after all my telling the girls never to be on deck like that. I only just avoided going in the water. Angela grabbed me, thank God, and dragged me back onto the deck.

Mikki was getting over 19 knots out of the boat with just the main up. When we put the reacher up Tanja pushed the speed to over 20 knots. How differently we all perceive danger now. Everybody is so much more confident of themselves and in everybody else's ability. Where we would take the spinaker down in 40 knots, now we take it down in 50 knots.

Rucanor is now 30 miles behind and *Schlussel* 19 miles. But *L'Esprit* is only a mile away.

January 2nd   41'00"S   154'09"E   1,271 miles to go

I called up *NCB Ireland* to wish Paul a happy birthday only to find they had broken their boom – again; they are very fed up indeed. We are now in a high pressure system. The strain of being so close all the time is getting to me. I know I had covered myself in Australia by telling people we probably wouldn't win this leg, but here we are with a very good chance. I am anxious we don't fall into a hole with no wind and throw this chance we have away. But I am much more confident in myself that we can win this one. My old neck problem has started.

January 3rd   41'00"S   158'10"E   1,081 miles to go

I was right about the strain. When I woke up my neck was a little bit better but I had such a stomach ache. So today I was completely out of action – in absolute agony for 12 hours. I just lay in my bunk and let Dawn take over. Claire was very worried – which hardly helped me. She asked me what I normally did when I got like this and I said I drink milk – fat chance of that. We had really dreadful wind and weather today. Ugh, ugh! I wish it was all

Jo and Dawn get the No. 1 Heavy ready to go up. When wet these sails are incredibly heavy to move.

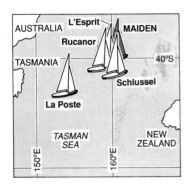

Maiden reaches the coast of New Zealand first and keeps her lead.

over. Everybody is the same – we none of us want to be out here a second longer than necessary. Today has been beating, beating.

January 4th   39'19"S   162'47"E   841 miles to go

We had a lot of wind today: we were beating with about 40 knots right on the nose. Absolutely dreadful: three reefs in with a No. 3.

L'Esprit was right next to us, suddenly. She was coming right out of the water as she shifted ahead. Then she passed ahead and swung to starboard. Right at that point she dropped her main – we found out the main halyard had gone. Her course was not as good as ours, though. We just carried on bashing our brains out.

They were steadily losing to us as the wind came. We then spotted them behind us and to starboard. We have been doing a straight course and they have basically circumnavigated us. The front went through: quite incredible. One minute it was behind us, the next ahead. When *British Defender* called up later to ask when it had gone through and I told him that it went through at 10:19am. He said back 'that definite, huh?' and I just said, 'right'.

L'Esprit had played her last card. In trying to take *Maiden* she had had to travel many more miles. The next day the French yacht was seven miles behind; slowly, but with growing confidence, Tracy knew she could win this, the 'impossible' leg.

January 5th   37'26"S   166'53"E   625 miles to go

The barometer was steadier this morning and the seas were less confused.

Today we sailed with *Schlussel* – again. When we first saw a boat off the starboard beam we weren't sure who they were. They dropped back with their spinnaker up, but we held our position against them the whole time we could see them. From what we could see they were pointing far too high. We lost them in the evening.

When we gybed this evening it was a bit hairy. Lots of wind.

January 6th   35'04"S   171'10"E   398 miles to go

We are racing a high pressure system. In the early evening we spotted land ahead – New Zealand! If only we can hold on. We

122

managed to reach with the spinnaker. At 8.00pm we rounded Cape Reinga at the tip of New Zealand: just about 200 miles left. We went quite into the coast which could have been a very stupid thing to do – we might have lost all the wind.

We have been pottering along to North Cape right under the cliffs. We came round at 10.00: we could see *Creightons* coming in. *L'Esprit* were nine miles, *Schlussel* 13 and *Rucanor* 30 miles behind. Everybody has been coming on deck and looking astern – it is almost as if we are sailing backwards, at least by the direction in which people keep looking.

January 7th Running down the east coast of North Island

As it got light this morning I thought we could start coming in; that's when we lost the wind and then, suddenly, I saw *L'Esprit* and *Rucanor* coming out. They couldn't see us because we were up sun. Then the wind shifted; they didn't use it as well as us. Phew! We managed to shake them off a little.

I decided we had to keep off as far as possible to keep the wind. We have been getting about eight knots from the boat. I have been praying all the time that *L'Esprit* and *Schlussel* would keep in close but I have had a nerve-racking day. All the division D boats are so close. I have been up now since Friday (about 48 hours).

We have had the spinnaker up, ghosting along. Then, just before the finish the wind really dropped. We cut inside the islands which is something I wouldn't have done unless I had had Mandi. Because she knows this area so well it was simple – and safe. When it got dark we had about 25 miles to go.

I forgot to report in to the Race Office at 25 miles. When I finally did at 15 miles, *L'Esprit* were just reporting their 25 miles to go. We knew then we had done it. In fact they were much closer – only six miles because they had got their position wrong.

Mandi's local knowledge came in handy.

Maiden made the line just 57 minutes ahead of *L'Esprit*, at 12.27am on the morning of the 8th January. Tracy, now very tired, knew she had done more than win the leg. She believed that she might well have won the Whitbread now.

The half dozen yachts and launches surrounding her as her crew flaked down the mainsail and stowed the spinnaker had all left Princes' Wharf a couple of hours earlier. There had been a Sunday evening bustle – no more. The wharfage in Auckland opens more or less directly on to the town; access to the Whitbread areas, the arrival pontoon, the yachts themselves, was relatively free and easy.

Maiden's shore crew, with the Royal Jordanian girls, powered away from *Maiden* to make final preparations for *Maiden's* berthing. When the launch turned back into the area of Princes' Wharf one of the team casually remarked about the number of birds settled on the roof of the wharf's main shed. 'That's not a flock of birds,' came the reply, 'that's people!'

In the two hours away something in the order of 14,000 people had gathered – they occupied every inch of space on the dockside, they crowded along the roofs of the buildings, they spilled over into the streets of Auckland. This was the scene, eerily silent, that *Maiden* glided into, a half hour after finishing the leg.

'It was just unbelievable,' said Tracy later. 'We just could not grasp how many people had come to see us in.' For New Zealand rigger, Mandi Swan, it was the crowning moment of her Race. She admitted that after this the rest of the Whitbread would be just like a delivery. There was something of this feeling for all of them. The City of Sails had taken *Maiden* to their hearts.

There was more to this triumphal entry. Before she left Fremantle, Tracy had admitted she felt it unlikely they could win the third leg. The expected wind conditions, with a lot of beating, the shortness of the leg, the tactical considerations and her own tiredness, all would seem to conspire against success. To triumph here, then, was pure magic.

Auckland had always been a very special place for Tracy. In her first Whitbread, in 1985, it had been here that she had come after her first leg on *Atlantic Privateer*, itself the unexpected winner of the leg. She had recalled just how big a welcome Kiwis could put on, never fully believing it was going to happen for her. Now it had.

She knew that she had been nominated for Yachtsman of the Year – an award given by the Association of British Yachting Journalists. But 1989 had been a busy year for British yachts and, in truth, she never thought she would win. To add to her general euphoria, Howard took her on one side, shortly after this arrival, and told her: 'you've won it'. Tracy had no need to ask what.

On Tuesday, January 19th, in front of television cameras beaming their signals back to the London International Boat Show live, Peter Montgomery, a veteran New Zealand radio and television yachting commentator, stood on the Whitbread stage by the dock and related the story of the Yachtsman of the Year Award. He pointed out it had never been won by a woman in its 35 years. Finally, Peter read out the names of previous winners. Tracy, unashamedly, started weeping. The names included Adlard Coles, Eric Hiscock, Sir Francis Chichester, Sir Alec Rose, Edward Heath, Rob James, Robin Knox-Johnston, Chay Blyth, Eric Tabarly, Harold Cudmore.

The award signalled many things, not least as it was handed to Tracy by Peter Blake, the lion of New Zealand yachting, a friend and the skipper of *Steinlager II*, which would win the Race for the maxis. Above all, for *Maiden* it meant that the project had finally been handed the most public accolade of a serious professional organisation. It was for her tenacity in putting the project together that Tracy had – in part – been given the prize.

The award was vindicated by *Maiden*'s third leg win – but the decision had been taken after *Maiden* had won the second leg only. For Howard and Tracy it was more than that, though.

I turned round and looked at the crew and the shore team.
Without them I could not have reached this point, got this award.
It made us all feel very, very proud.

A Day in the Life of Maiden

❛While we are sailing everything is moving. The yacht is bouncing from wave to wave and, depending on the wind, it is either corkscrewing from side to side, or over on its ear – or both.

On this leg the wind was blowing largely on one or other side. You thought you had your balance and then you'd over-correct and crash into something. I think we collected more bangs and bruises than on any other leg.

Everything is so hard to do. Say you are in the top bunk on the windward side, the first thing you have to do is to work out how to get from there to the floor without breaking your neck. When the bunk is braced up there is very little room anyway. It's like planning a campaign. Then, when you do manage to get out you invariably hit your shins on the metal frame round the sails.

If the boat has tacked in the night you'd find someone would have moved your boots or your socks: you can't find them anywhere. These little things become really important. Getting dressed is always a nightmare, trying to balance yourself with one hand while putting on layer after layer of clothing. Of course, we never fully undressed, keeping on a couple of layers of thermals. But you have to take most of your clothes off because otherwise you simply get colder and colder. When you come off watch you have to spend about another half hour getting out of those same clothes.

Once I got my clothes on I would stagger along to the nav station – collecting a cup of something warm from Jo in the galley. In the nav station I'd have to try to hold down all my charts, ruler, dividers, pencil as the boat thrashed around. You have to be a contortionist as well as a navigator: hanging on to everything and plotting the positions. And as it is the communications centre, the electrical breakers are here, and many of the boat's other main switches; people are constantly asking me to switch this on, switch that off!

One of the hardest things I have to cope with is working on GMT (Greenwich Mean Time) whatever local time we had on deck. So my life was always weirdly at variance with the girls. For weather faxes, for radio communication with home, for satellite passes and even for the chat shows, all those were operating on GMT. It makes things very confusing. On this leg, for instance, I am twelve hours behind everyone on the boat. I get into port and suffer from jet lag!

There is no privacy on board – and it doesn't matter to us. For instance, in hot weather after a couple of days I really think none of us 'see' whether the person they are talking to has clothes on or not. I am not sure whether the boys on the other yachts are quite so relaxed although they all strip off like us. But I think, maybe, they value their privacy in a way we don't seem to worry about. Women, in this respect, are much more adaptable.

Life goes on all through the sailing. There's Jo just opposite me, cooking lunch. But at any moment we might all be called out on deck to get sails up or down or cope with some emergency or other.

Just now, for instance. I was waiting to call in to the duty boat – *Equity and Law* – when we were all called up on deck. I had been feeling the boat about to go, right on the edge for some time, as I was sitting here. Suddenly we are all on deck changing the spinnaker. That was over, I came back down and then, wallop, we finally broached.

When I got back on the radio I heard all the other division D yachts explain why they had failed to call in like us: broached, wave down hatch, mainsail blown out – then us, broached. To cap it all, and really this made the whole thing very funny, when I apologised to *Equity and Law* they said, 'don't worry we weren't listening as we've just broached too.'

Then we're back to what we were doing before – for the lucky ones, a few hours snatched sleep. You get used to sleeping for short periods – if you are lucky for as much as three hours.

When I am in my nav station, I have reached the point where I can feel everything that is going on: I no longer have to look to know who is steering, who is on the winches, what sails we have up, how the boat is moving through the water – even whether we are on course or not. I feel I am at the centre of this small universe.

That makes it strange when I – or any of us – get to hear what's happening in the world outside. We often listen to the BBC World Service and, particularly in this Race, so much seems to have been going on out there – like the Berlin wall coming down. You feel detached from it all, though obviously excited by the good news, brought down hard by the bad.

We miss some things terribly, though, being out here. I miss cold milk and apples – something to crunch on. The freeze-dried food we eat to save boat weight and space. The first time you eat it you think it is OK but what gets to you is the lack of variety. We have a choice of four types of breakfast, five lunches and about a dozen suppers. But, remember, that's for the whole Race.

Because the food is re-constituted with water, it is very mushy so your teeth and gums suffer: when you get back on land it's agony when you first bite on something hard – or when you eat an ice-cream.

We all miss different things. Some of the girls miss meat; some fish. We don't angle for fresh fish because the line in the water would slow us down – although only about 0.3 of a knot that makes a lot of difference over 33,000 miles.

On leg two we put a lot of chocolate on board – but that was to help keep our energy levels up. The Southern Ocean is a great place for a diet. It's the cold and the pain.

But, although we are in the fresh air, it is not necessarily healthy. Wounds don't heal easily. Our skins suffer terribly from boils and sores – partly not changing clothes for weeks at a time, partly the salt and the accumulated dirt. Curiously, your hair doesn't seem to suffer from not being washed. I suppose it is the natural oil staying in place instead of being washed out.

We are physically very strong now. Yet when we get into port we can hardly stagger up the road before we are exhausted. The top of your body is being used all the time but from the waist down, you waste away. I have taken to doing leg exercises on the floor just outside the nav station.

All in all, life on trans-ocean races is very hard but we are all so comfortable with each other. It is that wonderful feeling of being a team, being together, fighting and conquering these elemental conditions that wins every time. **,**

Tracy on her crew

Angela and I didn't get on temperamentally, at first, because we are so alike, but we have had plenty of time to talk it over and sort it out. Now we get on fine. She is great on deck and inventive when it comes to solving problems down below. She laughs a lot and is bubbly and lively, often putting on one-woman shows on deck to cheer us up.

Her worst point – she keeps on disagreeing with me! Her best – she makes people happy.

Claire is a wonderful doctor, very practical and confident. She learned to sail more quickly than anyone I have ever known. Her obsession with learning has driven her to find out everything that has been going on and why. She has never shown if she has been down or sad; she has kept a happy face throughout.

Her worst point: no sympathy for the injured! Her best point: her irrepressible good nature.

Dawn is one of those few people who push themselves to the limit all the time – and then, when you ask for a bit more, gives it. She is a practical person and a logical sailor. It takes time to get to know her but when you do it is worth the effort. She has become one of my very closest friends during this Race.

Time after time she saved us from disaster with the generator, the water-maker (her personal no. 1 hate!). Her talent for bodging repairs is amazing. Her worst attribute is eating peanut butter and jelly sandwiches!

Jeni has been the hardest to get to know, but that has been because she is getting to know herself. She didn't have much sailing experience when she joined *Maiden* but she is now competent and confident in all aspects of sailing. When Jeni smiles everyone smiles. She does not suffer fools gladly and is as tough on herself.

Her talent is her patience to dissect any problem with great care and to understand how to reach a solution.

Her worst point is that she is a brilliant mathematician and she puts me to shame as I'm still counting on my fingers!

Jo has been my best friend since school. She has the wonderful quality of seeing good in everyone; consequently, she is always getting stamped on. Then she picks herself up and starts again with a smile. She is, really, a good person, bouncy, sparkling, kind and a very good and solid friend. Jo has been the saviour of the nav station equipment: she laughs when I get angry with it and stops me breaking anything when I am in a temper.

Her talent is in making people feel good; her worst point is, definitely, laughing when you are trying to lose your temper!

Mandi is the joker of the crew, a character and a half. She laughs at herself more than at others. She does everything in a different way, whatever it might be, to everyone else. She would stand out in a crowd just because of that. She is either very quiet or exceptionally loud and funny. She is, incidentally, an extremely talented rigger, very conscientious at her work.

Her talent is in breaking into pregnant pauses while her worst point is totally ignoring you, should she feel like it.

Michèle has been a constant source of surprises. I had feared she would miss her friend Marie-Claude but she is so professional that this has not affected her sailing. She has given 100 per cent all the time and she has taught the less experienced of the crew valuable lessons. She is fearless yet sensible. She has learned to speak English in a year and she has a great sense of humour.

Her worst point is her inability to open up. Her best point is her wonderful misuse of words, accompanied by an infectious laugh.

Mikki joined late but managed to fit in immediately. A very experienced sailor she never pushed her ideas on anyone else but she has made herself a valuable part of the team. She has a very dry sense of humour that has had me in stitches in some horrendous conditions. She is such a lovely open person I feel very close to her now, even though she is the only person I've ever met to match my temper.

Her best point is her warmth and sincerity. Her worst? She doesn't sulk as long as me after an argument!

Nancy was the first to join *Maiden* and she has helped me through some rough times – as well as help me re-design the boat at refit. Nancy is one of the nicest people I have ever met. She is easy going open and warm. She puts up with anyone, anywhere, any time. She is delightfully eccentric – the only person I know who can combine knitting with sailing. But there is a lot more to Nancy than meets the eye. She is a very talented sailor.

Her greatest talent is in saying the wrong thing at the wrong time. Her worst point is in forgiving you and making you feel even worse!

Sally is the most dependable person I know, she is as solid as a rock. You know that when you need someone or things get really tough, Sally will be there, no matter what. She has had a tough few years recently and yet she still finds time for everyone. She'll listen even when you know you're being boring. She is funny and witty – always seeing the amusing in everything. But – never – get on her wrong side.

Her greatest talent is in making you feel that what you are doing is worth the effort. Her worst point, funnily enough, is her honesty, especially in crowded places!

Sarah slotted in quietly and confidently, although it was difficult to do just the third leg with the crew already a tight knit group. She was good humoured and always did her share. We all have enjoyed her company very much.

Tanja doesn't stop moving and she is into everything one hundred per cent. If I had to use a phrase to describe her it would be 'perpetual motion'. She never does things by halves and, as a perfectionist, she expects the best from everyone else around. Tanja is fun on shore with what appears to be a mild character but woe betide you if you step on her toes on the boat.

She is a very talented sailmaker.

Her greatest talent? mixing up her sentences in English; her worst point – she's a dentist!

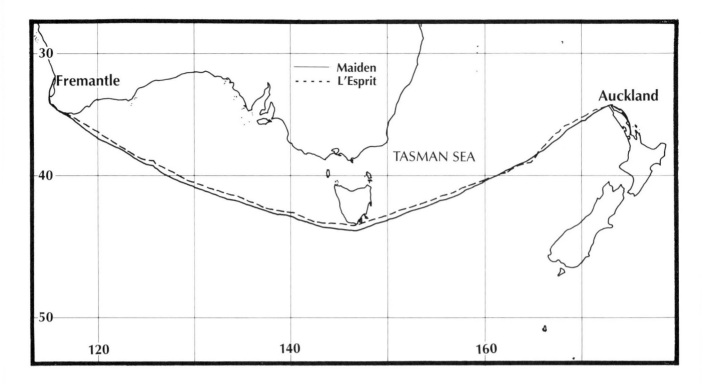

The map shows the routes of Maiden (solid line) and L'Esprit (dashed line) between Fremantle and Auckland, crossing the Tasman Sea past Tasmania.

A Summary of Leg Three: Half a World Away

Everyone knew this would be a difficult leg to complete. The weather patterns were bound to be uncertain, the tactics adopted by each yacht critical in deciding who would get into Auckland first. The maxis all knew the biggest fight would once again be between *Steinlager* and its skipper, Peter Blake, and *Fisher and Paykel*, with Grant Dalton, both desperate to grab a victory into their home port. The New Zealand ketches were to spend their entire time at sea more or less match racing across to New Zealand.

Half way through the leg the leading six yachts were within 35 miles of each other and were setting record speeds. Fehlmann's yacht had rudder problems. He had reported that whilst sailing in choppy seas, all the pressure and tension gauges on the steering system had started flashing red. The crew had also heard cracking noises, similar to those that had been heard 18 months previously when the rudder axle had broken. As a result he had decided to ease off a little.

Lawrie Smith was heading more to the east, working up to the coast of New Zealand, gambling that the dice would fall his way; with a couple of sails blown out, and hairline cracks in the boom, he could only gamble so far, though. He also expressed the opinion that *Merit*'s rudder problems were a bluff: *Rothmans* had suddenly spotted them on the horizon that day (December 31st). As Smith said, for a yacht that is reportedly being sailed at less than 100 per cent, their speed was surprising.

In the end it was perhaps a foregone conclusion: the Kiwis did it again. But there was a lot of drama in their approach – and a squall which determined that Blakey – once again – would win the leg for the maxis. On their way down the east shore of New Zealand, and fighting for the lead, Blake had picked up a local weather forecast by listening to local sailors discussing the weather. As a result he shortened sail.

It was an example of just how well he had planned to win the race. Grant Dalton never heard the broadcast. As a result, when the squall hit, *Steinlager* roared through it while *Fisher and Paykel* nearly lost a spinnaker as it threatened to blow under the boat. The line, then, was crossed by *Steinlager*, then *Fisher and Paykel* – only half a mile behind. Twenty miles back behind the leaders, when *Merit* finally crossed the line, she had just managed to beat *Rothmans*, holding on to her overall second place.

Much as they had into Fremantle, these two yachts engaged in another gybing duel – 25 this time. That final squall gave *Merit* the ten-minute break it needed.

The rest of the maxi fleet came in all affected in different ways by the squalls. *British Defender* was caught out and trailed in behind *The Card*, *Fortuna*, and *Martela*. But *British Defender* did beat *Charles Jourdan* which had suffered a hit by a whale in the week before, opening up a two foot gash in the side. It meant they could only keep going on a starboard tack. *Charles Jourdan* was followed into Auckland by the luckless *NCBI* with her broken boom in 12th place, behind both *Fazisi* and *Gatorade*.

More spectacular damage was sustained by *UBF*: her mast came down five days before the finish when a section of the Cobalt rigging parted midway across the Tasman Sea. The crew managed to rig a jury system.

The rest of the maxis arrived – *Belmont*, *Liverpool Enterprise*, then *Equity and Law* in division C. Then, shortly ahead of *Maiden*, came *Creightons Naturally*. She was being dogged by bad luck too. In rough weather, south of Australia, they had lost all steering and they had to sail more than 1,000 miles using their emergency tiller linked by ropes to the main winches. It meant that, once again, they had been beaten by the veteran yacht, *With Integrity*; the latter managed to complete the third leg undamaged.

But between the first maxis, and the rest of the fleet, Auckland crowds were really getting ready to welcome one yacht: *Maiden*. Her welcome, in the early hours of a chilly Monday morning, was nearly as great as the one they had given for the Kiwi ketches. They were welcoming one of their own – Mandi Swan – and the considerable achievement of the yacht in fighting off the challenges of *Schlussel* and *L'Esprit*.

At this point, half way through the Race, *Maiden* had scored a double: not only was she leading division D; she was now the overall leader in the combined division C and D on corrected time.

That Aucklanders knew: what they had no inkling of at that stage was that they were also welcoming a woman – Tracy – whose life was about to change for all time through the public recognition back in England, of what she and her crew had done. Tracy's Yachtsman of the Year Award, handed to her on a grey New Zealand day, could not have been awarded in a more appreciative place.

The City of Sails took to the Maidens as if they were all Kiwis. Tracy had been familiar with the city from the previous Race. For Mandi Swan it was home and she, of course, was treated like a conquering hero.

But all the girls found the atmosphere to their liking. They were feted everywhere. Their time in New Zealand also coincided with the Commonwealth Games – and Tracy was given a signal honour in being one of the final carriers of the Queen's Baton at the opening ceremony.

This was beamed back live to Britain and it gave those many people back home who had hardly heard of *Maiden* and Tracy Edwards a tantalising glimpse of a girl who was, from this point on, on her way back home.

CHAPTER 9

A Cook's Tour

When Tracy won the Yachtsman of the Year Award, Howard said, 'it's the first time the award has gone to a boat nigger.'

Tracy has been one for years – even her first home in Hamble was called Ibna House, after the International Boat Niggers Association (now, rather lamely but more politely, called the International Boat Workers Association).

Because we live in hypersensitive times the very phrase 'boat nigger' conjures up something unpleasant, even racialist. But boat niggers call themselves that because they perceive themselves as the hardworking element in a luxury trade – yachts. They are the workers; the owners, the charterers and the guests are the 'nobs'.

> Just the very word 'yacht' makes people think of rich, over-indulged people cruising about with nothing better to do.
> But that is only one side of it. The other side is hard, dedicated, professional people who know the boats, the wind and the weather inside out. As I sailed around the world as crew I began to get to know and admire them. More than anything I wanted to be one of them.

When Tracy discovered luxury sailing in the Caribbean in the Christmas of 1982, she believed herself to be in paradise. She had just completed her first Atlantic crossing on *Southern Star* but, as she was only helping to deliver it, she had to leave it once they berthed in Antigua.

Then on her first Sunday in Antigua she had gone to a cricket match and there had witnessed a man streaking across the pitch with a cricket pullover pulled up over his rump.

'Piggy' (Paul van Bekk) was to be her first skipper in the Caribbean on a yacht called *Sealestial* (what else!). She worked for him and his girlfriend, Jo-jo, in the same way she had worked in the years before on motor-yachts. But she was gaining valuable experience of how a large sailing yacht was run.

Big yachts are intrinsically more frightening than motor yachts or even large commercial ships. The danger comes from the amount of heavy gear which is, necessarily, not secured but changing as the wind changes or the yacht has to alter course. The engine room, if you like, is on deck with all the moving parts exposed.

Safe working – which is everything – comes with experience in all conditions. Although working as a boat nigger in the Caribbean was, for Tracy, geared to the charter trade, with the customers wanting a good time above all, she nevertheless could not help learning how things worked. And she wanted, badly, to learn.

Those experiences proved even more critical when she helped a friend, Julian Gildersleeve, deliver a yacht, *White Quailo*, from the Caribbean to the Mediterranean in the summer of 1983 to take part in the Swan Regatta in Sardinia.

> Two days out Julian Gildersleeve, the skipper, said: 'Can you navigate?' I said no. 'What are you going to do if I fall over the side then?' he said. I was dumbstruck. I hadn't a clue.
>
> In the next two days he taught me how to do celestial navigation and then said: 'OK, now get us to Spain.' It was the beginning of my greatest fascination. Offered any job on a boat I will choose, as I did on *Maiden*, to navigate.

They travelled over through the Azores, leaving their yacht's name painted, with a suitable motif, on the harbour wall in Horta, as thousands of yachts had done before. Off Spain they ran into very

Like others before me, I paint our battle emblem on the harbour wall.

133

'Shag' – the original ocean racer.

bad weather; they rode it out at sea and then pushed on to Palma.

For the first time Tracy was thrown into the offshore racing fray. From the very start she adored it and the people, many of them old friends and acquaintances, whom she now met in a different context. They taught her some of the hardest lessons she had ever learned. She would come back exhausted but triumphant. Among the very hardest of her task masters was Kym 'Shag' Morton.

'Shag', who once, worlds apart in space and time, had been a typesetter in Australia, is one of ocean racing's legends. Tough, resourceful, taciturn, he has a fearsome reputation for saying and doing what he pleases.

Tracy went back to the Caribbean again, chartering, racing, not thinking too much about the future. She invited her mother and brother over when there was a gap in the charters. Pat Edwards remembered the trip mainly for having to overcome her fears about sailing and the sea.

Trevor, her young brother, who went there to work, remembers how organised Tracy was; and how she bullied him to get his act together. Trevor was taken on as a steward but he had great trouble remembering all the cutlery and plates to lay out. Fortunately he had a charter party who soon began to sympathise more with him than with Tracy's desire to make sure it all ran smoothly.

'They used to ask for paper plates', he laughs now. 'It meant they didn't break if I dropped them and there was no washing up. I used to say "are you telling me you are insisting on having paper plates?" and they would say "yes".'

Life looked sweet. Tracy was settled and, on the surface, happy. But, by the spring of 1985 she was getting restless. It was then she had picked up a book on the yacht she was then on. It was called *Cape Horn to Port*; what happened next took her right through 1985 and half of 1986 on the Whitbread.

She discovered, quickly, that women were a rarity in Whitbread races, most easily acceptable as cooks. Undaunted, she took on the job as cook on a battered veteran of the Race, a yacht which was to go on doing the Whitbread like an old war horse, changing its name every time.

As *Great Britain II* it had been skippered by Chay Blyth and been in the first Whitbread. In 1985 it was about to take part in its fourth as *Norsk Data*, skippered by Bob Salmon. (And there it was again in the fifth, as one of the cruising entries, *With Integrity*.)

Tracy did not get on with Salmon at all. She worried about the way the yacht was funded (partly through getting most of the crew to pay for the privilege of being there) and she worried about the crew's ability, and understanding of safety. But, in the absence of any other 'ride' she took the ticket and went.

Four years later, looking back, Tracy pondered on the curious way she fell into her first Whitbread:

> That's how it started – no burning ambition, although I knew my career was on boats, and that I wanted to do *something*. After I talked to Bob about going with him – in the Caribbean – I jumped on to another yacht, *Jubilation*, and went up to the States and did some racing up there, and then delivered that same boat I was on back to England. I joined Bob and the yacht in Plymouth. I nearly ended up not doing the Race because I just could not get on with Bob Salmon. On top of that, the boat didn't have any money. I stupidly used to buy food for the crew. They had paid £2,000 a leg to do the Race and they were sitting on the boat with no food, no pocket money, no nothing.

During those summer months she had plenty of time to worry over her decision, and to continue to regret it. She was living in Hamble on the south coast, the Mecca for yachtsmen from all over the world. Many of the Whitbread boats were gathering there, with many of her friends aboard.

Tracy says: 'I used to talk to my friends on the other big yachts (the maxis in the coming Race) – it was like a dream world. I'd come back to the Hamble and go on their boats and we'd talk about all the new stuff they had on board and then I'd get a feel for the Race again . . . But, it was all up and down, all the time.'

The only time Bob and Tracy sailed together before the Whitbread was when they brought the boat from Plymouth to Hamble. She remembers thinking, '"Oh my God, this is a disaster." But once I am in something I find it very difficult to back out, even if a voice somewhere is telling me deep down not to do it. Another reason was that my friends were doing the Race and I thought at least I'll see them at the stops and that would get me going for the next leg.'

There was another problem which infuriated Tracy, as a professional, doing the Race as a serious sailor.

> It was that, as far as the rest of them were concerned, they were chartering the boat: I was the cook. As far as I was concerned I was a racing cook working for a racing crew. I put my point

On *Norsk Data*.

135

across that I was not going to pander to them, that was not what I was there for, I was there for the sailing. I was cook because that was the only way I could get on the boat. It was as simple as that, but they didn't understand anything about professional sailing. They thought that anyone who was a sailor was an idiot – these were my friends they were talking about. But they had all come from college, from university, and when they found out that I left school at 16, that strengthened their view that all sailors were stupid. It was this whole attitude – that they had paid their money and they were going to get the best out of it. Yet the sad thing was that they were missing all that they were supposed to be there for. It used to frustrate me so much.

When the yacht arrived in Cape Town, Tracy made a difficult decision. She went to Bob Salmon and told him she was leaving. Now a race of a different kind began. Tracy had packed her bags and left *Norsk Data*, but she knew that if she could not get another berth in another yacht she would have to swallow her pride, and her fears, and get back on board Salmon's yacht: doing the Race was the important thing. Fate intervened in a most unlikely way.

The doctor from *Atlantic Privateer*, Julian Fuller, came up to me. *Privateer* had the craziest bunch of guys on it, and it had been hot favourite to win. It was also the yacht I was most in love with – just its design. Karl, my friend on *Norsk Data*, and I were sitting in Cape Yacht Club. He had just been told he didn't have a place on *Drum* and he was heartbroken because he knew then that he'd have to get back on board *Norsk Data* – that boat. I was trying to console him by pointing out there would be other stops. I had decided that, rather than get back on *Norsk Data*, if I didn't get another boat in Cape Town, I was going to fly on to the next stop and try there. Anyway, Julian came in and said to me: 'Are you definitely off *Norsk Data*? I'll tell you a little secret – the cook on *Privateer* (James Lutz) has just had a stroke, I've just taken him to hospital.' I said 'Thanks very much Julian,' and I went to see Shag.

She had never forgotten what a hellish time he had given her in Sardinia. But, to her, he was a hero of the first magnitude. There was a problem, however: she knew he thought that taking women on long ocean races was madness. He had frequently and violently expressed this opinion to anyone who cared to listen.

Atlantic Privateer was a personal entry of its nominal skipper and owner, the South African millionaire, Padda Kuttel. He had gathered around him a bunch of the toughest, roughest racing yachtsmen in the world, largely South African.

The yacht's reputation was already a legend of male chauvinism and general squalor. Padda had recruited David Bongers as joint skipper, and Kym 'Shag' Morton as his sailing master. Their intention was to win – at all costs – and they were well in front on the first leg when they lost their mast. The acrimony that followed their abortive attempt to repair the rig ended by their having to take fuel on board from a passing freighter and declaring themselves *hors de combat*, before limping into Cape Town. Their scratching from this leg destroyed their chance of winning the Whitbread.

The blame for the disaster with the mast had fallen on David Bongers. Tracy is among many people who believe that blame to be wrongly placed. Nonetheless, Bongers left in disgust when *Privateer* docked at the Cape. It was to this boat she now dragged herself, knowing full well the kind of reception she was likely to get.

> Shag was actually the guy who taught me to race years and years ago and he is a very good friend of mine. I went on board and said 'Shag, you need a haircut, I'm going to give you a haircut.' So I sat him down and then said, 'Shag, how would you feel about having a girl on board?' He said: 'Forget it, before the thought even enters your mind, because I do not take women on ocean races.' I said, 'Well Shag, this means so much to me that I am going to try and get on board this boat and I just thought I'd warn you that I'm going to do anything I can.'

Shag's memories of Tracy in Cape Town also reflect her determination to get on *Privateer*. She was a great sailor, he says and, whilst they needed a cook, they also wanted someone who had the right sea experience. His doubts were over the advisability of having a woman – and a slight one at that – on a yacht as large as *Privateer*. He knew too, as did Tracy, that the men on *Privateer* were 'all pretty hard sailors'. What he had not anticipated, perhaps, was just how determined Tracy was to get off *Norsk Data* and onto *Privateer*. In Tracy, Shag had finally met his match. It was an experience he was never to forget nor, for a while, forgive.

Tracy went off to see the owner, Padda Kuttel. She had written out an entire set of menus for the next leg, with details on the stocking of the food, the prices, the weights, everything she could think of.

When she confronted Padda with this carefully researched master plan, she insisted to him that she was not only the best person he could employ, she was the only one around. Kuttel's reaction was to ask how Shag felt about it. Tracy decided to tell the truth – not that she would have been able to keep it from him. 'He doesn't want me on the boat,' she confessed. To her astonishment Kuttel laughed: 'Well, this should be quite interesting,' he said, 'you're on.'

When I told Shag he just said. 'It's going to be totally different from what you think. All these guys are great in port, but you don't know what it's like to sail with them. At the next port you'll be off.' As soon as he said that, of course, I had to do the whole thing. I could never go back on that. I got onto *Atlantic Privateer* the day we left. I had forgotten to get my passport checked. Customs arrived saying 'Where's Tracy Edwards's passport?' I had all the crew waiting for the girl who forgot to get her passport checked. I had to leave my passport – they promised to bring it out in a speedboat. The crew were rather bemused by it – we were all hung over. I got all emotional and I realised I had got onto a boat with a bunch of people that maybe I didn't know so well. I began to wonder that, maybe, I should have gone with people I knew.

They were the most professional crew I have ever worked with. It was so high-powered. When we were two miles behind one day, everyone's mood sank in a deep depression – and these guys were animals. I really had to fight to keep my head above the water. Another thing was that instead of turning on each other, some of them turned on the cook. In that boat the galley was right in the middle, it was viewable from every point. Not only would they complain to me, they'd expect me to be there to look after them when they needed a bit of attention.

But I did feel, much as I hated their guts at times, that I had my little family, 17 elder brothers, and when I was really desperate one of them would come up and say 'here, come on, don't let it get to you'. Shag made me cry a good few times. I told people the last race was difficult but I've never before said why. We had been going through rough weather and the spinnaker had to be taken down – fast. There was a sudden call for all hands on deck. I had slumped on my bunk down below two or three hours before and rushed up as I heard the call.

As I put my head up through the hatch one of the guys put his hand on top of my head, pushed it down and slammed the hatch shut. I couldn't believe it. I stood there slamming my fists against the hatch and yelling, 'Let me out, let me out.'

Later, when the crisis was over he came down and said, 'What did you want?' I screamed at him, 'I'm one of the crew, for God's sake. There was a call for all hands. I wanted to help.' He looked really surprised. 'Tracy,' he said, 'I was thinking of you. I didn't want you to get hurt.'

The first leg on *Privateer* was a real tester for me, finding out what it was really like on a full-on maxi racer. It was a brilliant leg, the best of the whole race. It was excellent sailing; we did very well, we came first over the line into New Zealand.

I think if it hadn't been such a spectacular ending I'd have been iffy about staying on the boat; it had been very difficult. Also the food was dreadful: this new freeze-dried stuff I'd bought and stocked the whole boat up with was atrocious. I couldn't eat it. I was living on Mars bars. It was so disgusting. It became a standing joke: but there was nothing I could do about it.

'Basic' Bill, a legend in his own lunch-time.

But that entry into Auckland was to prove a turning point, for Tracy, for the yacht, and for the rest of the crew. From all her memories of the last Race, the hours leading up to that night-time crossing of the second leg finish line stand out in her mind.

'When we were coming into New Zealand we spotted *NZI Enterprise* (one of the two New Zealand entries aiming for her home port). We spent the whole next 24 hours sailing with them down the coast – just amazing. We could see them all the time. Then suddenly, there were all these motor boats coming out at us with drunken Kiwis throwing beer cans at us and saying have a drink.'

In an uncanny preview of what would happen to her four years later, as she steered *Maiden* towards that extraordinary welcome, *Atlantic Privateer* also finished in the early hours of the morning.

We actually finished at one. As it got darker and darker all you could see were thousands and thousands of red and green lights; someone had a spotlight on our spinnaker and on the *NZI* spinnaker behind us. They were getting closer and closer. After 7,000 miles the two yachts were just over seven minutes apart. The tension was fantastic. We were listening to the commentary on Radio Auckland. Then we crossed the line and the gun went.

As we were motoring in *NZI* motored alongside. Many of us were crying, release of tension – winning – we were all just standing along the guard rail just looking at the guys on *NZI Enterprise*, not saying a word. Some of them were crying too. We were saying, 'We had to win one leg', and they were saying 'Well done, but we wish it hadn't been this one.'

We came in and the whole of the harbour was wall to wall with people. They had 25,000 people packed in. There was a nine mile traffic jam into Auckland. Just people everywhere, boats, shouting, laughter. I remember it like a film. I remember thinking that night, I want to remember every sight, sound, smell, touch. If only I could have bottled it and now open it up whenever I feel low.

To do the Race, Tracy had left a previous boyfriend, Scotty, a one-time skipper of *Jubilation*, back in the Caribbean. Knowing what was ahead of her, and expecting she would have changed, or met someone else, in the time-honoured sea-faring fashion, he had told her not to expect him to be around when – if – she got back. A neat role reversal of an old tradition that was about to have a surprising ending.

Tracy, hardly believing it was possible to be so high, having survived the rigours of the Southern Ocean, now stared in the darkness at the thousands lining the dockside. There she saw Scotty.

It was all too much, I didn't know if I could get any higher without exploding. When I crossed the line with *Atlantic Privateer* in New Zealand I was the first girl competitor in the Whitbread to finish first, which was brilliant, and which the guys were quite proud of too.

It was the high spot of *Atlantic Privateer's* Race. From then on, things got bad. After an overlong six-week wait in Auckland, the yachts set off for Cape Horn.

We really cocked it up, and had a dreadful, dreadful Race. We went to 61 degrees south, a really bad decision. There was a chance it could have been all right, but as we ran down south we watched all the other maxis go north and then we had a terrible time trying to beat back up again.

We got to the point where we were timing each helmsman and whoever did the fastest time got the most on the helm. The last 24 hours into Punta del Este (in Uruguay) were a nightmare; the tension was unbelievable.

We kept hearing where everyone was; we were eight hours out when *UBS* crossed the finishing line, and *Drum* crossed right after her. We got in and we didn't feel like seeing anyone. We were glad for the *Drum* guys because they had had a really rough time: no money, the boat turning over, falling apart. It took a lot of guts for them to get back on and sail it from South Africa.

But Tracy had passed that most legendary of sailing landmarks: Cape Horn. Tracy could call herself a sailor now; she wears a ring in her left ear, as the old salts did, as an everlasting reminder of that moment.

She had now begun to bully the *Privateer* watch captains to let her help to work the boat. She was learning a different game, the ultimate in yacht racing on what has remained, for her, the ultimate of racing yachts.

You choose what you want to do. I could have been continuously cooking, and I didn't have to do any watches. But I got so sick of going up on deck with people saying 'don't touch that', so I joined Paul's watch (the cook, like the skipper on a racing yacht does not have to be a part of either watch). Paul Standbridge is now a really good friend of mine. I used to join his watch. Basically I used to hassle him until he told me what was going on.

The first person I talked to about doing the Whitbread with an all-female crew was Paul. I asked him if he remembered that there had been a girl who tried to put together an all-female crew before the last race. I asked him if he thought that if she'd done it sooner it would have been possible.

Paul has changed a lot since then, but at the time he just said 'Don't be so stupid.' But I kept on pestering him all the time. Finally he said, 'Look, do you really want to do it? Is that what you are talking about?' I remember saying 'I don't know, I don't know if I could sail with women, it's the one thing that really puts me off, I suppose it would be interesting to try.'

We used to have big battles about letting me steer. I think I got to about twice. I enjoyed working the pit (the central area where the sails are controlled). I got a lot of work done and I learned a lot. By the time I got back to England I was well into doing watches.

CHAPTER 10

To the Edge

LEG FOUR

FROM AUCKLAND TO

PUNTA DEL ESTE, URUGUAY,

6,255 NAUTICAL MILES,

FEBRUARY 4TH, 1990–

MARCH 6TH, 1990

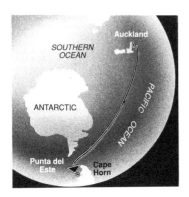

Auckland had been a high spot in every sense. Fêted wherever they went, the Maidens returned to the race confident they could keep up their winning run. But the Whitbread is a very long and arduous race: it is a worldwide survival course in which endurance – and luck, lots of luck – always play a part. Leg Four was to prove the hardest leg they had raced so far. And whilst, towards the end of it, Tracy might berate the Gods for being less than fair, mortals watching from the shore had already decided that a combination of over-confidence, as well as injury, had done more to hinder them than any cast of fate. Others in the Race, as it turned out, fared even worse. All this was still to come, though, as the *Maiden* skipper and crew headed joyfully back to their yacht, on the morning of February 4th, 1990.

February 4th   The Start from Auckland

The dock was teeming with people. The whole area was solid, they were all over the wharf. There was absolute chaos on the pontoon – cameras all over the place. We waited until *Steinlager* (next to them on the pontoons) had left; we were out at 11.20am.

The cheering and clapping that went with us as we pulled away was incredible. We motored out to the start and I was very impressed at how clear the start area was. It was a lovely day although there was not much wind. We got the main up at 12.30 and turned the engine off. *Rucanor* had problems with their main and changed to the Dacron one: tee hee – take no prisoners. When we got the headsail up the wind just died.

We had a lousy start with Michèle and Dawn disagreeing over tactics. Dawn took over the steering: I should have said something

but didn't – I was just too relaxed for once. Anyway off we went, tacking up to the first mark. Needless to say, all the spectator boats crowded in and made life hell, chopping up the water. Then *The Card* hit an anchored yacht and lost her mizen-mast. They managed to cut it free and carried on; poor things.

We went round the first mark last in class. *Liverpool Enterprise*, *Creightons* and *With Integrity* overtook us soon after. So, we were last. LAST! The wind died and then the maxis which had gone inshore got stuck with no wind too. We almost overtook them. The spectator boats were still appearing every so often. Finally, as the wind died to nothing, they left us in peace.

Most of us (the yachts) were in sight of each other during the night – which was warm and pleasant. But the wind just kept on going up and down; we were going nowhere fast. I slept like a log.

February 5th

Up late – 6.30. I just couldn't wake up. There was not a breath of wind, we were doing a knot. All division D were very close with the maxis on the horizon.

It was very hot; everyone was relaxed and happy. In the afternoon the wind started to come up: Cyclone Nancy might hit

Looking for the first mark in a sea of boats.

143

us but Cyclone Ofa will miss us. I can't decide whether to dive south or go gradually. What, I wonder, will *L'Esprit* do? They seem to be faster than us in these conditions but the weather is so wishy washy we will stick with them until something definite comes up.

There is a good atmosphere on the boat: lots of happy chatter, mostly about men! I slept in the afternoon. I am doing lots of thinking about the future – it's crossroads time. I got up and the wind was up; *L'Esprit* began to move, slowly, away from us. *Schlussel* is to leeward and *Rucanor* on the horizon in front, *La Poste* to weather with *L'Esprit*.

We waited for *L'Esprit* to gybe; of course they waited until dark but we saw them anyway and went with them. After we followed they proceeded to take miles from us; we were heading straight for East Cape. The wind was getting up though.

February 6th 38'19"S 179'33"E 5,483 miles to go

Everyone on great form today: lots of jokes and laughing, a perfect atmosphere. The wind slowly came up, and all the boats drew apart again. We kept *Schlussel* and *Rucanor* behind but we just can't seem to pass *La Poste*. Cyclones Nancy and Ofa are heading our way: two choices of where to go. We are following *Merit*. We crossed the Dateline today: back in the West!

Although it was cool and cloudy this morning, it cleared and ended up by being hot. When I got up the chart room (her nav station) was in a mess – again. I don't know who messes around in here but I wish they'd stop. Nothing gets to me as much as knowing that someone has been mucking around in my nav station. But we had pancakes for breakfast which cheered me up. *La Poste* was two miles ahead this morning so the main task was to get in front of them. Michèle said 'We'll have them for lunch,' and so we did, modestly putting our tops on as we went past. The wind stayed variable all day, but it was nice sailing with the flanker up, cruising at around 8–9 knots.

In the late afternoon the wind died and started to come aft; we gybed three times before dinner. Tanja injured her ear: she's got a hole in the back or something. Angela's filling dropped out and she also fell down the hatch – not her day. I broke my bracelet and lost it.

Our gybing is getting better: the atmosphere is still absolutely wonderful, we are so comfortable with each other. We are called

Maiden the love boat this time, as there are so many pining women on board. So we're looking forward to SBS – Sleaze Bar Speed (the Sleaze Bar was the favourite in Punta del Este).

I am doing so much thinking about Simon, getting married and the future. My brain hurts. I just don't know what to do. Each day we tackle someone's love life. Eleven women giving advice: it's hysterical. You end up even more confused than before.

Meanwhile: I spent an agonising evening trying to work out whether to go east or south. The wind is right behind; I decided to wait and see where *L'Esprit* was when we did the chat show.

February 7th   44'46"S   171'09"W

The weather was much colder today: everything was grey, damp, cloudy. We saw our first albatross: a lone comment from the cockpit 'yep, we're back'. The mood on board is still unbelievably good, better than ever before. Everyone is so happy with everyone else, it is almost impossible to describe. It feels as if going back to sea is coming home.

Not once have I seen any agitation or loss of patience by anyone.

At 14.00 I was asleep after the chat show. We had caught up on both *Rucanor* and *L'Esprit*, who I could see on the horizon in front. Claire woke me up to say *Rucanor* had hit a whale and were calling us on the VHF. I spoke to Bruno who was very upset. The thing has damaged their rudder, taking some off the bottom and loosening the quadrant so the stock was swinging freely in its bearing.

Changing headsails – a wet, cold job for the girls on the foredeck.

They had been taking in water, but after they had stabilised the quadrant it had stopped and they were able to pump out. There had been no other visible damage, Bruno said. However, they had lost their radio tuner and they asked if we could call the Race Committee which we did.

They are going to have to go back to Wellington for repairs – poor guys, what a shame. It's bad for us too, as we now only have *L'Esprit* to race. *Rucanor* will lose at least six days (they actually lost more and were, in the end, forced to retire from this leg in order to get to Uruguay in time for the start of the fifth one).

I called the Race Office again, who had the message totally wrong. I spent the whole afternoon on the radio. I checked with Wellington that they could take *Rucanor* and then called the guys back. They have 300 hours fuel with 400 to go to Wellington. They

145

had dived and found the skeg was damaged.

Apart from all this it was an incredibly boring day. No wind but we have caught up *L'Esprit* who have had even less. Strange day, with what wind there was nearly coming aft and then going right on the nose, and from 19 knots to 9 in seconds. The sun was out for a while, but then it got cloudy. We are on the right side of the high and we should get the low tomorrow. The maxis have all shot off with lots of wind – as usual. Our ETA is now March 5th. Jo started us on the freeze-dried food today so dieting is getting easier. I am also exercising every day – good girl.

We nearly ran an albatross over: it was very funny watching it take off, looking extremely indignant.

February 11th   50'51"S   159'41"W   4,478 miles to go

The weather has been really mild, with the sun blazing down in the past three days. Skip (Novak on *Fazisi*) says they are getting warm weather at 54'S; I can't believe it. I have fouled up very badly on the navigation by not going south as fast as possible. *L'Esprit* is now 52 miles in front.

Everyone is being really good about it, but I really feel like I have let everyone down. I feel very low. Still, the warm weather helps although the lack of wind puts a lot of strain on everyone. This high pressure is attached to us by elastic, I think. *L'Esprit* always seems to have more wind.

We have had problems with the mast screws coming undone – and on the boom and gooseneck. As the weather is so mild we have been able to botch them up: we are checking them every day. *Rucanor* has reached Wellington and should be leaving

Eat your heart out Jane Fonda! Aerobics in the Southern Ocean.

tomorrow. *NCBI* have broken their boom – AGAIN! It's crazy.

I still can't decide whether to be really radical and go south, or follow *L'Esprit*. I took a chance today by going further south; I hope it pays off. If it doesn't we will have lost miles for nothing.

Everyone has gone on a diet although Jo is doing such a good job it is very difficult. It now looks as if we won't get to Punta until March 9th, which gives us only six days before the re-start. Who ever thought these timings up for lengths of leg? *Rucanor* may not even make it before the re-start.

Down here, meanwhile, iceberg city is coming up at 56'S and from 140'W to 11'W. Hell. I don't know what to worry about next. I just wish this blasted Race was over.

February 12th   53'19"S   156'32"W

We actually had some wind today from the front that is passing over us. But, of course, it was right behind and we were going dead downwind and not managing course most of the time – and with lousy speeds. It is still quite mild – about 9°C, and it's sunny when there are no squalls. Every time a squall went through we had to gybe.

I got some weather maps through. There is no more wind further south and the centre of the low coming up is 57' so we are now heading for 59' instead of 60'. It will mean a shorter course, because I can't see us going to 60'S at all. We should take some miles from *Schlussel* and *L'Esprit* today and tomorrow.

The compasses are messing us about again. Sometimes they go back to normal, sometimes they are 10' out both ways. Scream. I wonder what it is like to set a course and know you are going to do it? Our seven person gybes are getting really good with no shouting: very smooth.

The front went through during the chat show with about 35 knots of wind from behind. Then it swung around 100' in a couple of minutes and started going north. I ran up on deck and told them to get the spinnaker down and to gybe. I got the positions and zoomed back and did the runner. The deck was being lashed by driving, freezing rain.

Dawn crash gybed and Mikki got hit on the head and was unconscious for about five minutes. She's OK, but a bit wobbly and she has an horrific lump on her head. We got back on course and put the flanker up. There was chaos on deck – knitting (halyards and sheets) everywhere.

February 13th   54'54"S   150'54"W   4,151 miles to go.

We should have had truckloads of wind today from the low, but we just had enough to keep moving, although it built up during the day. It was much colder; we closed the aft hatch and put the heater on for the first time. There are still blue skies and brilliant clear sunshine. The air is so clear, clean and fresh. And the atmosphere on board is still so good.

We took 16 miles from *L'Esprit* which helped. They have gone a little further south but are doing the same course as us. The girls on deck have been making up Valentine's messages for the rest of the fleet; I hope they don't expect me to read them out. Lots of laughter anyway.

I spoke to *Rucanor* this evening; Bruno was quite pleased that I called. All I did was to welcome them back and ask them how they were doing; the girls send their love. He told me that *Fisher and Paykel*'s shore manager, David Glenn, had been incredibly helpful, arranging for all kinds of facilities in Wellington to make sure they got repaired as fast as possible. It makes this race worthwhile, when things like that can still happen.

I turned the radar on tonight: first iceberg watch coming up. The moon is bright which is good. I have changed my routine so I will be up during the night from now on. I called Simon – he's OK.

February 15th   57'41"S   139'04"W   3,576 miles to go

Well, I screwed up big-time today. I went too far south, so that leaves *L'Esprit* ten miles north with loads of wind and us with nothing. It is incredible. I can't believe their luck and my stupidity. We ought to have gone east. We lost 21 miles to them and they are now 82 in front. I've never felt more like giving up in my life. I just have to try and pull myself out of it. The girls are being great – really helping by not being sulky.

Anyway I'm trying not to be depressed and we are looking forward to the lows coming up from behind, although with our present run of luck they'll probably go right round us and hit *L'Esprit*. Oh God, I hope everyone is not disappointed in us if we lose this Leg. I feel I have let everyone down – all the people who believe in us. The girls, God bless them, still trust me (God help 'em).

The weather today was absolutely dreadful: there was no wind but we were all over the place with loads of squalls, cold, cold rain and lots of sail changes. The wind, when it was there, was bitterly cold too even though there is still sunshine.

We saw two icebergs this morning and one this afternoon – pretty big but far away. We have come through the biggest patch. The moon has been perfect for watching: right in front and out all night.

February 18th   58′39″S   118′03″W   2,927 miles to go

The last two days have been the worst of all our lives – the vote is unanimous. Yesterday, early morning, the wind started building with the front coming through but, of course, it was from the wrong direction. We had to close reach, bloody uncomfortable with the waves on the quarter lifting the boat with a lurch.

When they came over the boat they did so with a vengeance. The girls were soaked to the skin, hands freezing, feet numb. It was back to the Southern Ocean with surprising swiftness. Did we ever complain it was mild?

I had come too far south; the compasses are 50 degrees out again and I spent all of yesterday trying to find the right course. We ended up steering 5 degrees higher than we should. The moon last night was hidden behind cloud, so I had to do seven hours radar watch. The wind just would not come aft; the boat was soaked, the bilges were swimming. Then the generator went off; no heater to dry clothes either as the exhaust is constantly under water.

We have been wondering if there is water in the generator exhaust. I managed to make some calls. Dawn changed the filter – nothing. Power is very low.

And then this morning Tanja woke me to tell me Michèle had badly injured her back. The wave coming in on the port quarter hit her, threw her backwards bending her back. It has broken the wheel, so the force must have been tremendous. The boat is still on its ear with the wind forward; Michèle is now laid up – for a few days at least.

Claire is not sure how bad it is; I just pray she is OK. Mikki's taking the watch now. We have had no power all morning (the radar had to be on all night) so Dawn and Jeni have been spending all that time trying to get the generator on and the engine going.

Angela and Nancy have spent most of their time hand-pumping the bilges after Angela had hand-rigged a pump. Water has been pouring down the mast; the sails down here are absolutely

The buckled wheel shows the incredible force of the wave that injured Michèle.

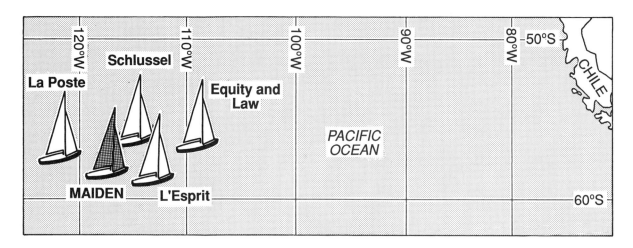

La Poste | Schlussel | Equity and Law | 120°W | 110°W | 100°W | 90°W | 80°W | 50°S | CHILE

PACIFIC OCEAN

MAIDEN | L'Esprit | 60°S

The light winds have affected *Maiden* badly. She limps towards Cape Horn only just in front of *La Poste*.

saturated. It is freezing and, of course, we have no heater.

Everyone's clothes are soaked through; there are no lights. I am navigating by torchlight. I told *L'Esprit* on the chat show all that had happened and asked them to pass it on to Race HQ to ask them to call our office, as we can't afford to use the extra power. He was really helpful.

Schlussel, who are nearest, as standing by on six megs. Then *British Defender* called to say there were good medical facilities in the Falklands. *La Poste* came in to say not to forget that they were behind us if we needed help. *With Integrity* offered to turn back to give us spare batteries. Everyone is so sweet! Mind you, as far as *L'Esprit* goes, 125 miles ahead, they can afford to be, although to be fair they offered to turn back as well – sweethearts.

The Card called us up and Roger (Nilson, the skipper and a medical doctor) offered his advice. Dawn and Jeni got up for their watch and Jeni, instead of having a watch off (as she is entitled to) elected to go on deck so Dawn could work on the engine again. It is amazing how emergencies bring out the best in everyone.

Dawn, with Nancy's help, got the engine going after bleeding it; great. We should be able to start charging the batteries now. We turned everything off. Nancy and I did the bilges again. Jo kept everyone amused. But we have all solemnly decided that we will not be doing the Race again and that we would remind each other of the last two days if anyone thought, seriously, that they might. A dreadful evil day.

Whilst all this has been going on things were flying all over the place. Doing anything – sleeping, going to the loo – involves a fair chance of injury when conditions are this bad. It is an endless hassle. We are staying on an easterly course so we don't end up on the wrong side of the low, even though *L'Esprit* has gone south again and taken miles from us.

Roll on the end of this awful Race, when the only person who will have to rely on me is me. I hate all this responsibility; it's too nerve-racking. Every chat show is like a death sentence.

The batteries were re-charged enough this evening for me to make calls and use the radar. The wind is still doing the same although the waves are better. I had a very silly five minutes with both Angela and Claire. We talked about how the men would turn their boats around for us out here when they'd never think of opening a door for us on shore. In the end we were weak with laughter; that cheered us up.

February 19th   58'52"S   111'18"W   2,832 miles to go

Early this morning the wind finally came aft. Unfortunately it dropped as well. Then I made mistake number three: we headed south again thinking that the low was passing over us as it showed that on the weather charts. Wrong: it was just beginning and I should have worked that out; *L'Esprit* did and went north. We ended up too close to the centre with no wind. I figured we could do a great circle route and wait for the next low, not knowing that this one hadn't gone over. We are really stuffed now.

Funnily, it was a lovely day for sailing; the wind dropped this evening. *L'Esprit* had taken another 17 miles. We have to start hoping they get caught going up the coast; there is a small chance of that. Dawn appears to be totally fed up with me (not half as much as I am with myself). I am going through a serious self-hate period.

February 21st   58'53"S   95'39"W   2,252 miles to go

The last two days have just been frustrating: one thing after another, being in the wrong place at the wrong time, trying to get a bit further north to get the wind. *L'Esprit* has been taking miles out of us, and so has *Schlussel*.

Michèle is much better and she is going on watch again, but doing very little. She and Tanja have been in great spirits, though. The other boats still all call up to find out if we are OK and how Michèle is. We have now got a better course, which means less banging and crashing about which was driving us all crazy. I have changed Sally to Dawn's watch to compensate for Mikki doing

Michèle's turn. *La Poste* were getting 60–70 knots from 220'. Jesus – we'll probably get that tomorrow.

February 22nd   58'12"S   87'03"W   2,059 miles to go

Well it finally looks like the Southern Ocean down here: massive swell and waves and with a very impressive sky with huge clouds, 30 knots of wind with us hurtling along with a poled-out reacher. Dawn gybed this morning and the wind has come a little bit more forward. We should go round the Horn on Saturday night or Sunday morning. I still can't get any weather charts from Buenos Aires.

I have started trying Antarctica. I found out from the other boats that the New Zealand weather charts are wrong. Great; all the boats doing badly have been using them; all the boats doing well have been using satellite weather pictures.

Steinlager and *F and P* went round the Horn yesterday, *NCBI* will go round today with a whole load of others. I just hope we don't end up going round in the dark with 70 knots of wind; it would be our luck, as things are right now.

February 23rd   57'59"S   82'53"W   1,924 miles to go

Nice day's sailing with the spinnaker up. Real Southern Ocean stuff: lovely, a huge long swell and an angry sky. We got a good wind angle, maybe a bit close but good speed. The Horn is now on the schedule for lunch-time Sunday. Sarah-Jane tells me everyone has left southern Chile so there will be no pictures; poor Tim must really be upset. We are too: we were looking forward to getting some great pictures of an historical event.

The atmosphere on board was much lighter today, especially as we are now taking miles from *L'Esprit*. I had a long series of talks with Jo which cheered me up no end. Angela has bruised her ribs and hurt her arm in a fall. Everyone else is fine, but we are all looking forward to finally going north.

Maiden had been 1,300 miles from Cape Horn while Tracy was going through this process of self-doubt and self-torture. She had always been prone to this; whilst in Australia – and even more in New Zealand – she had begun to believe more fully in herself, now all the misgivings crowded in. She felt trapped, unable to break out of the

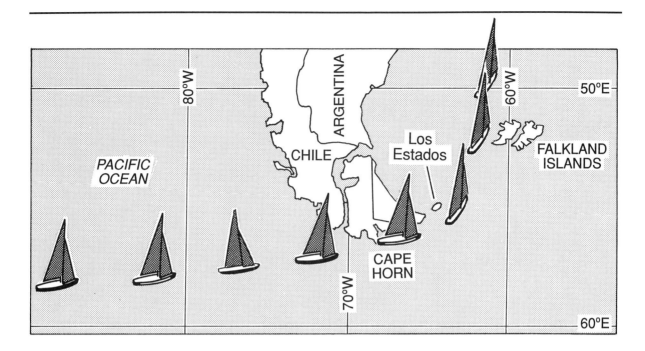

doldrums into which *Maiden* had fallen, or to lift her own spirits.

Now the crew came together, weaving a web of support about her. Tracy had always had her doubts about the 11 women who sailed on *Maiden*: not in terms of their ability but whether, when the fight was really on, they would rally to her, or turn against her. They rallied. Whatever else Tracy, or the crew, would remember about Leg Four, they would none of them forget how close they all felt, how strong the bonds had become that linked them all.

Leg Four became the leg they just had to survive; get through it and we can start again, they began to say. Struggling to Cape Horn was an epic voyage in its own right, although the Horn (passed by *Maiden* on Sunday, February 25th) chose to show its friendliest face for the historic passage of the all-women yacht. Even so, the nightmare of the days that followed (see Chapter 1), when Tracy was convinced *Maiden* had developed a serious leak, when Black Tuesday (February 27th) was succeeded by Bloody Wednesday, demonstrated again how hazardous the Whitbread could be – right up to the final finishing line.

But by then, when *Maiden* had to heave to close by the Falkland Islands and pump out, it was clear *Maiden* could not win Leg Four and would, certainly crawl in a bad third, having lost, as Tracy feared she would, the overall lead to *L'Esprit*.

Now came the long climb out of the southern latitudes along the coast of Argentina.

Maiden's track around Cape Horn shows how we went outside Los Estados Island, losing valuable hours, and I believe, the whole leg.

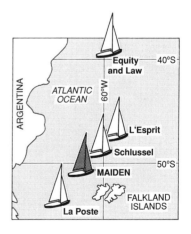

Maiden beats around the Falklands, leaking badly in heavy weather. *L'Esprit* takes off again.

153

March 3rd   44'15"S   58'42"W   704 miles to go

The last few days have been very strange. It is difficult to describe: a calm acceptance of the fact that we won't win this leg; replacing the need to win with the need to get everything possible out of what has happened. It has been the worst leg, weather wise, sailing wise, position wise.

Yet, everyone agrees that it has been the most interesting, the best atmosphere. We have noticed more about ourselves and what is around us, the people we are with. I feel almost a calm relief at not winning – no, that's not quite right. Not relief, just more calm than I thought I could be. I am not feeling aggressive or angry (very odd for me). I'm sleeping well, my dreams are peaceful, happy and comfortable and my stomach is fine (all equally unlikely).

I have sorted out my emotions, my thoughts, my fears, and come to terms with them. I feel grown up – finally. Adult enough to face defeat fairly and squarely, at a time when my inferiority complex should be at its most painful, its worst. In fact all that seems to have vanished. It's crazy. At the point when I will have to stand up and tell the world that I have messed it up, I feel I will be stronger than when I was telling them how we won.

I feel as if I have done the spring cleaning and now I'm patiently sitting down waiting for the sun to shine through the window so that I can see the results. Today has been slow, a pretty mindless day, although it picked up tonight. The seabirds have been amazing and tonight I saw a seal. It was a beautiful sunset.

Three days later, early in the morning of March 6th, with a hot day beginning on shore and the sea sparkling, *Maiden* danced her way into Punta del Este for the second time during the Whitbread. A huge crowd – much larger than in October – had gathered on the jetty to see the girls in; their defeat at sea was treated as a triumph on shore.

Curiously mirroring what Tracy had felt, many of the other Whitbread crews now appeared to treat the *Maiden* crew as equals at last: there is nothing like adversity to bring people together and for many of the yachts this had been a long hard leg.

The damage to *Maiden* proved to be less than everyone had feared, so during the ten days they had in port, it was possible for everyone to relax. Never very far from the back of their minds, how-

ever, was the knowledge that the girls were now 17 hours behind *L'Esprit*. It was the same position they had been in the last time in Punta. The difference was that they had won two legs and tasted victory.

Skipper and crew were much more hardened this time, and despite some initial gloom by Tracy over their chances of pulling back the time, she and the girls knew it was still possible.

Weary and sad, we arrive in Punta to a rapturous welcome.

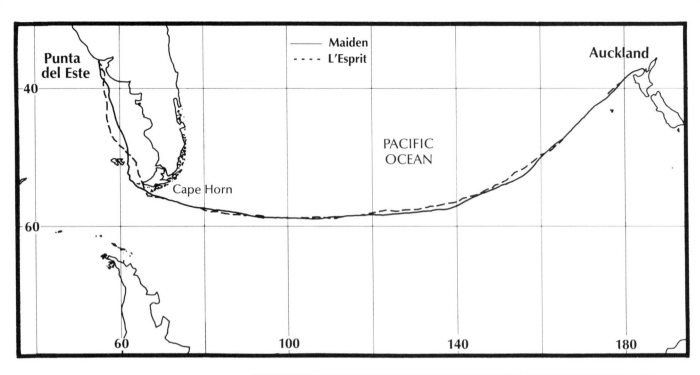

Punta
del Este

40

——— Maiden
- - - - L'Esprit

Auckland

PACIFIC
OCEAN

Cape Horn

60

60   100   140   180

A Summary of Leg Four: Double Jeopardy

Rick Tomlinson, a professional photographer doing this leg on *The Card*, wrote one word in his diary for day after day of this leg: boring. Ironic in one sense because it had been *The Card* which provided the second most dramatic incident on the leg, only moments after the start.

Cutting too close to an anchored spectator yacht in Auckland Harbour, *The Card*'s wash had bounced the yacht so that she jerked forward entangling her mast in *The Card*'s mizen which was instantly wrenched out of the deck. Desperate efforts had cut it free and a quick decision by Roger Nilson had determined *The Card* would sail the rest of the leg as a sloop – eventually coming in a creditable sixth place.

But the most dramatic incident was not played out until much later. On Monday, February 28th, *Martela OF*, the leading Finnish maxi on this leg, sent a Mayday to say her keel had dropped off, some 400 miles short of Punta del Este. That this was a possibility had been known for several days; the shock of it happening (at the same time *Maiden* believed she might be sinking) created consternation in the Race offices in Punta.

By a miracle the accident happened in daylight; all the crew were able to scramble onto the hull and sit there for five hours until *Merit* and *Charles Jourdan*, both of whom had turned back, came to their rescue.

The Argentines, who had been asked to mount an emergency operation, had been nowhere in sight. A plane eventually overflew the upturned hull as the crew were being taken off by *Merit* and *Charles Jourdan*. The subsequent South American farce of the abortive attempt by the Argentine coastguard to salvage *Martela* was itself upstaged when a Uruguayan fishing boat found the yacht, sailing upside down in the Falklands Current, the water acting like a wind on her still set sails.

While this drama was taking place off the Argentine coast, the first three maxis had arrived in Punta. It was no surprise to anyone that Peter Blake, for the fourth time, led *Steinlager* across the line first, in a 50 knot gale but only 21 minutes in front of Grant Dalton and *Fisher and Paykel*. The two ketches had kept this match race up across the whole distance from New Zealand.

Lawrie Smith and *Rothmans* plunged over the line 12 hours later with Smith believing, perhaps for the first time since he had been trounced into Punta in October, that he now knew how to beat Blake. *Rothmans* was followed by *Merit* and *Charles Jourdan*, both yachts laden with Finns from *Martela* and both anxious to start negotiations with the International Jury over the compensation they would be allowed for having turned back for the rescue.

As the yachts came in, one by one, it was clear, though, that for most of them the leg had been disappointing. Apart from the leaders, most thought they had been facing indifferent winds which had prevented them from performing at their best.

The other major complaint was the damage many yachts had sustained. *Rothmans* reported they had broken their boom – as had *NCBI* for the third time. Threatening noises were beginning to be made against a number of manufacturers. What *Martela* crew said about Speedwave, the manufacturers of their keel was, of course, unprintable. A view was growing that there was a long way to go in quality control for many of those engaged in building yachts or their parts. And crew were angry that gear could fail so easily.

Much of the problem – and it afflicted *Maiden*'s gear – was that equipment had been made for offshore races, but not a world distance offshore race, even though that had been specified in the orders. If this Whitbread had shown anything at all, it was in the need for the yachting industry, world-wide, to look again at its standards.

Punta del Este, though, was a treat. In October, when last the Race had touched its shores, it had been a resort town gearing up for the summer. Now, in late February and early March, the delights of the port were open for all. The town was full of holiday-makers having a good time and the atmosphere was electric. What Punta – or Uruguay – lacked in economic success, or in some amenities, it more than made up for in its welcome. The town hopped and bopped to a Lambada beat, not fully coming alive until around midnight, not going to bed until 4.00 or 5.00 in the morning.

It was a tonic, and the Whitbread racers, weary from their long toils in the oceans of the world took it, wholeheartedly. For this was the last stop-over where everyone was within hailing distance and where the sponsors' hype did not penetrate. The States would be all hard sell; after that, in England, everyone knew that this vast caravan would begin to break up as soon as it hit Southampton.

Punta became the last party before the end. Sadness, just a tinge, crept into the margins of the town; and would not go away.

CHAPTER 11

Against all odds

The *Maiden* project was only a glimmer in Tracy's mind when she finished the 1985/86 Whitbread Race. The conception and birth were to prove long and hard.

After recovering from the last Race, Tracy's first approach was to Admiral Charles Williams, chairman of the Race Committee, then and now. Williams, ever the Corinthian was enthusiastic.

> I asked him if there were any rules against an all-female crew doing the Whitbread and he said no. Then I asked him what his attitude would be if I was to enter an all-woman crew with me as skipper. He said he'd have to go away and have a long think about it – which he advised me to do as well. He said go and talk to other people who have put Whitbread projects together. If you follow all the safety requirements you can. I went away for a month and thought and thought. At that time I did not know.

She did what any girl might have done in the circumstances: she went and talked to her mum. She told Pat of her plan to do the next Race as a skipper of her own yacht. If Pat felt incredulous she did not show it. As always, when her children came to her with a plan, she sat down and talked it through, concentrating on their true desires and feelings.

With Tracy she said: 'you've never stuck at anything, do you think you could stick at this for four years?' It was a good question but asked too early. Tracy shook her head: she didn't know, she simply did not know.

> I really wasn't a hundred percent definite until I met Howard. I felt it was important for me to do something with my life – other

than just going from boat to boat. I knew I wasn't qualified enough to get a job as a skipper. I'd have to get the boat and learn as I went along.

She was 22 soon to be 23; many young women at her age had hardly ventured out of their village or town; she had criss-crossed the Atlantic, raced in a yacht all round the world. If she believed she had achieved very little, and had done little with her life, it was because she had – and has – a terribly hard outlook on herself.

The first Whitbread was a great moment of change for her. Previously she had drifted in an Eden, partly of her making, but largely as a place stumbled upon, an accidental paradise. Could she really commit herself to one great project? In the summer of 1986 her main concern was the time it would take. Quite possibly had she known the effort involved, the tears that would be shed, she would have turned away.

There was another factor, one she simply had never encountered before. Tracy has her strengths but she has her weaknesses, too. To convince a world highly sceptical of women on yachts, Tracy would have to change herself out of recognition, or find a partner. It was the first piece of luck – and luck has adhered to this project like a permanent glue from its first stages – that she found a partner.

Howard Gibbons is as different from Tracy in personality as can be imagined. And that was to prove crucial in the future, because they complemented each other.

Howard was not a professional yachtie, however. He had for some years worked as a sports journalist. The turning point came when he had been offered a job on a south coast newspaper. Before he joined he went to the Caribbean to sail with a friend, Eric Woolger. He was asked if he wanted to help deliver a yacht, *Mystère of England.*

Soon after the newspaper received a postcard from him saying he no longer wanted to take the job. Howard had drifted since then, knowing he was never likely to want to settle into a desk-bound job, loving the sailing when he could get it, looking for a lucky break. When it came, he didn't recognise it at first.

Howard's memory of meeting Tracy is hazy – as is her's. Not long after the end of the 1985–86 Whitbread a mutual friend, Syd Janes told Howard that Tracy was talking about doing the 1989–90 Whitbread with an all-female crew. Janes had at that time been asked by Tracy to build the boat Patrick Banfield was designing.

Janes asked Howard if he might be interested in helping Tracy with the PR and publicity she would need and to help her find the sponsors. Howard agreed to talk and he and Syd went to Pat Edwards's house, then in Reading, to talk to Tracy.

They found Tracy was more and more convinced that it could be done. But her doubts in herself kept crowding in. To anyone who doesn't sail – and for quite a few that do – the idea that anyone who hasn't had an enormous amount of experience as a skipper in charge of a yacht could seriously consider sailing one round the world must seem insane.

Yet it is not as mad as it sounds. Tracy's own story is instructive. It is also not so unusual, if you forget the idea of the round the world race and imagine just a yacht, just a newly minted skipper. The art of managing a yacht and its crew comes down to the ability to pick the right people, and to be able to get them to mould together.

But in the summer of 1986 Tracy's immediate quest was to find the reason to do it all again – as a leader rather than a follower.

Tracy kept pondering on the last time a woman had tried to put a yacht into the Whitbread.

> I had very bad reports about that earlier attempt by a woman and when everyone else laghed about it I'm afraid I did too. But she played the women's lib card which I hate.
>
> When we got in one of the girls from another boat came up to me, a girl from *Baiaa Viking*, Eva. She said, 'Tracy we've been talking about doing an all-female crew and we'd like you to skipper it, you have the experience of a maxi and the years'. I said there is no way on God's earth that I could skipper an all-female crew. I'd never skippered a boat in my life for a start. Then I was still thinking, I suppose, of running the *project* rather than running the boat.
>
> It was something that kept nagging away; if I still had to put my finger on it it would be a mixture of things. The thing is that I've never had a problem getting on yachts. I've sailed with some brilliant boats and brilliant skippers. I did keep thinking about it.
>
> I went into the Olde Ship in Bursledon one night and all the guys from *Privateer* were there and I thought if I make the sugestion and anyone laughs at me that will be it; really at that point the whole project hinged on whether I was going to be laughed at. So I walked in and said what would you say if I said I was going to put an all-female crew together to do the next

Above: Jeni and Mikki marvel at the incredible crowds at Auckland to see us off.

Below: The first mark is directly in front of the square-rigger and we had to find it! Then, just 6,250 miles to go as we leave New Zealand.

Working on the foredeck meant
climbing the rigging under any
circumstances day or night.

Left: Blizzard conditions in the Southern Ocean. Feet and hands are frozen and unworkable. Masks and goggles are worn to try and prevent severe and scarring frostbite on our faces.

Right (above):   The loneliest place on earth: the Southern Ocean lives up to its reputation for cold, bleak, stormy conditions.

Right (below):   Iceberg! Impressive during the day at a distance; terrifying at night when they are just a dot on the radar – if they showed at all.

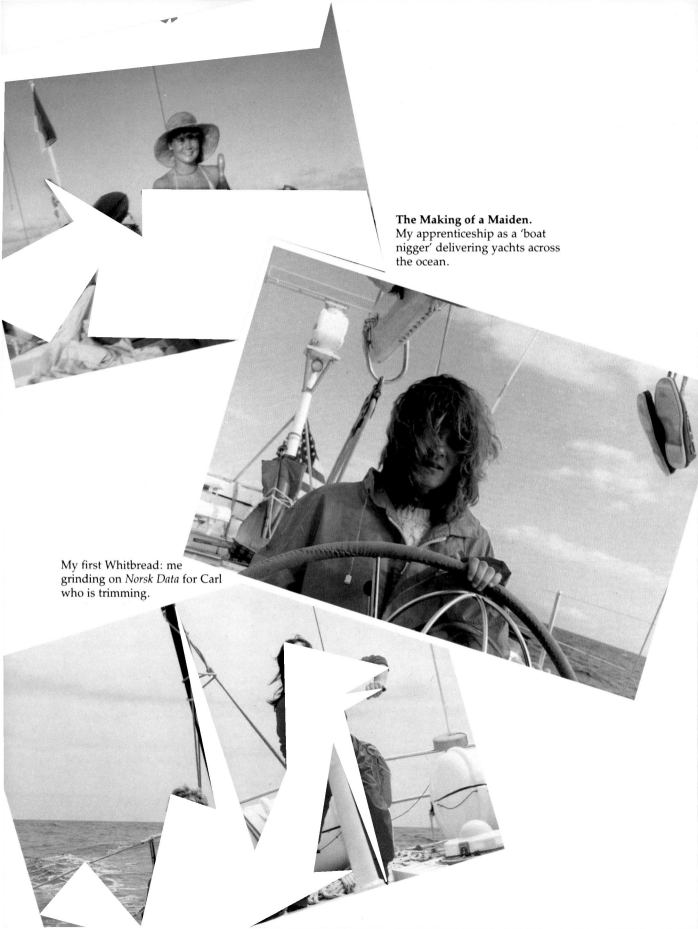

The Making of a Maiden.
My apprenticeship as a 'boat nigger' delivering yachts across the ocean.

My first Whitbread: me grinding on *Norsk Data* for Carl who is trimming.

Rucanor and *L'Esprit* in New Zealand during the 85/86 Race – little did I know then that they would be my main rivals in the next Whitbread.

Ian Martin lets me ride shotgun on *Atlantic Privateer* – I can hardly see over the top of the wheel.

The Making of *Maiden*.
The longest and most thorough
refit meant re-planing
everything except the hull.
Even that had to be repaired;
when the yacht arrived from
Cape Town it had holes in it.
Nancy, Jeni, Mandi, Michèle, Jo
and I worked night and day
with Duncan and Jonny on the
shore team to get *Maiden* ready
for her christening on
September 20th 1988.

Left (above): A great moment – the Duchess of York prepares to christen *Maiden Great Britain*.

Left (below): The Duchess takes the helm of *Maiden* on a day sail in The Solent, while I guide her past the shallow water.

Right: Maidens ahoy! The first *Maiden* symbol on one of our original spinnakers as we practice in The Solent.

Left: Fast down-wind in heavy conditions: *Maiden* loved it and so did we.

Right: **The Final Leg.** *Above*: Dawn over the Atlantic.

Below: Pampering Marvin: he got fed prawns while we had freeze-dried fish!

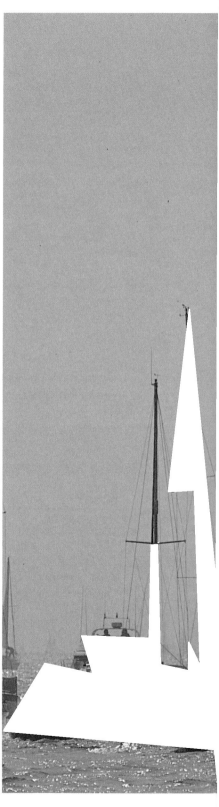

Left (above):   The needles in sight AT LAST. Little did we know the wind was just about to die completely.

Left (below): Gybing up Southampton water at the finish was hampered by the many boats besides us, so we took to indicating before we turned.

Right: Maiden's final few moments of sailing in the race, with our lovely 0.75 spinnaker.

The Maidens Triumphant.

Whitbread; they all looked round and said well if a woman was
going to do it I suppose it would be you.

So, when she met Syd Janes and Howard Gibbons at her mother's
house Tracy had seriously decided to do it. As she ruefully admits
now, had she realised just what she was getting into she might never
have taken that fatal first step. The first meeting between Howard
and Tracy had them agreeing that when she was ready Howard
would help with the publicity. He thought he could manage one day
a week.

To put the plan into practice, Tracy bought a house in Hamble.
Her decision to do that had profound implications, many of which
she could not see at the time. The reality of the next Race was a million miles away, in every sense. But Tracy, first and foremost, was a
boat nigger and Hamble the British Mecca for boat niggers. From
Britain, America, Australia, New Zealand, and from everywhere in
between they would come, as the race seasons unfolded, year by
year.

When she moved into Hamble Manor Court, into a modern
detached four-bedroomed airy house, Howard came round. It was
August, 1986. There was nothing in the house, he recalls, apart from
a kettle, a tv – and a wastepaper bin. We needed that for the rubbish,
he said much later; there was to be a lot of rubbish, he laughed.

Tracy remembers that day well:

Our first day, and Howard arrived with a typewriter and a desk.
He didn't have a chair, I upturned a bin for him to sit on. We
started from there. At that point I still didn't know if I wanted to
do it, if I was going to be able to stick it, what sort of person it
took to do it and if that sort of person was me. I didn't know if
Howard was the right person to help.

He reminded me of someone who had his finger in everything
and I don't particularly like people like that, people who make
you feel that they are maybe thinking of something else while they
are talking to you. He always used to be like that and I used to
think 'Oh God, am I going to last four years with this man?' But it
has worked out well, to become one of the best partnerships that
I have known about. We have been through a lot together and he
is the best friend I could ever have.

Like Tracy he kept many of his thoughts to himself, early on. But,
like her, one day just before the start of the race, he would be heard

161

to say 'stop it, just stop it all'. Tracy had said that frequently during the summer of 1989, similar words along the lines of 'Oh God, what have I got into; what have I gone and *done*?

From the start, however, Howard was convinced there would be no problem in selling the story to the press. It was so obviously a winner. Of all the great sporting adventure stories left in 1986 there were a few not yet achieved by women. There was Mount Everest, the North and South Poles – and the Whitbread. In the years that followed, as it turned out, all the others were conquered by all-women teams. By 1989 only the Whitbread was left; for those few who studied such things, the Whitbread remained the biggest challenge of them all.

In many ways putting together the project was no different from putting together a major expedition to any of those other wild places. There were horrendous financial mountains to climb, enormous obstacles of indifference and scepticism to surmount. There were questions of equipment; and of what kind, including the yacht. And there was the question of the crew: where would the girls come from; how would they be assessed; how – most important – would they manage to get along?

Although the problems of getting her crew together were in the future, they would become important immediately any announcement was made. The publicity would generate the interest and then the applications would come. Of that Tracy and Howard were sure. In the event they never had to advertise a single position for crew. Hundreds of women wrote from all over the world. Many had to be turned down.

Howard and Tracy decided their first official announcement should come at the impending Southampton International Boat Show early in September. Both knew it was important to be the first project to declare, for certain, that they would be contenders in the next Whitbread.

Already it was clear that the stakes in that race would be much, much higher than they had been in 1985–86. The size of sponsorships was growing, as was international interest in the Race. The big money was coming in. To be first, and to be different, they fondly imagined, would be enough. Tracy had done her first costings; assuming she would have to build a yacht especially for the Race, the total had soared to about £2 million. We were so naive, she was to say later.

Fortuitously, Howard knew the owner of a restaurant, Geddes, more or less opposite the Boat Show. Steve Grimble provided his restaurant free, throwing in coffee for the assembled reporters and television crews. Both Tracy and Howard recall that they had very good coverage from that day. The first hurdle had been crossed with apparent ease.

Patrick Banfield, who had been on *Drum* and whom Tracy had assumed would be her project manager had, meanwhile, had decided to go to Australia to be part of the America's Cup. He, too, had wanted to be part of the project – to design her yacht or act as project manager. It was his departure which changed the degree to which Howard became involved. Tracy had assumed Banfield would be a major part of the effort to raise the sponsorship money. Now he had left Howard stepped into the breach.

It was Howard who set about organising the first proper proposal to be sent out to potential sponsors. They had not yet thought of a name so everything went under the ponderous title of the 'First All-Female Whitbread Challenge'. As well as writing the proposal, Howard had to research a list of likely companies, get addresses. Tracy, meanwhile, was phoning all her cronies from the yachting world, picking their brains, asking for advice. One of the most helpful was Dirk Nauta, the Dutch skipper of *Phillips Innovator*, one of the yachts in the 1985–86 Whitbread and, subsequently skipper of *Equity and Law II* in the 1989–90 Race.

He was not the only one who dropped in. What kept both Tracy and Howard going in those early days – and later – was the camaraderie of other potential skippers and crew, all seeking sponsors, all seeking boats. Skip Novak would stop by to borrow Tracy's car – sometimes for days on end as he travelled around Britain. Grant Dalton who, before he got Fisher and Paykel to put the money up, could not sometimes afford the price of a taxi into Southampton and who would ask Tracy the time of the buses.

Pippa Blake, Peter's wife came by to say hello; others slept on Tracy's floor, grateful for her proximity to the Hamble River and for her hospitality. The boat-niggers grapevine kept her and Howard informed of others' progress toward raising money: all of them treated her as an equal in this critical period; all were willing listeners and providers of advice.

What eventually emerged from all this early activity was a massive document – almost a complete book – detailing everything they could think of about the next race, its route, the budgets for building Tracy's dream yacht. With hindsight, Howard could see the mistake in all this. Landed on corporate desks it simply contained far too much information. No one could absorb its central message.

Disaster strikes Howard as Mildred, the computer, gaily wipes 48 hours' worth of sponsorship proposals.

That message was slowly emerging back in Hamble. One of Tracy's friends from the last Whitbread, Neil Cheston, who had been a sail trimmer on *Drum*, had come up with the name for the project: *Maiden Great Britain*. The name for the yacht, they thought, then, would be dependent on the sponsor they got. With the name came the idea of forming a proper company, to put the project on a fully professional basis, and, incidentally, to recover VAT on any items they bought.

Tracy had believed from the very beginning that if her idea was to work it had to be 'professional'. Even at this stage there had been murmurings in the yachting press about the lunacy of her plans. Although she has eschewed throughout the label of feminist, she has fervently upheld the notion that for the whole enterprise to succeed – on her terms – it would have to demonstrate to a highly sceptical yachting world that women were capable of putting together a Whitbread yacht as fully funded as any all-male project. More than that, that women were capable of organising and running such a project to the same level of efficiency and competence, long before the yacht ever reached the start line.

To help start the company Tracy gratefully received a gift of £2,000 from her new boyfriend, Simon Lawrence, who lived next door to her in Hamble Manor Court.

He was not a yachtsman. His interests would give her the chance to escape, whenever she wished, from the often claustrophobic atmosphere in Hamble, to fresher unknown places. She could talk to him as an objective observer of her activities. Simon's support, as she was often to say was crucial.

She was to be lucky in other ways. Several local benefactors did come up with quite substantial sums at times where the whole project might have collapsed. But gifts were never her nor Howard's goal: they wanted proper accreditation from sponsors, not even a whiff of charity.

What both she and Howard slowly came to realise, however, was that to get an offer of any money from a commercial backer at all, was not going to be as half as easy as they had imagined.

Early in 1987, at the Earl's Court Boat Show in London, Tracy's touching naivety was publicly displayed when a potential sponsor let them down. She climbed on a chair at the press conference Howard had arranged, ostensibly to announce the sponsor had agreed to pay £250,000 to get the project started, only to angrily declaim she had been let down. Charles Williams witnessed that outburst and saw within it the seeds of Tracy's possible destruction.

Quietly, he took her aside and offered her help. As a result she went to his house, tucked away just behind the sea-front at Lee-on-Solent for 'lessons' in how to behave at press and other conferences. 'I invited her round and we actually did a few rehearsals of precisely how she should present herself,' he remembers. Press conferences aside, the real issue was how she might come across to a sponsor.

'I told her to wait outside the door and then to come in and then we rehearsed that and her saying her little piece. We even got to the point of me being very aggressive when she opened the door and saying "What do you want?",' he recalls.

That Williams bothered at all is testament to the growing response among those who took the trouble to find out that Tracy had psyched herself up sufficiently to look like a possible contender. Williams saw that early on. 'She is a very, very determined young lady with the most astonishing management capability. Although she is this tiny girl, and she doesn't throw her weight around, she has attracted a most incredibly powerful team around her. She's a natural leader. It's amazing really.'

Even so, few outside a small group of people suspected Tracy had the power to form the team she eventually did. In the early part of 1987 the first checks against the whole idea were beginning to materialise. The canter to the start line was slowing to a trot. Press interest, high a few months before was waning as Howard was unable to offer anything other than fond hopes and impossible dreams. Howard's recollections of these early days were of a heady period before that first Christmas, followed by a sudden bump, when their first real sponsorship prospect pulled out.

Their Earl's Court Boat Show annoucement had said that Tony Castro, a brilliant yacht designer from Hamble, with an international reputation, was going to design the yacht. It ought to have added that a financial services organisation was going to put up the first quarter of a million. Tracy and Howard felt bitter about the way they were treated but it was a valuable lesson.

The company appeared to use them just to get its name in the papers – and at no cost. Many others would try to do the same. The lesson for the nascent *Maiden Great Britain* team, was that in business – especially big business – fairness does not play a part.

In February, 1987, came what turned out to be a very lucky break. The Whitbread organisers had persuaded Prince Andrew to give the prizes at the end of the fifth Whitbread Race, in London in 1990. They invited him to lunch with Tracy and Peter Blake, then the ex-skipper of *Lion New Zealand*. Over lunch the Duchess of York, who

MAIDEN GREAT BRITAIN
The First All Female Whitbread Challenge 1989-1990

Luckily, the Duchess of York did!
This was our original logo.

sat opposite to Tracy, expressed great interest in what she was trying to do. After the lunch had ended and people were just standing around, Tracy remembers asking the Duchess's equerry if he thought she would launch her yacht.

'Why don't you ask her yourself?' he said. Tracy stalked the Duchess and then made her request, point blank. 'I thought you'd never ask!' replied the Duchess. It was a small but significant victory, the importance of which no one could know at the time. For when the Duchess came to do her duty it was to be her first public engagement after the birth of her baby, Beatrice. The result put the christening of *Maiden Great Britain* on the front page of every major newspaper in the country.

That was not all. The Duchess eventually decided that *Maiden Great Britain* was worth her personal support, as a largely British effort and, it seems, simply because she liked Tracy and the others. What began as a formal relationship turned, during 1989, into something much closer to genuine friendship.

By the end of 1987 Tracy had begun to borrow money on her house. MGB had already tried to sell off various boating items to a local chandlers; Howard was working just for his expenses. Worst of all, Tracy knew all this meant there could only be a certain amount of time before she had to sell the house. The dream was becoming a nightmare. At the Earl's Court Boat Show at the start of 1988 they announced the impending crisis. For the first time there was public talk of closing the operation down. Tracy recalls it all: 'By that January I wanted to give up,' she says.

The financial crisis exploded on February 1st. The crew house they were renting was abandoned, the crew that had been formed by then were disbanded; from then on only Howard and Tracy remained. 'We were really down. There was just the two of us; it was quiet, and we got more done,' says Tracy.

Howard remembers it too: 'Somebody made a joke the other day about the meat packing factory,' he said, 'they were looking it up in the telephone directory.' I said 'Don't laugh because I was actually thinking about going to work in it in the evening for money.' That's what it was like. Then some other prospect came along and that kept us going for a bit longer – even when they didn't come up with the money.'

I used to sleep at night with a notepad and pencil at my side. I often get ideas late at night and it helps me to remember everything next day. One night I woke up about 2am and thought, 'That's it! What we need is a *boat*. Of course no one takes us seriously. Anyone can come along with a set of plans and *say* they're going to do the Whitbread. We have to have the boat to show them what we're going to do it in, to make it real.'

The next morning Howard arrived and said 'Is anything going on?' I said, 'Yes, Howard, we're going to buy a boat.' His face dropped. I think he thought I finally had gone mad.

Sarah-Jane, cheerful as always.

To finance it Tracy decided, finally, to sell her house and did. They got in touch with a local yacht broker, Malcolm Lee at Berthon's in Lymington, who fairly quickly found the yacht they thought would suit Tracy. She had been called *Disque D'Or III*, was a 58 foot sloop, had raced in the 1981–82 Whitbread; in fact, in all the Races she had contested, she had always had a result. But, in a sad condition, she was at that stage laid up in Cape Town.

In April Tracy flew down to have a look. Although she was trying to be rational she admits she simply fell in love with the yacht. As so little was happening on the sponsorship front Howard had taken time out to go and sail in Antigua Race Week. Tracy phoned him there. The sponsors were Prestige Kitchens. They had called the yacht *Prestige* and had wanted £150,000 but Tracy had beaten them down to £135,000. Offer them £100,000 said Howard. They settled, in the end, for £115,000.

At the last moment one of the friendly benefactors the project has stepped in. She was given a donation of £125,000 to buy the yacht and ship it back to Southampton.

When *Prestige*, now about to become *Maiden*, arrived in June and Tracy took people to see it few dared say what they thought. The yacht was a dreadful mess. To get it into any kind of shape an enormous amount of work was going to have to be done – and quickly. Tracy began to re-assemble her crew and a shore team which was to include Duncan Walker, a local boat builder.

That summer of 1988 grew more and more hectic. Sarah-Jane Ingram joined the team and became shore manager, working closely with Howard on PR. In July the project took over Ferryside Cottage in Hamble, as the crew house. Known across the world as the 'Pink House', its colour seemed singularly appropriate for an all-woman crew. It continued to provide a secure home: equipped with numerous rooms, bathrooms and showers, with its outlook over the Hamble River, it could not have been better placed. And it was just a few yards from where Tracy lived in Ibna House.

Ian ('Poodle') put a chock under the rudder before removing it from the boat.

The task facing them all was a daunting one. When the girls first got on the yacht Tracy's instruction to them was, in effect, to demolish it from the inside out. After that they could rebuild her.

The yacht that was to become *Maiden* was in a terrible state. Nancy was scraping away inside the hull when she came across some old carpet. When she pulled it she realised to her horror it was carpet from the chocks on which the yacht was resting: there was a hole clean through the hull.

On another occasion Nancy again was pulling at some headboards in the old galley when a shower of dead cockroaches fell on her head. Like a scene from *Indiana Jones and the Temple of Doom*, laughed Howard later.

As work progressed on stripping the yacht bare, Tracy, along with Tony Castro the yacht designer, Nancy Hills and many others, were working out what to put back – and where. The exterior of the yacht had to be substantially modified, to begin with.

On deck it was decided to add new winches for the control of sails and halyards; and to put on two 'grinders' – the devices used on the largest yachts to help raise sails at speed.

Below, much more drastic work went on. The boat was completely re-wired, re-plumbed, given a brand-new set of electronic equipment. Needless to say, the galley sink was new, too.

On a yacht of *Maiden*'s size such sophistication would normally be dispensed with, but although the girls were stronger than average (men as well as women) it was decided they could do with a little bit more mechanical assistance.

Duncan cut holes in the deck and worked out an elaborate system of gearing. This meant that thereafter climbing into the top aft bunks on the yacht would be fraught with difficulty as these gears hung down under the deck.

But it was the sheer workload that counted. As the time for the re-launch came nearer and nearer it seemed the yacht could not be ready. Tracy remembers friends – other yachties – coming through, looking at the state *Maiden* was in, and offering to help for a couple of days.

Bit by bit we got her together. The engine went off for overhaul. We worked day and night rebuilding her to our design. People at the marina would come and help, giving up days and weekends to help us. I remember every one of them. Slowly *Maiden* took shape.

Not everyone was happy about our project. It put a lot of

people's backs up. God knows why they objected so strongly. I suppose they felt that a group of women were getting above themselves. There would be snide comments. Often, a couple of girls would go into the pub to hear some drunken lout shouting, 'Watch out, here come the stupid tarts from *Maiden*. Gonna sail round the world are we loves?'

In the summer of 1988 people started getting at me. I still don't know who it was. It started with abusive phone-calls from a group of men. They came at all hours of the day and night. I had petrol and oil poured on the grass in front of the house.

Someone stole my truck (I had stupidly left the keys in it, a habit which has lost me two cars) and ran into a wall. The police came to my house and arrested me. I became very frightened; so much so that I eventually asked my brother to come and stay with me. I was terrified someone would damage the boat.

Trevor racing cars, before lack of sponsorship stopped him.

By the end of August it seemed everything was happening. Tracy – and the office – moved in with Simon. She and the crew worked flat out for 24 hours a day.

And a truly big corporation was looking at them: Digital Equipment, the world's second largest computer company, had already sent its director of corporate communications and its sponsorship manager to have a look at the yacht and the gathering crew, which by now had swollen to include a doctor, Louise Dubras, as well as a Dutch girl, Tanja Visser. They were greatly impressed by the activity and commitment they saw.

Their immediate response was that DE should put in £500,000 from the British division with a recommendation to the US parent company that other parts of the company's worldwide operation should add another £300,000. Howard was so encouraged by this that he began to worry about how quickly they could change the name of the yacht from *Maiden Great Britain* to *Digital Dancer*.

In the event it became clear no decision would be forthcoming by the time the Duchess arrived. In June Howard had contacted Buckingham Palace to remind them that the Duchess of York had agreed to christen Tracy's yacht, whenever it was ready. The Palace had earlier told him that the Duchess would be unable to fulfill what had been only a tentative arrangement because she had meanwhile become pregnant. Tracy and Howard wrote what they described as an 'impassioned' letter begging her and her advisers to reconsider. The Duchess agreed and the date was set for the christening: September 20th. (As the yacht was not new it could not be 'launched'.)

The name was kept untouched. By now there was frantic work to get the yacht ready; the girls working seven days a week to give the outside of the yacht sufficient 'gloss' for the photographs they knew would be seen across the world. Activity was at fever pitch. Getting materials, however, was speeded up no end when suppliers, claiming they were too busy, were told it was for a Royal visit.

And then, on the afternoon of the day before the christening Tracy was in the office when the phone rang. She picked it up, incuriously. It was the chairman of Royal Jordanian airlines, Ali Ghandour. He had seen the proposal, and had watched some film of them all on television, announcing the Duchess' visit. As a result, he said, they'd like to put £100,000 into MGB immediately.

As she recalls that phone call Tracy remembers how distracted by the impending Royal visit she was.

> I just said 'oh, thanks very much, but I must rush now' and I put the phone down. We were all so busy. I turned to Howard and said Royal Jordanian have just offered us £100,000 and he said 'Oh, good' and that was it.

The Duchess came and christened *Maiden Great Britain* the next day. At the ceremony she was given a bottle of Mumm champagne. Whether by design or accident she uttered the immortal words, made famous by Elaine Strich in Mumm's television advert: 'Oh, Mumm's champagne, this is far too good to waste on a ship. . .' It caught the headlines the next morning. In fact the event was in every national newspaper. But the really important event of the day had gone un-sung and un-noticed. MGB, though even they didn't know it at the time, had found *the* sponsor.

The Duchess of York has been a great supporter of *Maiden* ever since she found out about the project.

CHAPTER 12

Doldrums

Punta del Este in March: the last stop where the Whitbread crews could truly relax in a holiday atmosphere. They needed to. The long haul ahead past the coast of South America and through the Caribbean looked on the map – and even more so on the globe – like a horrible uphill climb.

No-one was expecting the winds to be much other than light. Any yacht – and that included *Maiden* – which did not go well in light airs, or which went badly to windward, could expect a slow trip.

Maiden, having now lost her overall lead to *L'Esprit* in Leg Four, was prepared for a hard fight. But Tracy knew in her heart it would take a fairly monumental mistake by Patrick Tabarly on *L'Esprit* to put her back in the lead; either that or a completely unexpected weather pattern. As March 17th approached, she steeled herself for the coming month, still brooding over the mistakes on Leg Four.

March 20th   29'50"S   46'23"W

We had a very good start – got over the line in front of both *Steinlager* and *Merit*. Then we loused up badly at the first buoy. We didn't get the spinnaker down fast enough and *Rucanor* caught us. *L'Esprit* pulled away at that point and, by the time we were out of sight of land, both of them – through better tactics – had pulled away, so they were almost over the horizon. That left us, *Schlussel* and *La Poste* fighting it out.

I went too far out. We kept everybody on the radar and I went much further than any of them with the result that *L'Esprit*, *Rucanor* and *Schlussel* all took miles from us. I should have edged out gradually. The whole point was that I thought there would be more wind – wrong again, we had the same wind only we did a longer route. Wonderful!

LEG FIVE

PUNTA DEL ESTE, URUGUAY

TO FORT LAUDERDALE, USA

5,475 NAUTICAL MILES,

MARCH 17TH, 1990–

APRIL 14TH, 1990

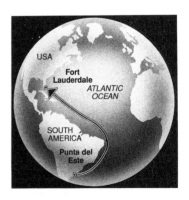

The start of Leg 5: here we go again!

The wind so far has been flukey, light variable and the weather fax information is totally unpredictable. We have been losing and gaining alternately. It is the same with the maxis –it's just a lottery and it's likely to continue like this until we get through the Doldrums.

But everyone is in good form, sailing the boat well. It is now hot every day so the clothes are off. God, it is good not to have to wear clothes.

All the talk now is of the last stop – and of the end of the Race. This feels like a particularly stupid extra leg. We all want to be racing home – I certainly do. I am dying to get on with my life. Oh well, only two months to go. It is hard to believe that we have already sailed 24,000 miles and been around the bottom of the world.

If we were heading home now it would be perfect. I am terrified of screwing up again and losing this leg, then drawing out the agony on the last leg. I am so frightened that I'll let everyone down.

The twin aims for this leg are: (1) to win by lots of hours; (2) to get back into shape. All of us feel totally wrecked by the last two months.

March 21st   27'32"S   44'14"W

I woke in a pretty bad mood and went up on deck to find Angela and Mandi asleep with no-one trimming the sails. Fantastic! I don't know why the hell I'm so worried about us winning. I told Michèle and she agreed not to let it happen again.

The chat show certainly brightened things up. I told Peter Blake about Dee having problems with the Pink House (she was trying to book it for *Steinlager* for when they returned to England). He said it must be our reputation. I said of course not. Then he said two of his guys sent love to two of ours.

Next, Juan from *L'Esprit* called to say all eight of his crew sent their regards to all 12 of mine; I returned the compliment. Then he said if we caught up he'd have the gin and tonics waiting. I said they could invite us to their equator party. Very funny, it really cheered us all up.

Although we are way ahead of *Schlussel*, *L'Esprit* and *Rucanor* took loads out of us. We are not doing too well. It was a hot day with light winds; we had the No. 1 up. The wind was all over the place, heading us a lot of the time. It is exactly what we don't want. Boring, boring, boring – and it is only the fifth day!

The wind still would not swing aft, although according to the weather fax it should free us. But considering the times they put them out, I wouldn't be surprised if they were wrong. They were ten minutes late yesterday, and ten minutes early today. Unbelievable: what did they do? Go home early?

I had a really good talk with Tanja this evening. Everyone is getting on very well, as usual. There is a relaxed atmosphere, even though we're not doing so well.

March 22nd   25'16"S   42'10"W

The wind gradually came up. The sea was getting difficult. We spent all day beating or just cracking off the wind. It still won't let us go. The weather was really hot and humid and heavy. I found it impossibe to sleep properly. Truckloads of wind and it's all on the nose; what a waste.

L'Esprit took miles from us; everyone did. It is so frustrating. Horrible day and my neck has gone again – very painful (and marvellous fun when you're beating). I hope we can get round the point without tacking – the oilfields are just past that.

Finally, the wind did free us in the evening. We were doing a great course at eight knots. Then the squalls started and every time one passed we were pushed further into the shore – just what we don't want. I just hope this dreadful weather isn't the result of us being too close to the coast. It's ironic, we lost miles to get out and now we're the furthest in and losing more miles. It seems we can't win!

Will I ever do anything right again? I feel like a useless idiot. Beating drives us all mad. Jo is so down doing the washing up, that I said we'd have a rota once the weather improves. Doing anything is awful in these conditions.

We are going round the corner tonight if we possibly can. I am only sleeping a couple of hours at a time and then getting up to do the positions – it's making me very tired. No music, everyone subdued.

March 23rd   23'01"S   40'30"W

We are still beating our brains out and not doing the course most of the time. We are moving really slowly as well: SCREAM!!! I bet *L'Esprit* is reaching gaily along at 8 knots. When will this wind swing?

An uneventful day. We should have come up onto the wind as much as possible today, as tonight we couldn't get round the oilfield. We got to the oilfields at dusk and spent the night tacking through the restricted area. I wanted to tack out when the wind was right; Michèle reckoned we should wait until we got closer. I should have done what I thought. I'm not blaming her, but us going so close to the rigs affected what happened later.

It is still my fault. When the wind came round to 070 we tacked out and, instead of tacking back and forth as we should, I decided to keep going as the wind was swinging in the right direction. As I'd only slept four hours in the previous 24, I decided to go to bed at midnight, after we'd dodged the last ship and oil rig. We were doing 090 (the course was 070).

When I got up at 4.00am I thought the world was coming to an end. The boat was shaking itself to pieces and the main was flogging badly. We had a squall with 50 knots of wind. A good way to start the day. All three watches were on deck along with Angela who had swapped with Jo for the day. They were trying to get a reef in. We managed to get the No. 1 down and changed it for the No. 3, bareheaded.

The wind and the rain were incredible; it really hurt your face. I plotted the course and checked we had been steering 090: the plot showed 110. We had been going east for four hours. Needless to say at that precise moment the wind swung round and we started doing 080 so I didn't tack.

March 24th 21'37"S 38'51"W

50 knot squall meets *Maiden*: a good way to start the day.

I should have. I got up at 6.00am and we were in a really bad position. But that was the least of our problems as it turned out.

The Kevlar main had flogged so badly that the luff had shredded away from the slides at the head. We took a reef and got the Spectra main up on deck while Jo started filming. Thank God we took a spare main.

The girls put the battens in the Spectra. At that time I was trying to work out what had gone wrong with the compasses. Meanwhile our mysterious leak is back when we are heeled over on the starboard side (that is, once again, on the port tack). Nancy went below and started pumping the bilges.

Another great weekend coming up. There were heavy seas and a good wind but in the wrong direction. Anyway, I steered while the girls got the main down and put the No. 1 up instead of the No. 3. They packed the main and put it down below.

The next problem was that four of the slides had got stuck in the mainsail track. Tanja had to go up the rig in very heavy

175

conditions, twice, to get a strap round them. She got too tired and battered, so Mandi went up and finished the job.

The wind swung round drastically and we tacked while Tanja was up the rig. We were DOING COURSE. Bloody hell! I gave the wheel to Dawn and rushed down for the chat show. We weren't doing as badly as I thought – but it was bad enough. Juan called up and said he was sorry to hear about the main. He gave me his 'you can catch up' speech and wished us courage which was very sweet.

Schlussel and *La Poste* must have had a bad night as well, from what I could tell. Back on deck I took the wheel again for Dawn. They finally got the slides down, amidst much cheering and clapping. Tanja and Mandi were bashed, bruised and tired. We got the Spectra main up and slowly but surely – hey presto – we were doing the course at 7 knots.

It was a great wind; we stuck the No. 3 up with a reef in the main. I went to bed at 10.00am. When I got up at 12.00 the wind had gone forward . . . ARRGGHH! Are we going to beat for the rest of our lives?

The compasses are definitely out: we've been steering 060 but travelling 070. I told Dawn to come up to 050. Oh God. The wind was still forward and we couldn't do the course.

It has also been wet and the water is very salty; everyone and everything is encrusted with it. The watches on deck left the others to sleep a bit longer and then all changed together at 14.00 when Angela did the lunch. Poor Michèle's Walkman has drowned in the bilge water. Everyone de-salted in a row before eating – a very funny sight. Music on, off we go.

March 25th   19'48"S   37'14"W
March 26th   16'58"S   37'21"W   (18.00hrs)

Both days we have spent tacking in light breezes. Wherever we tried to go the wind came from there. We are doing the closest tack possible. *L'Esprit* is further out than us, which is a shame. Finally, on the evening of the 26th the wind swung aft on the starboard tack and picked up and off we went. *L'Esprit* and *Rucanor* had blitzed us by this time. *Maiden* is such a dog in these conditions. Humour on board – amazingly – is still good, and the atmosphere great. Sailing tonight is good: eight knots in the right direction with a scatter of stars –beautiful.

March 27th   15'08"S   36'40"W

We had a silly day today. Positions are pretty much the same. At the chat show, Juan said that he'd expect us to be red but as he came from near Africa he was brown already and going black. *Liverpool Enterprise* thought we were talking about someone banging their head – their radio is so bad!

Just after the positions the wind was right down and we were going round in circles (the other boats are the same). Suddenly, this huge squall came over. Everyone was on deck like a shot washing in the rain, laughing and shouting. We jostled to stand under the main while Sal tipped it and we rinsed under it. It would have been very funny for an onlooker. Eight naked women giggling like crazy and screaming with laughter.

But it was a wonderful pleasure; the water was so cold and refreshing; lovely. After us we washed the boat down. Poor old *Maiden*, so salt-encrusted. Everybody let the sun dry them. Then it was back to no wind, round and round. Very, very HOT.

We got the spinnaker up just before lunch, bumbling along. Yet the atmosphere is so good on board – as if we are all sisters – no secrets, no inhibitions. It is such a lovely feeling not to have to worry about clothes – or what you look like. No-one even notices any more. Total freedom. I wonder what the other boats would think if they could see us: ugh, probably.

March 31st   04'32"S   35'59"W

It is difficult to describe the utter feeling of despair and desolation I feel when I work out the positions after the chat show. When the figure comes up on the calculator to indicate how many miles ahead *L'Esprit* and *Rucanor* are, my heart drops into my stomach. It is a really physical thing like a blow in the guts – or that sinking feeling you get when someone you are crazy about leaves you. The pain, that breathless emptiness.

To say that I have let everyone down would be the understatement of the century. There is this to be said for single-handed sailing, I suppose: you don't have anyone to answer to, you don't have to watch the looks of hope on 11 faces as you come up on deck to read the positions, only to see them turn to misery. Even worse are the forced smiles and sympathy for the navigator. ('How can she get us so far behind?', they think but they say, 'Never mind, there's still a long way to go.')

They are great, my crew, they help me so much to feel positive. It's difficult. I feel about as positive as a cat in Battersea Dogs' Home at feeding time. Dawn and Michèle are terrific: they never stop pushing the boat. The girls won't give up. I know why I am not a single-handed sailor!

The last few days have been just a blur of hot with little or no breeze, loads of current close in to the Brazilian coast. That helped us to get round. *Schlussel* and *Maiden* have been in sight of each other for three days now. Close battle. They asked on the VHF if we knew how they and us could beat *L'Esprit* and *Rucanor*. Nancy suggested Exocet missiles.

Everyone is now brown and lean; the diets are going well. No-one is peeling yet – except me! I have swapped the watches over so the girls can sleep six hours each night. It's better than rolling around in your own sweat in the daytime.

The talk on this leg is not of men (well, not much) but of food: Big Macs, Kentucky fried chicken, salad bars, Chuck's Steakhouse (a famous restaurant in Fort Lauderdale), BBQs etc. Junk food rules. Everyone is looking forward to Fort Lauderdale: the last stop, so let's go for it.

There is a lot of talk as well about 'what am I going to do at the end of the Race?' It's like leaving home all over again. Everyone, to tell the truth, is a bit lost. I am sure something will turn up for everyone.

The girls are taking turns at washing up in the evenings now, as Jo looks like she just spent six hours in a sauna by the time she had done dinner. I have to put the fan on the instruments for two hours a day to stop them melting.

Evenings though are lovely and cool, with clear starry skies. We saw loads of dolphins today – the normal grey ones at last. They are so lovely.

April 1st   02'12"S   38'21"W

I got up every two hours in the night to check our course, as the current is no longer pushing us as hard as it was. Just as I was getting up for the last time, absolutely exhausted (now I know why most boats have a skipper *and* a navigator), I noticed we were no longer doing the course.

Tanja was steering 5' higher as the course had been passed along like Chinese Whispers. I went berserk. Then I tried to trace back to when the course had been changed and to log between the two fixes. What a crazy waste of eight hours. I just sat in the nav station and burst into tears. It felt good –like I should have done it at the end of the last leg. If the guys could see me now I know they'd say, 'I told you so, women can't handle it.' Well, I'm glad I'm not a guy and don't have to pretend not to want to cry occasionally. It was the final straw. The last leg, the failures, the last stop, our loss of all these miles, this leg, my own stupidity, everything all bundled into one.

We started taking miles back from *Rucanor* and *L'Esprit* today which was some consolation. It looks as if my taking a more northerly course compared with them has paid off. Bruno still talks on the radio to Juan about how wonderful it is to be racing each other, and how they'll get drunk when they get in. They all talk in French so Michèle translates.

L'Esprit is a real problem – trying to beat them on the last leg so we can win overall. The last leg is too short to put that many hours between us. I shouldn't think about it because it makes me so angry with myself.

We should have won the last leg, there is no excuse. At least on this leg there is good reason. The girls are all enjoying this leg and there has been some excellent sailing. It's like being in heaven, reaching with the spinnaker up and doing 9–10 knots.

Jeni hangs on for dear life at the end of the spinnaker pole.

As they crossed the equator, Tracy could see that the light winds and slow conditions were giving *L'Esprit* and *Rucanor* a big advantage.

Music is blaring out, there's a blazing sun, blue sky and white puffy clouds racing against us. The sea is a deep, deep blue, there's white surf all around and tropical sea-birds. Perfect. Everyone is looking so healthy and brown. Everyone is losing weight. (Come to think about it, I seem to be the only one who isn't losing anything.)

Apart from the problem with the main, *Maiden* seemed in good order. Leg Five was always going to be a problem, though. The course the girls had to steer along the coast of South America until they were able to bear off through the Caribbean, was the worst point of sailing for them: they hated beating, hard on the wind. The girls loathed it as the boat buried its nose, unable to shake away the combination of wind and water.

So they lolled, fretted, cursed while Tracy wracked her brains hour by hour trying to work a course that would take them out of these frustrating days as quickly as possible. The combination of the disasters of Leg Four, the knowledge that Patrick Tabarly on *L'Esprit* was inching his yacht ahead on both distance and, crucially, time, nagged like a toothache.

Then, on April 3rd the girls noticed a crack had developed in the boom, just behind the point where the vang joined it – an area of maximum stress. Bearing in mind the number of yachts whose booms had broken, it was an additional source of concern for Tracy. Michèle, meanwhile, set to work out how to effect a jury repair.

April 5th   08'53"N   49'21"W

However, coming a little further north than *L'Esprit* and *Rucanor* has paid off: we've taken 80 miles from them in five days. There is high pressure to the north of us which should make the wind swing aft. It's been forward for a while which has been good for speed – three sail reaching.

But now it is the eternal problem until it swings round: course or speed? *L'Esprit* and *Rucanor* are doing course now and we have come down a bit. I hope it swings quickly. The last few days have been very pleasant, with us reaching in heavy conditions at times: *Maiden* loves it. We are 1,000 miles from Antigua where we turn the corner for Fort Lauderdale.

It hasn't been so hot down below in the past couple of days, and everyone has been sleeping like the dead. I can't get enough

sleep at the moment – don't know why. I feel so drained, trying to figure one step ahead of the other boats the whole time. I suppose I can't switch off when I'm sleeping.

The crack in the boom is getting bigger. Michèle is making plates for it today to strengthen it behind the vang saddle, as it seems to be weak there, and as the boom pumps the crack works and gets bigger. The boom looks like a patchwork quilt; will they ever get it right?

The reacher is slightly torn at the clew but should last until we can take it down and mend it. The Genoa staysail is very effective and gives us an extra half knot.

Last night there were loads of flying fish on the boat. One landed on Sally and she went berserk. Everyone else just cracked up laughing. This morning *Maiden* looked like a fishing boat; they were everywhere. Maybe we should cook them – if we are able to gut them quickly. The sun is out again today after two cloudy days. Roll on Fort Lauderdale: clean, still beds and lots of junk food.

I am duty boat today and I can hear the charter boats in the Caribbean talking on six megs. It makes me feel even more homesick but a little stronger, too, to be racing past my other world. I'll try and call Antigua when we go past.

7th April   13'46"N   56'13"W

We've managed to keep the wind for the past two days although this afternoon the wind has come aft and dropped a bit. It was cloudy yesterday, but today has been blazing with a hot sun, although there has been a cool breeze. The night before last, after I had finished doing the chat show, I had calls from two old friends of mine. Phil Wade on a boat called *Gandalph* and Peter Mullins on a motor boat, *Chaptiva III*.

Phil was on *Drum* and stayed with me in Hamble for a while. Peter was chartering in Antigua when I was. It was great to hear from them. Peter gave me times and frequencies for English Harbour so yesterday, at lunch-time, I called and got *Crackerjack*, another boat I know. The skipper, Peter, told me to try again in an hour; we had a good long talk.

Then I called *English Harbour* – I told them I would call today and could they get Jol Byerly to the the radio. Jol and Judy have lived in Antigua for years and have a yacht brokerage. I lived with them when I had no boat and no job. They've always looked after me and been there when I needed them. Two dear friends. By this time I was missing Antigua like crazy.

When Jol did come on the radio I had a terrible lump in my throat. I wanted to turn the boat in and head for security. We had a good chat and I said I'd try and get down from Fort Lauderdale for a couple of days. I know I'd really love to although I just don't know if I'll have the time. (In fact, for the first time since the Race began, she did take those days off, had a short break and flew down to Antigua.)

It certainly cheered me up to hear all my old friends. I'll try and call again tomorrow. We should go round Antigua at lunchtime on Monday. I heard today that the front maxis are just two days away from the finish. *Merit* is 250 miles behind *Steinlager* which made me feel better. Everyone makes mistakes except Mike Quilter (navigator, *Steinlager*).

Friday 13th April   25'05"N   75'25"W

What an apt date. We lost truckloads to *L'Esprit* and *Rucanor* last night and now we are close reaching with awkward waves and 20–25 knots of wind. Ugh! Ugh! Ugh! I wish I'd washed my hair yesterday. So does everyone else. As it happened, I did mine this morning. What a palava – you need danger money. Oh well, the sun is shining through the clouds when it can and there are streaks of blue in the distance.

We are now doing 9 knots towards the last corner – 90 miles away. Life isn't so bad. The wind finally came up this morning after

12 hours of us sitting still with only three knots. *L'Esprit* and *Rucanor* had 15 knots from the *NE*. We consequently lost all the hard-earned miles we had taken from them over the past ten days.

I still can't get over the fact that a mistake in the first 100 miles has put us this far out at this end. Both of them will be in this afternoon: scream! Everyone was quiet last night but now we are moving again we are all happy. I'm duty boat today, which is a pain as I have to listen to the radio and hear all the charter boats saying where they are going today and how they won't leave harbour if waves come over the bow. Jeese!

The last few days have been excruciatingly boring. Dead downwind with 18–20 knots. You can feel your mind and body turning to jelly. So you do puzzle books and exercise frantically but of course it's not enough. Our course has been slightly more northerly than the others since South America and it paid off.

We clawed miles back from *L'Esprit* and *Rucanor*. *Schlussel* seems to be attached to us by a piece of elastic. *La Poste*, is a couple of hundred miles behind. Now I know what they must feel like all the time. What a disaster of a leg.

As we went round Antigua on the morning of April 9th, loads more of my old friends all called up. Peter Mullins and Jol Byerly called again; Robbie Cook from the slipway (he was once a member of this project); Stuart on *Enchanta*; various others. It was great, they are like a second family. They all said how proud of me they were. They all had a part in getting me here. All of them, and many others: Piggy and Jo who changed my attitude towards boats; Jol and Judy who looked after me and advised me; Julian Gildersleeve who suggested I do the last Whitbread; Robbie Cook who helped me with the project. All of them, too numerous to mention, got me here.

So here we were, sailing past saying, 'We've done it.' It was a proud moment for us and everyone felt it. Jol was organising a boat to come out and see us, but we went past too early and they missed us. The thought was there, though. I must try and get down to Antigua from Fort Lauderdale. I haven't taken a holiday in any of the stops yet.

Just past the Caribbean we saw a massive whale surfacing and we had to change course to miss it.

A couple of nights ago I heard a really strange noise. The girls on deck were all imitating an ambulance: nee naw, nee naw, nee naw. I went up to investigate and I discovered Dawn flicking a flying fish back into the water with one of Jo's galley spoons.

They all explained it was the 'flying fish emergency unit'. I laughed till I cried – they were deadly serious about it. I think I can seriously say we are all looking forward to getting in – and then some!

There was one surprise left – one which the girls had been keeping for Howard Gibbons. When *Maiden* coasted across the horizon outside the entrance to Fort Lauderdale, the welcoming party was on *Mystère of England*, a yacht which figured largely in the first meeting between him and Tracy. Howard was amazed, then delighted, to see the whole *Maiden* crew in swimsuits.

Of all the stopovers, Fort Lauderdale was the one and only place to spring this surprise. The local media loved it – and so did the British press who had long given up hoping that the Maidens would ever let their hair down in this fashion. As Tracy said later, 'Well, if you are going to come fourth (*Schlussel* just beat them in), do it in swimsuits.' It was an option which could only have been effective for the first all-women crew. Having shaken off forever any doubts about their ability they could afford to relax the image a little; and they did.

Shorts off, swimsuits on as we come in to Fort Lauderdale.

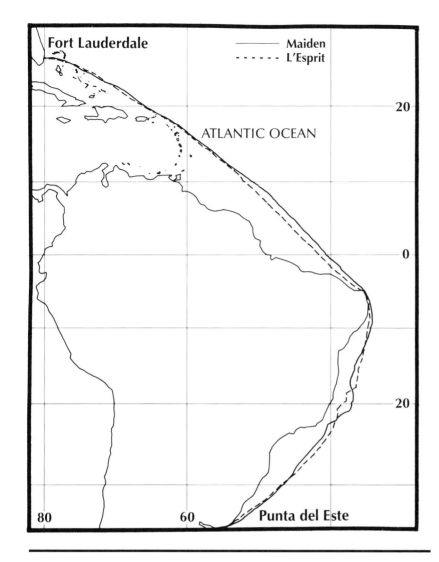

Fort Lauderdale

Maiden
- - - - - L'Esprit

20

ATLANTIC OCEAN

0

20

80   60   Punta del Este

A Summary of Leg Five: Sunshine Sailors

Steinlager won Leg Five for the maxis. By now this was no surprise. The Race for the maxis seemed to have come down to only the time gap between the two New Zealand ketches as *Fisher and Paykel* arrived in Lauderdale in second place.

Yet, for just a while, off the coast of South America, *Rothmans* had taken the lead. And then lost it. By Lauderdale Lawrie Smith and his star crew were 54 hours behind Peter Blake's Kiwis; *Fisher and Paykel* had slipped to 35 hours behind. Pierre Fehlmann and *Merit* came fourth, making a race for third place overall the one possible excitement for the last leg among the division A yachts.

Everyone hauled into Fort Lauderdale and agreed the fifth leg had been dull from a sailing point of view. It was perhaps best summed up by John Chittenden, the skipper of *Creightons Naturally* who said he thought the leg had been the Atlantic equivalent of crossing the Serpentine: 'We half expected someone to come out with deckchairs for us,' he said.

It had been a long dull meander along the Brazilian coast, across the Equator for the second time. As with the fourth leg (and to some extent the first) the winds were generally light with one or two sharp and nasty squalls. No yacht in this leg reported any major damage.

There were no excuses for those who came after the first four in the maxi division. Tracy most certainly did not excuse *Maiden's* fourth place, although by now everyone who had followed the race in division D knew that nothing but strong winds would help the girls on their way.

Florida was basking in spring sunshine. The yachts pulled into Pier Sixty Six for the welcome, such that it was. Then they scattered, either into the adjacent berths of the marina or off in one or other of the hundreds of canals that make Fort Lauderdale the Venice of the USA.

For *Maiden*, whose crew and skipper stayed at the luxurious Embassy Suite, just down the road from Pier Sixty Six, it was a reflective time. Their entry into the States had been a supreme example of professional PR. Of all the Whitbread yachts and crew, *Maiden* got the cream in Florida.

But there were niggles. Nance Frank chose this moment to re-emerge, saying she would be in the next Race with the first all-woman *maxi* crew, herself as skipper. Tracy was outraged, with all her doubts and fears about this Californian woman coming crowding around. Most infuriating for her, was the false identification of the nebulous Frank plans with her own boat and crew. But there was another, more serious point.

Tracy argued that no one who had not sailed a leg of a Whitbread before – and preferably one of the Southern Ocean legs – should be allowed to skipper a yacht in a future Race. Many had so argued before, expressing amazement that more or less anyone could put a yacht into the Race.

What Tracy had feared all along was that a badly organised, or a poorly experienced, crew of women would jeopardise her own achievements – and set the place of women in ocean racing back once more. 'We are special,' she said for the first time in the States. 'It's not just our being first, it's being who we are.' She knew, too, that in the next Whitbread the stakes would be a lot higher, for her and for any other all-woman crew.

The future of the Whitbread was decided in Fort Lauderdale. The brewery announced they would be sponsoring the next Race. They also announced, to Tracy's delight, that there would be a new 'Whitbread' class of 60ft yachts, whose design was yet to be agreed. After all her previous doubts, this clinched one thing in her mind.

She sat with Howard Gibbons one morning in Pier Sixty Six and asked him whether he would be her project manager if – if, she stressed – she were to take part in the next Race. Yes, he said, if you want me. Tears filled her eyes. It was the best kind of answer for the future of what had now become universally acknowledged in the Race as the best team of all.

Another team became final in Lauderdale. Howard Gibbons married Elizabeth Green, which is to say Nancy Hill's sister, Lizzie. They got married on *Maiden*, as Tracy had promised, though not at sea, to save the guests from possible *mal de mer*.

It was a very public ceremony and one which simply reinforced the growing realisation that now the whole *Maiden* project was very much in the eyes of the media. After all the efforts to get the very idea of *Maiden* established, it now seemed as if the world could not get enough of the reality.

CHAPTER 13

Racing Certainty

The Royal Jordanian offer to *Maiden* in 1988 had come just in time. Although it was initially a short term deal – £100,000 for a winter race programme – it was to be the saviour of the entire project.

With enough money to ensure the yacht was fully kitted out, at least for the next few months, the race shifted back to the yard in Hamble where all speed was put on to get *Maiden* ready for her first test: the Spanish-run Route of Discovery Race from Cadiz, near Gibraltar, to Santo Domingo in the Dominican Republic. The race more or less followed the route taken by Christopher Columbus, who doubtless would have been astonished that a couple of dozen yachts would be following in his track 500 years later, one of them to be crewed entirely by women.

Tracy was beginning to feel pressured, though, by opinions still being expressed by a sceptical yachting press, one of whose members believed the girls should be physically stopped from sailing anywhere.

As a result, in the week before they were due to set sail to Spain, she suffered an agony of stomach disorders and a crippling stiff neck, the latter so bad she had to wear a surgical collar. Lying in bed in her house, she looked frail and, for what she had planned, dangerously unwell. As her doctor said then, and was to repeat: if you want to be relieved of the burden of going at all keep on like this and I'll put you in hospital for six months. It was medicine of an unconventional kind.

The day came, bright and sunny. An excited crowd of supporters gathered by the Royal Southern Yacht Club, in Hamble – families of Tracy and her crew, reporters, camera crews, and some delighted members of Royal Jordanian, along with Howard, and the shore team. Everyone embarked on the launch as *Maiden* came swanning

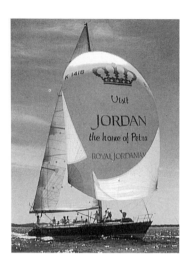

Maiden with her new sponsor's spinnaker.

down the river. She came briefly alongside and then was off, the launch fussing in her train. A couple of spinnaker runs down The Solent to show off her Royal Jordanian colours and then she turned west for the first time under her all-women crew and sailed away.

What few people knew was that there was a stowaway on board: the yacht was still suffering from many mechanical problems and Duncan Walker had shipped aboard. All through the farewells he had remained a prisoner below; the doubters would have had a field day had they caught a glimpse of him. In the run down to Spain he became the first of a very small and privileged group of men to have sailed with the girls.

Maiden got away to a good start on the afternoon of December 4th and, in fairly stiff conditions, plunged on towards the Canaries, their first mark. So far, their performance had been good but not as good as Tracy had believed they could achieve, even at this stage. As the days passed, she was growing in confidence, but that shift in herself was about to be challenged in the most dramatic way.

They swept into the bay off Las Palmas on the night of December 9th to round a mark. It was strange for all of them to be able to see people promenading on the shore whilst knowing they now had 3,000 miles of the Atlantic ahead; it was unsettling as well.

More unsettling still, their weather fax had broken. Ocean-going racing yachts have increasingly begun to rely on equipment such as this, to give them detailed and up-to-date information on where the best winds might lie, as well as providing information on unsettled or stormy conditions. The system was devised for commercial shipping, tied in to weather routeing advice.

Much controversy has arisen among yachts people about the ethics of using shore-based advice during a race. The purists argue it destroys the seamanship aspect altogether. But the technology is there and is used. *Maiden* had had it installed; now it had failed.

Tracy could make one of two decisions. She could have applied a conventional rule of thumb and followed the pack – the yachts ahead and around her whose equipment was still working. Alternatively, she could break that rule and follow the old sailing ship route to find the trade winds which blow across the Atlantic. Marie-Claude told her to go North, Tracy went South. Her argument for doing that was to be that the weather suited to the biggest maxi yachts would not necessarily help them. In any case, as they opened up an inevitable lead, the weather information which would get them to change course one way or another, would not help her anyway.

Another day passed and *Maiden* now lost the wind she had had; the yacht rolled on the Atlantic swell. Tracy's comfort, such as it was, had been that one other contestant had followed them, *With Integrity*, skippered by Andy Coghill, and a Whitbread cruising entry.

It was scant comfort, though, to have a yacht the MGB crew looked down on following in their wake. The yacht was by now dropping back in its race position from fifth to 13th. There were only 20 yachts in the race.

Tracy had aimed to hit the trades at a latitude of 20' south; *Maiden* had now reached that point, by dribs and drabs of wind and current. The wind ruffled the surface of the water, caught its breath, much as the skipper and crew were doing, breathed a little harder, then gathered its skirts for a romping, rolling 25 knots of gorgeous north-easterlies. They were truly on their way.

Far to the north the pack now found themselves beset by headwinds and storms. From leading the way they now began to drop back, spinnakers blown out, egos dented. One or two began to come further south. The daily positions were showing Tracy and her crew creeping back into the race and then, incredibly, beginning to open out a lead.

It took them 19 days to cross and, despite their progress, they could never have hoped to be first over the line. As with the Whitbread the maxis would always cross first. So when they turned into the busy commercial harbour in Santo Domingo it was no surprise for them to see the dockside lined with male crews off those maxis. What was a surprise to her, tinged at first with disbelief, was what they were shouting: 'You're first, you're first,' they choroused. (This was an estimate of their handicap-adjusted position.)

The final race result was that *Maiden* came second, beating all the other Whitbread yachts, including – and this was a sweet moment for Tracy – Pierre Fehlmann, the winner of the 1985–86 Whitbread Race. At a reception in the Spanish embassy, the hundreds of male crew applauded when the girls turned up in striking black and white dresses, chaperoned by a Howard Gibbons aglow with pride and emotion. 'When we came in,' said Howard later, 'you could have heard a pin drop; they were astonished at the transformation.'

But *Maiden* and her team were not allowed an unalloyed victory. Just before they had been about to set out for the reception, whilst everyone was gathered in the hotel lobby, a man in a dark suit, wearing a black tie approached Howard. 'Which one is Tracy Edwards?'

he asked. The British Honorary Consul for the Dominican Republic brought very sad news.

He took her aside to tell her that Sally Creaser's mother had been taken suddenly ill with a rare form of meningitis and had, equally suddenly, died. Thinking fast Tracy got hold of Louise and told her before she said anything to Sally. Then she broke the news. Sally, the strong-willed, heart-of-oak sailor, the life and soul of *Maiden*'s joke factory, was shattered. When the others went, she and Louise stayed, while arrangements were made to get her home the next day.

Maiden had been prepared for an immediate departure to Antigua after the reception; that, too, had to be delayed. When they finally reached Antigua, Tracy sent Marie-Claude home for a holiday. Her misgivings had set in after the mate had violently lost her temper with one of the crew.

The start of 1989 – the year of the Whitbread – was gloomy for other reasons. Despite the money from Royal Jordanian, there was no other major sponsor in view. Digital, after a second long and apparently committed look at MGB, pulled out for good in a letter sent on February 2nd, 1989. Over 300 prospective sponsors in various parts of the food and drinks industries showed interest one by one and then faded away, as did others from a diverse range including the shipping, clothing, perfume and pharmaceuticals industries.

Because of the 'Ruta' result, MGB were now going back to companies that had earlier rejected them, pointing out the result Tracy had got was the best result for a British yacht in a trans-ocean race for many years. Still, the interest from a British company failed to materialise.

With the yacht arriving back from its trans-Atlantic delivery, Howard and Tracy were faced with a terrible choice. Every avenue they had explored had apparently gone cold. Now, the yacht would need to be hauled out for a major re-fit – the critical major re-fit – before the Whitbread, only eight months away. The cost would be vast.

We began to see the whole project crashing down,' says Tracy. 'We were back to where we were a year ago – a half-finished boat, a £100,000 overdraft (at that time – it grew bigger). The bank wouldn't lend us any more money to finish the boat. Howard and I were liable for that overdraft. We were both going into a cold sweat. We started pussy-footing around for a while before we thought out what we had to do.'

Howard decided he had to approach the Jordanians again. They were enthusiastic, but asked for more detailed costing. Then the wait began: all through the early spring nothing appeared to be happening; meanwhile, the bills were pouring in.

It was with a heavy heart, then, that Howard set off for Portsmouth, on Wednesday, May 10, with Sarah-Jane Ingram in tow. On the way down, Sarah-Jane asked Howard what excuses he was going to deploy as to why the money had still not arrived. They drove into the Nat West Business Centre car park and walked in trepidation through the door. Paul Emmerson, the manager, was waiting for them.

'Well,' he said, 'you must be feeling very pleased.' Howard looked blank. 'Pardon?' he said. 'About the money,' explained Emmerson, 'how much exactly were you expecting they'd send?'

Howard felt the floor move under him. Not to be put out, even under these circumstances, he parried back: 'Oh, just about what they've sent,' he said smiling. In the end he had to confess he didn't exactly know. Emmerson, grinning broadly, told him it would pay off their overdraft and leave enough over to get them and the yacht to the start line.

At last, after three years of intense and often bitter struggle, *Maiden* was a racing certainty in the 1989–90 Whitbread. Pausing only to put the bulk of the money left over from paying off the overdraft into a short-term high interest account, Howard and Sarah-Jane hurried from the bank, found an off-licence, bought the obligatory champagne, and drove as fast as they dared back to Hamble. Work on *Maiden* in the yard came to a halt. That night everyone got roaringly drunk. Now, at last, they all knew they would be in the Race.

In June, Tracy, Howard, and Keith Webb, the local designer of the yacht's colours (and those of the Royal Jordanian) flew off to Jordan to meet their official main sponsors.

'When we saw the hotel in Amman – the Plaza – we just hoped Royal Jordanian were going to pay for it.'

In her hotel room Tracy put in a call to the Royal Palace; the King had not known she was coming but her luck was in; he was in town.

She had first met him just before the start of the previous Whitbread in 1985. She had been on *Jubilation*, in the States, waiting to deliver it to England, when the skipper of another yacht, *Excalibur*, asked if she would do him a favour. Would she come and act as a stewardess for a day charter?

We didn't know who it was, they wouldn't tell us, but we knew it had to be someone very important because the security people were all over us; they searched the yacht, they checked the hull.

I was standing at the rail with the skipper, when they all arrived. He said 'Who are they, I know their faces?' and I said, 'That's King Hussein of Jordan.'

The day charter was a great success. Later, after lunch, Tracy was doing the washing-up. To her great surprise, King Hussein appeared. 'Let me help you,' he said. They talked and Tracy told him of her life as a sailor, and how she was going to sail in the coming Whitbread. 'The King was very interested; as a pilot he was particularly intrigued by the navigation side,' says Tracy.

As they left at the end of the day the King turned to her: 'I'm passing through London,' he said. 'Give me your mother's phone number and I'll tell her I've seen you and that you are all right.' Tracy hesitated but she gave the number. 'And you stay in touch, too,' said the King. 'I am very interested to know how you get on.'

King Hussein made that call. Pat Edwards still remembers it. 'I was just about to laugh it off as a joke and say "Oh, yes, and I'm the Queen of Sheba," when something told me it was real. It's Tracy, you see – with her anything is possible.'

Tracy and the King stayed in touch. It is a friendship Tracy values for that as much as for anything else. In Amman, though, first came the business of the sponsors. All three found themselves at the Royal Jordanian offices to meet the chairman, Mr Ali Ghandour.

When we got into Mr Ghandour's office we all sat down and watched the *Maiden* video in the boardroom. Just after it started I suddenly remembered there was a sequence with some of the girls topless and I sat thinking 'How can I stop this?' It came up on screen and there was dead silence.

We got a lot done – the meeting did last the whole three hours. Afterwards we all went for lunch and toasted the success of the whole venture. At four there was a car waiting for me, and I was taken straight to the Royal Palace. I met the King and we talked and he asked me how everything was going. He is amazing – he always remembers everything. We talked for a while and then he said 'I'm going to take you on a tour of Amman.' He called in an aide and arranged for a helicopter. Then he said, 'I'll arrange for Howard and Keith to be picked up and brought over.'

Back at the Plaza, Howard and Keith, unknowing objects of royal attention and command, were lazing by the pool, oblivious to the world. A hotel porter rushed up and shrieked: 'It's the Palace on the phone, quick.' Howard tore into the lobby, found the phone, got the message. He and Keith managed to get out of bathing costumes and into suits just before the palace car arrived. Swept away in a royal Mercedes they stared at each other. 'Is this really happening?' mouthed Keith.

In the Palace, King Hussein had asked Tracy how long they were in Jordan. When he found out he called his aide: 'I want them to have a helicopter for three or four days, with a crew. And can you tell the Royal Palace in Aqaba that Tracy and her friends will be staying as my guests for the weekend.'

When Howard and Keith walked in His Majesty said 'Howard, it's good to see you. Keith, you do such wonderful designs for *Maiden*.' I could see the looks on their faces. Then, after we had talked, the King said, 'Right, we are going to go and tour around Amman.' Now, *I* knew it was going to be in the helicopter but they didn't. We walked outside and there was a Mercedes waiting. Howard and Keith got in the back and the King got in the driving seat. I looked at Howard and he was mouthing at Keith, 'The King is going to chauffeur us around Amman in his car!'

Well, in fact he flew us in his helicopter. We had a wonderful trip all over the city and then he flew us down to the Dead Sea. As we went below sea level he called to me and said, 'Look at the altimeter, this is the only time in the next year I want to see you below sea level!'

The Duchess of York at the helm of *Maiden*.

Back home another royal occasion was in the offing. Ever since she had christened the yacht the previous September, the Duchess of York – Fergie – had kept her interest in *Maiden*. She had been invited for a sail and it was finally arranged for Monday, July 10th. Ali Ghandour was to fly in from Amman for the visit. The day dawned bright and hot.

Tracy met the Duchess, just up the road from Hamble village. She was very nervous but when the helicopter door slid open there was Fergie, grinning and wearing a *Maiden* sweat shirt. 'How's it all going?' she asked. Tracy felt herself relax.

The sail that followed went perfectly. The Duchess was determined to put everyone at ease and, during lunch, undertook to hand round the food. The wind, which had been fitful earlier, picked

Ali Ghandour was the driving force behind the sponsorship of *Maiden* by Royal Jordainian airlines.

up and the yacht kicked up her heels and sang her way down The Solent. 'I'll be on the start line, cheering you all on,' was the Duchess's parting shot.

Once the royal visit was over, a different kind of corporate frenzy took over. There had been an agreement with Royal Jordanian that there would now be a formal announcement about sponsorship at the start of Cowes Week. Howard had arranged for a reception in the Castle Rock Yacht Club in Cowes on July 29th. He and Tracy both felt this was the right place to make this most significant of announcements. It also smacked of the kind of style *Maiden* was now claiming for its own. It had also been the place where Tracy had made an announcement in 1987 that she certainly would be a Whitbread entry.

The project was still called *Maiden Great Britain* – often shortened to MGB – when the yacht was christened by the Duchess of York. But when Royal Jordanian airlines took on the sponsorship it seemed quite wrong to keep the full name. After some discussion with Ali Ghandour, it was decided to drop the *Great Britain*. Ghandour was insistent, though that as the Duchess had given the name *Maiden* at least should remain on the boat's side. When he left the company this mis-match between the sponsors and the boat's name was to cause much agony as Royal Jordanian felt they could not adequately get their involvement across as fully as they had hoped.

In the marquee on Cowes, Ali Ghandour made a speech – a clear statement about the Royal Jordanian interest; Tracy made her reply, standing among her crew, suddenly all looking very vulnerable in their dresses. She remembered only too well the time two years before, at the start of Cowes Week standing more or less in the same place, bravely telling a sceptical world that she would have a yacht and a crew ready on the start line. Now, finally she had done it.

CHAPTER 14

Coming Home

May 5th   3,837 miles to go.

I am so nervous. Talk about under pressure! If one more person had asked me if we could beat *L'Esprit* I would have screamed.

I had breakfast with Howard and we talked about what the hell we do about our desperate financial situation. It affects what I now want to do – the next Whitbread – because I don't want debts hanging over me. The new 60 foot class the Whitbread want to introduce sounds really exciting. I am also now thinking that if we don't win this Race, overall, I will have to try again with everything I have learned. If we can get an early sponsorship we could do the whole thing properly.

It would mean a new boat, a careful study of the weather, the sails – all the things we would need in order to win. I'm itching to get going already. I know we could win with a sponsor getting involved at the beginning.

It was boiling hot, very sweaty. I was getting into a worse and worse mood. Not a good way to start the last leg. The dock was teeming with people – they hadn't stopped the public from having access to the boats. We pushed our way through hundreds of jostling people.

We had roped off our end of the dock so at least people couldn't get that close. I retreated to the peace and quiet of the nav station and tried to gather my thoughts. The girls packed everything away and got the lines ready. Everything seemed to happen at once. The bridge went up and I decided to leave. I more or less had to throw a photographer off the boat who wouldn't get off.

By the time we were ready to go I was really worked up. When Howard gave me a hug I nearly burst into tears. Then it was 'lines

LEG SIX

FROM FORT LAUDERDALE, USA

TO SOUTHAMPTON,

3,837 NAUTICAL MILES,

MAY 5TH, 1990–

MAY 28TH, 1990

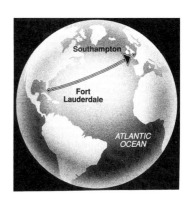

off' for the last time on this Race and we backed out. Everyone cheered.

Someone shouted 'Goodbye, Nance Frank!' and I thought, well, that just about says it all for this stop. We were out, though.

One yacht had anchored slap bang in the middle of the start line! But when we did cross the line it was the best we had ever done. We were at the right end and almost first over. We looked back to see the maxis bearing down on us. It was an impressive sight. We had a run to the first mark.

L'Esprit got round first. We were second, ahead of *Rucanor* and *Schlussel*. We headed out to the Gulf Stream with all our class going in the same direction. We kept *L'Esprit* in sight but with light winds *Rucanor* and *Schlussel* were soon abeam. It was easy to see what had happened on the last leg.

Slowly the spectator boats disappeared. I felt ill; Mandi did too. All four boats stayed together until the evening when *Schlussel* set off straight across – the shortest route. It's a huge gamble but they have nothing to lose and a lot to gain. *La Poste* followed her.

During the night the wind came aft and we gybed with *Rucanor*. We are still keeping the Gulf Stream. *L'Esprit* carried on eastwards. Then the wind came forward and we put a reacher up along with a staysail – still heading northwards.

May 6th   26° 45'N   79° 51'W

This morning, early, we were all within a mile of each other. Then, the most incredible thing happened. I had just got up and was wondering what to do next – go north or east – when we looked over to our left and there was a tornado heading straight for us.

We rather stupidly all stood there and gaped at it, mouths open. Then the spell broke. Michèle and two others rushed to get the headsail down and I started to get the leeward runner in. As it hit us I turned to see *L'Esprit* and *Rucanor* taking down their headsails. We were grabbed by the wind as if we were a toy and turned round in a complete circle. Totally powerless, we didn't have enough time to be scared.

We got control of the boat and got back on course just as the heavens opened stinging our faces and hands. We put the headsails back up and set off on the track of *Rucanor* while *L'Esprit* changed headsails. The wind came further forward and we took the staysail down and put the No 1 up. No one could believe what a crazy hour we had just had.

L'Esprit soon began to catch up in the light airs that followed the rain. They kept climbing (heading more north) while we stayed on 040°. *Rucanor* stayed with us for a while before dropping out of sight over the horizon in the evening.

During the night *L'Esprit* dropped down and stayed close to us, two miles ahead. Everyone on board is really tired and this leg doesn't feel like part of the Race. It is very odd and disjointed. It feels as if the finish was in America: the Race is so long! There has been a lot of sleeping going on, no music and not much talking. It's like a ghost ship. There is not the usual atmosphere.

Maybe we don't need words any more. Everyone is looking forward to the end of the Race but no one wants it to come. The thought of having to sell *Maiden*, having to pay off all our debts is very distressing to me.

I try not to worry too much hoping that something will turn up. I suppose all the girls are worried in one way or another about the future after the end of the Race. They are lost in their own thoughts – and fears – for their futures.

When the tornado hit us we were grabbed by the wind as if we were a toy.

197

I spoke to Juan on *L'Esprit* today about the tornado. He said it was very impressive to see us disappear inside it. They had been very worried – as had *Rucanor.*

May 7th   30° 20'N   79° 11'W

The wind built during the night and by early morning we were beating in huge seas, all feeling a bit the worse for wear. My stomach is really bad again. *L'Esprit* had a problem and dropped sharply off, ending up behind us. I can't see *Rucanor* at all.

I can't seem to find the Gulf Stream and we are being headed east anyway onto the circle course. Both *L'Esprit* and *Rucanor* have gone for the great circle route. I think it is the right thing.

The wind got lighter all day: difficult to keep any course at all so we just went for speed. Dawn finally got the generator going after two days trying. We ran the engine this morning. I went to switch the battery light off and turned the power off. The sat navs went as a result. They did start to take fixes later but it was tense. No wind all night.

May 8th   33° 59'N   74° 18'W

Messy Marvin on top of our primary port winch

Michèle had to fix the mast track again. It had probably been pushed out when we tacked without the runners on in the waterspout. When I plotted our position this morning we were way north because of steering high for speed. The wind was dead behind. I sat and thought about it and decided to carry on going north on a win all, lose all, basis. It means doing the exact opposite of *Schlussel.*

It's also to try to catch the low before either *L'Esprit* or *Rucanor;* to skirt over the Azores high; to stay further north and closer to the Stream; finally, to keep on northwards is our best point of sail right now.

I agonised for ages figuring we might lose some miles, then gain – but end up by losing. We went for it anyway. I missed the morning chat show because we were still fixing the mast. That meant I didn't know where the others were. We kept on north.

A bird landed on the boat today and stayed. We named him Messy Marvin. He's a plover of some sort. Sally has taken to feeding him and looking after him. He is really exhausted.

The wind is still all over the place – it's warm and pleasant, though. At the evening chat show we found out that my decision had paid off. I had got it right and we were in the lead. Yippee! The wind slowly came up during the night. We were steering high for speed. Marvin settled in the port steering well for the night.

May 9th   36° 47'N   71° 24'W

I woke to find Angela frantically pumping the bilges. One of the extra pipes that Dawn had used to try the generator had come off the sea cock and we had taken loads of water. Then I found out that Michèle had changed battery banks and turned the power off. Consequently, the sat navs didn't work all day.

Marvin has now taken up residence in the port steering well where I had to move him when we gybed this morning. He got really indignant when I picked him up. It's like having a child on board: the more brave he gets the more he gets into danger and mischief. Every time you have to do something on deck you have to check he's not going to get injured.

By this afternoon he had taken to flying round the boat and then coming back. We saw more waterspouts today but luckily didn't get hit by one. The wind picked up all day: we are doing a perfect course on this gybe with up to 30 knots of wind. That meant us romping along at 12 knots and occasionally surfing at 16–17 knots. Marvin loves it.

The day got greyer but it is still really warm. The second sat nav finally took a fix. Meanwhile, the next problem on the agenda is icebergs. Should we avoid the area altogether or go through – the shorter course. All it says on my chart is area of many icebergs. Does that mean more than we found in the Southern Ocean or just lots for the Atlantic? In the end I got an ice report from the Race Committee.

Disaster nearly struck this afternoon when Marvin went for a quick flying practice. He fell into the sea but got out again and came back on board – very clearly puzzled. I said to Claire that small birds like that ought not to be out in the ocean and she said that's very probably what they are saying about us.

May 10th   38° 37'N   67° 31'W

This was the day I lost us the sixth leg. I spent all morning trying to decide whether to carry on along the great circle route or to follow the Gulf Stream. The chat show didn't really tell us anything except that L'Esprit will eventually follow the Stream.

199

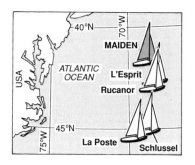

Maiden looked to be in a good position but Tracy knew she was in the wrong place: too far north and not enough East.

After dithering around I finally decided to go for the Stream. Unfortunately it was too late. We changed course and reached over for it – also trying to work our way north. What I should have done was to go straight over to it before (or tried for six hours).

So I spent the whole day trying to get into it with us being pushed too far north and not enough east. Can we go back to yesterday, please? Oh well, when I muck up, I certainly muck up big.

We reached along quite nicely all day. Marvin spent most of the time eating prawns and sitting on Sal's head. Then, in the afternoon, he headed for home. How did he know the wind would now blow him back to shore instead of away as it would have done before?

Maybe our luck went with him. The wind built all day coming forwards but it is unlikely come so far forward as to stop us reaching. There is a front to come through, though.

Then around 5.00 this afternoon we hit a whale: luckily it didn't damage anything, thank God. I think the whale must have been hurt. It just bounced along the side.

This evening the wind has really started trucking – close reaching now to get us to the Stream. The positions at the chat show were not good for us. *L'Esprit* is 21 miles ahead, *Rucanor* 9 behind. *Schlussel* has also taken some miles.

What happened next is a testament to the guts and bravery of *Maiden*'s crew. The girls had passed reefing lines through the first two outer reef line points in the mainsail (see diagram). When the new boom had arrived in Fort Lauderdale it only had four sheaves fitted at the clew, not the five needed for the third reefing line to be permanently fitted. In a rising gale, and at night, Tanja was sent up to get this vitally needed line in place.

As soon as it got dark all hell broke loose – of course. The wind came up to 35 knots. We put one reef in and changed to the medium reacher; we also dropped the staysail.

Then we put it back up and put another reef in the main and then took the staysail down and put the No 3 up. By now the sea was becoming much more violent with wind screaming through the rigging, waves over the deck and as high as the first spreaders. We had just about everyone on deck.

Tanja had to go up the mast and across the mainsail with ropes lashed to her on all sides to try and manoeuvre her to the third reef line. This is only the second time I have seen Tanja frightened. She got too tired to do it and the lines were in the wrong position for us to hold her so she had to come back down. The boat was leaping around in the growing waves. Tanja looked like a rag doll being flung around the mainsail. At times we could hardly see the torchlight through the blackness and driving rain. Trying to keep the boat going fast into the wind and keep Tanja alive was almost impossible.

Michèle went up – we had positioned the lines to hold her better. Meanwhile Jeni did a marathon couple of hours on the wheel and did a really good job. Dawn co-ordinated the whole thing, as professionally as ever. I stayed on the mainsheet, my neck giving me hell from having to look up the whole time. Nancy, Claire, Sally and Tanja were hauling on Michèle's safety lines.

We finally got her to the leech of the main. She hooked her feet round it and managed to pass the reef line through the hole. We got her back down OK and then she went out on the boom and secured the reefing line.

Tanja, then Michèle, had to climb across the mainsail in these conditions.

The whole operation took four hours. Everyone was shattered. Poor Jo had to wait for us to finish then heat the dinner up for the third time. The girls ate in relays. I finally got to bed after plotting our positions.

May 11th   39° 30'N   62° 10'W   2,576 miles to go

I was up again at midnight to plot the positions. The wind was gusting at over 40 knots but generally around 38 knots (Gale Force 8). The sea seemed to be better with a larger swell which is better for us and good for surfing.

The chat show unfortunately brought bad news. I was late as we were having more mast problems – it definitely must have been damaged in that waterspout. Anyway the situation was that *L'Esprit* was 50 miles in front, *Rucanor* 20 and *Schlussel* 70 behind.

I thought I had to have reached the lowest point of the entire Race when Tanja subsequently sat on the battery switch and – yes, you've guessed it – turned the power off. Off went the sat navs which had only just started working again at full strength. I didn't know whether to cry, scream or jump over the side. I screamed.

I just could not believe it. Just as we had reached the Gulf Stream and then fallen off I didn't know where we were. I can't remember ever having felt this unhappy. Empty, tired, devoid of all feelings. Really DOWN. Mind you, no one is enjoying this leg. The Race is too long and this all feels surplus – just a way of getting home.

I can't wait till the only person my decisions affect are me – and Simon. I'm looking forward to seeing him so much. Simon, my family and my home and the dogs. To be able to go to the pub, the local supermarket, to walk in my garden. Picking the milk up off the doorstep in the morning with the paper, having some coffee, listening to Radio One and reading the news. Heaven. Get me home!

The wind dropped after we had come off the course for more speed. What else? We took the third reef out. I had no way of knowing where we were as the current could be taking us north. I've given up praying for the sat navs to work. I've taken to threatening them with a hammer.

Maybe it worked because they took the next fix. So, I turned the top one off in case it happens again. Good thinking batman.

We spent the rest of the day in the Stream after we had located it – really good speeds, great sailing, great surfing. It got very foggy tonight. We are approaching the icebergs, so I hope it clears. Peter Blake suggested at this evening's chat show that we all listened on 6215.5, the emergency channel, while we go through the ice – as well as on 2182. We started right away as we are on radar watch for any ice.

May 12th 41° 21'N 58° 07'W 2,466 miles to go

The fog only cleared this morning. It is definitely getting much colder. I am so tired I made a decision to gybe, went back to sleep and then, when I woke up, couldn't remember saying it. Luckily it was the right thing to do. Maybe I should do all my navigation asleep as it can't be worse than when I'm awake.

When the fog went the sky cleared, the wind came forward and we put the reacher up. We are not in the Stream any more. The less said the better. The wind came aft during the morning and we spent the rest of it enjoying some very pleasant sailing. It's back to 'maybe I will do the next Whitbread' for most of us. Amazing how quickly you forget the bad stuff.

The morning chat show wasn't too bad either: we are holding our own against *L'Esprit*, although *Schlussel* is creeping up on us. A high pressure area will be over us tomorrow but it ought not to be too bad. A front and a low are following that.

I don't want to go too far north and get in the centre or on top of the low. Spirits are generally high today with only 11 days to go. Called Sarah-Jane tonight as well as Simon. They both sounded fine. SJ said England was cold and wet.

Simon said the house wasn't exactly finished and it could be a bit chilly with some windows and doors missing and a pile of rubble in the bedroom. 'I don't care,' I said. I'll try to phone mum tomorrow when I call Howard. The chat show tonight had lots of ice reports from the maxis. *Fisher and Paykel* is still in the lead. We had taken more from *Rucanor* and *L'Esprit*, as well as *Schlussel* and *La Poste*. So, we were very happy. I got very annoyed with all the French-speaking going on in our division – and said so.

May 13th 43° 17'N 53° 21'W 2,248 miles to go

During last night it was so cold no one could believe it. We thought we must be back in the Southern Ocean. There was a clear sky – which makes it worse. We are in the high now with a front to follow then the low. We had the spinnaker up for a while

Spirits could be amazingly high!

in the morning. It was quite pleasant until the wind came forward and started to rise. But the sea was surprisingly mild mannered.

This time five years ago I was going across this same route from St John's in Newfoundland to England on *Jubilation* to join *Norsk Data* for the last Whitbread. (Little did I know!) We had the same weather then.

The wind kept coming up all day. It got cloudy and dark but we had some great speeds. Reefs were going in and coming out faster than ever. Living conditions on the boat are bad. Everything is wet and freezing cold. One sleeping bag is not enough. The nav station is like a fridge again. Wet sails everywhere.

Dawn has finally found the problem with the water tanks. She fixed the filter and Jo can get water out of the taps. Poor old Jo has been going mad trying to pump it up.

At 6.00pm this evening we spotted a group of fishing boats on the horizon. When we got to about four miles away we could see six of them in a circle. I called to see if any of them had seen icebergs and the guy that came back told me they were searching for the body of a man who had gone missing – presumally fallen over the side. He had been in the water for four hours, poor sod, so it would be his body they are seeking, not him.

The water is so cold he would only have lasted about half an hour. He had apparently gone to the wheelhouse while they were eating dinner and hadn't been seen since then. They asked us to steer clear so we came up for four miles and then went back on the old course.

Everyone came out on deck to keep a look-out. It was a very sad sight and I felt we were intruders, trespassers.

We are going through the worst of the ice tonight. We may see some, I hope not. The sky is clear which is good and we have a moon. The temperature has dropped right down – on deck at 1°C, in the water 4°C. Brrrr! The boat is like a walk-in freezer.

We have taken miles from everyone today.

May 14th   44° 30'N   48° 53'W   2,022 miles to go

At 5.00am all hell broke loose. We tried to change down from the medium reacher to the No 3. The wind had got up to 29 knots. We had to run down for an hour because the No 3 came out of the headfoil in three places. We could not get it down and it tore at the luff. Everyone got drenched to the skin in icy water. We finally managed it and got it bagged.

Hot drinks provided by Jo kept everyone going. At watch changes there was a chance for a quick hello to people you would hardly otherwise see.

We will have lost a few miles doing all that. We put up the No 4 and reefed the main twice. Disgusting sailing – close-hauled, with an awkward sea. Wet, freezing, cold and miserable. The heater still won't work so no one can dry their clothes.

The wind did drop during the morning and, of course, we needed the No 3. Tanja and Mandi mended it but we lost speed for four hours. We had lost miles anyway, as I found at the morning chat show. Miserable day. The wind kept swinging between 350° and 020°: neither one thing nor the other. The girls are so fed up – but they are still not moaning. They just take it in turns to come down and thaw out.

Dawn actually got her hands frozen today and had to thaw them in hot water. Claire said if she'd stayed out any longer she would have been in danger of losing some fingers. It was agony as the circulation came back. It's the only time I have seen Dawn cry. Now her fingers are painful and swollen.

The wind dropped in the afternoon – just as we were leaving the Grand Banks. It means the sea is getting easier. We are still managing the great circle route – just. The chat show tonight was none too good. Lost to both *L'Esprit* and *Schlussel*. The weather charts look a bit dismal too: lots of highs coming our way.

There was very bad visibility tonight and we were all glued to the radar. Thick thick fog and it was very very cold.

May 15th   45° 36'N   44° 23'W   1,822 miles to go

I got to bed at 4.00am. The wind was down and went slightly aft later. The reacher went up and down as many times as we took reefs in and out. But the temperature went up drastically to 8°C. The sea is still at 4°C (this was why they were getting such bad fog).

When the fog cleared in the morning there was *Rucanor* on the horizon, just about 4 miles to leeward. We spent all day trying to overtake them. The chat show this morning was not too bad. At least the temperature is OK.

We really should be out of the iceberg belt tomorrow morning. Mandi went up and checked the rig: everything seems to be OK. The screws have stayed in and the piece of main track that Michèle repaired is holding its own.

After dinner the girls had a silly hour dancing on deck and generally being totally mad. Time to get back! We all talked about the first night in the King and Queen.

Mostly, we wondered if Tim (the landlord) would be pleased to see us or say 'Oh no, they're back!'

May 16th   46° 32'N   39° 38'W   1,598 miles to go

One week to go – I estimate. Visibility was not too good last night. It was very dark and the moon had trouble getting through. There is a huge high pressure system forming to the north. I hope it's going to move east. *L'Esprit* is holding her course so we will too.

The wind started to die by lunch-time and it's come forward this afternoon. We can no longer make course. We can see *Rucanor* about a mile ahead still trying to get above us. I have decided now to steer a direct great circle route for home.

The boat is like a Chinese laundry today: after all the wet and foggy conditions we had enough sun to put out all the girls' kit to dry – and the bunk cushions, everything.

Tonight the wind has dropped to nothing. *Rucanor*, of course, has gone.

May 17th   46° 50'N   35° 59'W   1,439 miles to go

The wind has dropped to nothing. It's cold, grey and damp. Horrible. We can't make course. We have been tacking the whole time, trying to go south but the way the wind direction is working we are still being pushed north. I just pray the wind will shift a little and release us.

Today everyone has been feeling pretty low. The girls are finding it very hard to keep their spirits up, although we are starting to get lots and lots of phone calls from home.

Schlussel is creeping up on us. I wonder if they are going to be a problem? By this evening the tacking was really getting to everyone. Each time we tack the watch below has to struggle to get from the windward bunks across to the leeward (to help balance the yacht). It's driving them mad and who could blame them.

The barometer is showing 1036 which is incredibly high.

May 18th   46° 43'N   33° 11'W   1,320 miles to go

I am beginning to get a terrible sinking feeling in my stomach about how long it will take us to get there. There was no wind, nothing. We are right in the high.

Today I think everyone realised that even at this speed we only have about a week left together. The music has got turned off and everyone has started chattering away like mad. You'd think that after nine months together we'd have nothing left to say: wrong, very wrong. The girls are all discussing their futures like crazy.

Also, whether we are going to do the next Race or not. When the wind came up we decided we would, when it died we all decided we wouldn't.

I asked Angela what she thought she'd learnt and she said: 'The world's round!'

The waves today were horrible. They sort of stood up so the boat kept slamming into them. The boat would just get moving and then stop.

May 20th   49° 16'N   26° 19'W   1,071 miles to go

The chat show this morning was like a manic depressives club. Everyone has realised how long it is going to take to get in. All the maxis are shooting off east because they can't get north; we're shooting off north because we can't get east. We saw loads of driftwood today – maybe off a deck cargo. As we get closer to England the rubbish in the water is getting worse. And a tanker has cleared its tanks near here and there is an oily scum on the water.

It's getting much warmer. Loads of dolphins.

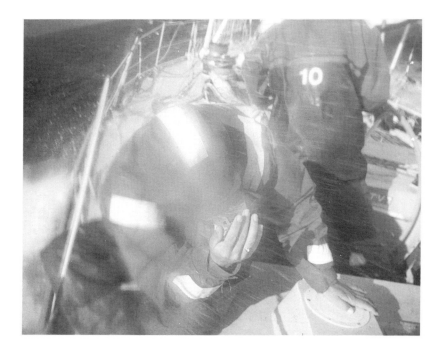

Sometimes, when the sea was up and the rain was falling in sheets, life seemed to be elsewhere.

207

May 21st   49° 49'N   22° 40'W   902 miles to go

An RAF Nimrod came out today and overflew us. They were looking for *Satquote* (*British Defender*). They took some photographs of us and we took some of them. As a result we started talking to *British Defender* and we decided to have a quiz just to keep our sanity.

The sea was like a mirror. We were doing 0.4 of a knot; the clouds stood still. We have reached an all-time low.

But, this evening, the sunset was incredible: the colours looked like oils splashed into the water. It was so still even the sails were not flapping.

May 22nd   49° 51'N   20° 33'W   790 miles to go

Schlussel has disappeared over the horizon but we have found *Rucanor* again.

Patience is wearing thin!

Maiden, caught in a high pressure area which went on and on, was sliding, rather than sailing, in the direction of the Channel. Apart from the appallingly slow progress, they were now running out of food.

But there were some surprises left. In sailing nothing is decided until a boat is safely in harbour. Two days after *Maiden* had expected to be in that happy state, she started to bash into awkward waves – still tacking.

May 24th   50° 55'N   13° 24'W   550 miles to go

We have been with *Rucanor* for days now. Still, the wind will not come right. The waves have been dreadful today.

Then, to cap it all, I phoned Howard who turned out to be at the *Fisher and Paykel* crew dinner (*F and P* had arrived on Tuesday, May 22nd). How nice for him – I could hear all the jollity in the background. Meanwhile we're just about out of food.

May 25th   50° 32'N   09° 35'W   389 miles to go

Home – please!

The wind has come up but it's in a lousy direction. But we have finally got upwind of *Rucanor*.

Then, when we were beating our brains out this power boat suddenly appeared with Jo's father (Norman) on board. Jo was completely over the moon at seeing her dad.

Our course was so bad today we saw Ireland (this meant they were far too north for the Channel).

May 26th 50° 15′N 06° 33′W 250 miles to go

Welcome to Black Saturday. For a start poor old Jo's bunk broke while she was in it. She just flew across the boat. She's very lucky not to have been hurt.

Water has started pouring into the bilges again. We have narrowed it down – at last – to one section of the boat. It has to be one of the cockpit drains but we can't get at it because of all the foam.

Nancy sat at one point for four hours on the bilge pump. I had gone to sleep while she was doing it; when I woke up she was still in the same place. We had to get all the sails on the deck – 22 – to get the boards up. Then the generator went (we *have* been here before).

Dawn started the engine to help with the pumps, put her hand in under it and got quite badly burned on one of the fan belts. It was at that moment the No 3 halyard broke.

Then we heard there was a boat in distress off the Scillies. For a time I thought we were the closest boat but we weren't.

By this afternoon the Scillies were six miles to starboard. We passed by the Seven Stones. We will just be able to make The Lizard. *Rucanor* is still ahead.

We are now being affected by the tide.

May 27th 50° 22′N 03° 01′W 150 miles to go

The wind direction couldn't be worse. Are we ever – ever – going to get home?

The sea is incredibly awkward, too. But we won a tacking duel with *Rucanor* and we got ahead by The Lizard.

What Bruno kept doing was to get me on the radio and then while he thought I was occupied, tack. But we caught him out and every time we saw them come up into the wind we were over. Unfortunately, there was no time to warn the watch below so they were flying out of their bunks all over the place.

This amazing tacking duel – as good as anything in the Race – went on all up the Channel, past Start Point, into Lyme Bay, past Portland Bill, across Weymouth Bay to Anvil Point.

Maiden was being constantly buzzed by planes and helicopters. Power boats came out and, thinking they were being kind, offered them food (they were now down to popcorn and water). The Race rules forbade their accepting even a biscuit. With all this going on, the *Maiden* crew never lost sight of what they were trying to achieve. After a nightmare leg, after 33,000 miles, they were racing *Maiden* like a dinghy, seeking the advantage on every twist and turn. It was a virtuoso display of their professional skills.

In the last 24 hours of *Maiden*'s race around the world she tacked 100 times (an average of one every fifteen minutes).

May 28th   Position: Ocean Village Marina   Distance to go: zero

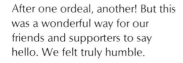

After one ordeal, another! But this was a wonderful way for our friends and supporters to say hello. We felt truly humble.

| We're home!

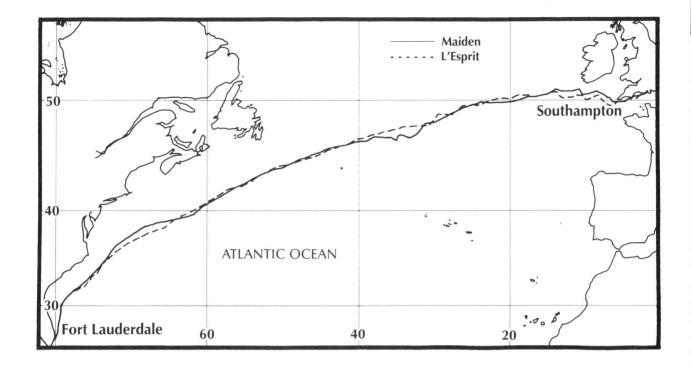

Maiden
L'Esprit

50
Southampton
40
ATLANTIC OCEAN
30
Fort Lauderdale   60   40   20

A Summary of Leg Six: Breaking Records

The Race was over. In division D *Maiden* came fourth in the leg – finally losing the battle with *Rucanor*, on the edge of The Solent. But *L'Esprit*, the real target for the *Maidens* had herself been beaten at the last moment by the German yacht *Schlussel*.

L'Esprit was, inevitably, first overall. Leg honours for first place would read *L'Esprit*, 3, *Maiden*, 2, *Schlussel*, 1. Well, everyone said, that seemed fair enough.

But *Maiden* had come second overall in her class. 'Next time,' said Tracy, 'we'll win.'

Maiden's fight with *Rucanor* lasted almost to the line. The fates cast against the girls. Tracy had planned to get to the Needles Channel to get the tide gate to sweep her into The Solent. But the wind picked up and both *Maiden* and *Rucanor* got there too early.

Then *Rucanor* hit the Shingles Bank and went aground. Tantalisingly close behind *Maiden* was tacking against a fierce tidal rip. Back and forward she went, making no ground. *Rucanor* floated off the Bank and, as the tidal flow abated, moved into The Solent ahead of *Maiden*. She stayed in front.

It hardly mattered. It was a Bank Holiday Monday. The weather that had frustrated *Maiden* and her fellow yachts for weeks, brought out the crowds – on land and on the water.

As she made her way through The Solent *Maiden* attracted a growing armada of yachts, power boats and dinghies. As she turned into Southampton Water, three miles from the finish line, she broke out her spinnaker for the last time on the Race. A huge cheer went up.

By now as many as six hundred boats were acting as her escort. *Maiden* crossed the line just on 11.00. The Royal Southampton Yacht Club had arranged a special 'gun' for her and the report was so loud it was heard in Hamble.

> I heard the gun and four years hard struggle ended in a deafening bang. I had expected that at this point I would cheer and throw my arms up. I didn't, I felt this deep pain within me, my throat ached and tears welled up in my eyes and poured down my face. Instead of the joy I was expected to feel I felt totally desolate as if life had stopped.
>
> Then as quickly as it came the feeling passed and I laughed as the girls hugged me. We took the sails down for the last time.

Immediately the RSYC support boat threw a hamper of hamburgers on board. A note said: diet free zone.

Then *Maiden* slowly, so slowly, motored up the Itchen and turned into Ocean Village Marina. A huge crowd – some newspapers suggested it was 50,000 strong – went wild.

Maiden was home, Tracy Edwards was the most famous woman in Britain, her future likely to be studded with glory. The little girl who had once run away had finally come home – with dignity, with grace, her faith vindicated, her courage emblazoned in a thousand headlines.

Maiden had not won the 1989–90 Whitbread Race overall in her division but it no longer mattered. The Whitbread's significance to Tracy Edwards and her crew was that it had given them a framework. Far more important than the Race, as the rest of the world began to realise as *Maiden* crossed the Atlantic, was that they were the first fully crewed female boat to have circumnavigated the globe.

The last great battle between *Steinlager II* and *Fisher and Paykel* was played out in this last leg. For *Steinlager* it nearly ended in disaster when, four days into the leg the crew heard a tremendous bang and found that the mizen port chain plates had parted. This fitting also housed the running backstay for the main mast and, Blake reported in secret to his project manager, 'the rig started swaying like a piece of spaghetti'.

Quick thinking by his crew, who crash gybed the boat so the strain was on the other side, was followed by an ingenious jury repair using part of the engine mounts to hold the shrouds to the deck. The bad luck which had dogged Blake in four previous Whitbreads had been prevented and, twelve days later it was *Steinlager* which led *Fisher and Paykel*, in sight but far enough behind, into The Solent and on to victory.

Both Kiwi ketches were greeted by an ecstatic crowd of 15,000 on Ocean Village, Southampton, when they docked. The crew of *Steinlager* were all in tears, as was their leader. 'Well,' said Pippa, his wife, 'you've done it.' The final 'distance' was 36 hours ahead of *Fisher and Paykel*. Both crews, however, repaired as one to the King and Queen in Hamble to celebrate a New Zealand double and to plan their next moves.

Behind this finale to an epic nine-month battle other dramas were unfolding. *Rothmans* also suffered damage to its rig, serious enough to have to put into port. Lawrie Smith suffered the final indignity of having to anchor his yacht off Lymington, in The Solent and only ten miles from the finish line when the tide headed him. *Merit* had stolen in to take third place – and a third overall behind the two ketches. *Merit* had suffered a broken stay but Fehlmann and his crew were determined to be the first of the sloops home.

It was the yacht rigs which bore the brunt of damage in this final dash across the Atlantic. Apart from *Steinlager*, *Rothmans* and *Merit*, *Gatorade*, the Italian entry suffered a broken top spreader. Worst of all, the ill-fated *Satquote British Defender* lost the top half of the mast altogether. Her painful progress across the 'pond' was to be compounded by the same huge high pressure zone which so sorely afflicted *Maiden*. She finally made it across the finish line two days after the girls.

So, they all came on home. The *Card* crossed fifth, a position they seemed to have made their own. The Finns arrived, the French, the Italians, the Irish – and the Russians, minus Skip Novak who had retired to Queensland to write a book about it all.

They did bring another American as crew – and as sponsor – to get them back to England. David Matthews had helped raise money for *Fazisi* which came eighth on the leg and eleventh overall. They'd be back, the crew all vowed, and no one disbelieved them any more. In the time it had taken for them to go around the world, their part of it had changed for ever.

The arrivals in Ocean Village were tinged with sadness. There was a delivery crew waiting on the dock for *Fisher and Paykel*. The yachts came in and then disappeared, seemingly almost as fast as they docked. Crews too, who had lived and worked so closely together for so long, suddenly were no longer around. An air of desolation overlaid the celebrations.

The late arrivals meant the Whitbread leg prize-giving was simply abandoned. The formal prize-giving for the whole Race was held in London on June 20th at Whitbread's Chiswell Street Brewery. The Duke of York handed out the awards, attended by the Duchess.

For *Maiden* there were one or two surprises. They knew they had won the second prize in division D, as well as the third prize for the combined division C and D. There was more, though. The whole crew won a prize donated by the Russians for the best crew competing for the first time. Tracy won a prize for being the leading girl on a first yacht on handicap. To everyone's delight Claire Russell won the most distinguished performance by a doctor award for her work with Bart van den Dwey in the Southern Ocean.

In her short summary speech the Duchess had a surprise, too. Singling out 'her' girls, she departed from her speech to give a short but clearly heartfelt panegyric on their achievements; the audience responded.

Four days later *Maiden* – the yacht – departed from her Hamble berth to go to a Dutch yacht brokers for sale. She left with an all-male crew. Neither Tracy nor her girls wanted to be on that last, sad voyage.

Writing in the early summer of 1990, it is too early to make anything other than a preliminary judgement on the 1989/90 Whitbread. It was probably too long; the handicap system destroyed any chance of their being a unified Race; the cruising class, as it was constituted, was a constant worry to all those involved.

But, as the veteran *Daily Mail* sport's commentator, Ian Wooldridge, wrote in that newspaper, shortly before *Maiden* arrived, to concentrate on details too much is to miss the central point. This Whitbread, like its predecessors, is the world's last great adventure to which pretty much anyone can aspire. To use an old cliché, if it did not exist someone would be compelled to invent it: if there is no cruising class in the next Race, it no longer matters.

The amateur Atlantic Race for Cruisers, the ARC, is being extended to a world 'race'. It will not be a rival to the Whitbread but it will fill the gap. The next Whitbread may only contain full-on racing crews but it, too, has to develop. It will remain a unique challenge for men and women, a lifetime's excitement crammed into nine months.

The Whitbread is said to change all those whose lives it touches. Oh yes, along with Tracy Edwards, I can vouch for that. Long may it be so.

CHAPTER 15

The True Glory

'It is not the beginning, but the continuing of the same until it be
thoroughly finished, that yieldeth, The True Glory . . .'
        Sir Francis Drake in a letter to Sir Francis Walsingham

At a stroke, Tracy Edwards entered a new realm: now, in truth,
could be seen the continuity of her voyage with those of the greatest
ever undertaken by British seamen. Drake, Raleigh, Frobisher, Hud-
son, Franklin, Shackleton: all of them would have recognised her.

In the past thirty years some of that tradition has returned: Francis
Chichester, Alec Rose, Naomi James, Clare Francis. But those latter
all sailed alone and at their leisure. Tracy chose to race on a high-
tech machine. Her achievement leapt over theirs to a farther past. In
the spirit of the great explorers, she had left the shores of England,
now to return, changed: older, wiser, and much, much happier.

> I remember sitting in a bar in Palma years ago with a guy called
> Sam who said I'd never stay on boats. I'd drift in and drift out and
> never learn. That stayed with me for a long time and I couldn't
> understand why. It was, of course, because I doubted myself.
>
> This doubting was to continue on and off throughout the
> project. During the Route of Discovery Race at the end of 1988, I
> wanted to go south and my first mate said I was mad and had to
> go north. It was a turning point.
>
> At the time, as she stood there judging me, as she shouted and
> screamed at the crew in her frustration, I withdrew and backed off,
> even though I knew I was right and she was wrong. The constant
> arguments with her over how we should sail the boat made me
> sick with worry.
>
> But, I knew I was right: I believed in that decision. Then the
> family strength took over. The doubting was at an end. We went

Tracy Edwards, M.B.E. When the letter came she was really excited, though she had first heard that she had been awarded the honour in Florida.

south. I looked back on all this as we neared Cape Horn. I had a call on the radio from Mike Plant on *Duracell*. He was doing the Globe Challenge single-handed race (around the world, non-stop).

He said he never thought he'd see the day when he was being followed round Cape Horn by a bunch of women. That remark, from that man, in that place, put all that had gone before neatly into perspective. I remembered the times I had been in the King and Queen in Hamble with Nancy right at the start of the whole thing, how we had dreamed and planned, planned and dreamed. We had so often imagined it that when we arrived at the Horn it had a dream-like quality. Mike's voice brought me back to earth – to where we were, what we had achieved.

When I first thought of entering the Whitbread with an all-female crew it was because I wanted to give other women the chance I had craved so much. It was a dream, too, to achieve what so many had dubbed 'impossible'. I did not get into all this to prove to others as much as I – and all the crew – wanted to prove to ourselves. We certainly did not want to be male clones.

We are women; we love sailing. That's all, that's it.

What I have ended up with is so much more than I could have hoped for. A new confidence, an inner strength and security. Most important of all, I belong to the *Maiden* family, the shore team as well as the crew. My ties with them and the eleven other women on *Maiden* have been forged out of agony, tears, fear and love and over 33,000 miles of faith and hope.

They trusted their lives with me; I trusted my life with them. I will *never* be the same again.

It was not all about us, about *Maiden*. You cannot travel these kind of distances at sea and not realise how fragile our existence is. Out there we have to rely on the weather, have constantly to learn how to read its moods. We are in an alien environment and we have to adjust to that, too.

Living on land you can get complacent about life, begin to believe we have it all cracked, that the natural world is ours to command and, once we have made a choice, nature will just knuckle down and obey. It's not true. Living within an ocean environment for all these months has taught us all how precious the planet is, how vital it is we preserve all aspects of the natural world.

I think it was a big surprise to us all, how close we all felt to nature and how disgusted we were at the litter that is now strewn around the oceans of the world. We felt guilty for the rest of mankind for that.

Yet although it was the wildest, most inhospitable place, we felt freest in the Southern Ocean. It was very lonely, but that's freedom's price. At one point I couldn't believe I was back there and I wondered if I'd ever go back again with just the whales and the albatrosses and icebergs for company. To that question I still have no certain answer. Is it too early? But I know that I might.

The most difficult thing to do after the Race is to sort out your thoughts and feelings. Although you have learned about yourself, what do you do about it? The answer – one answer – is that you crave to learn even more.

Part of the wanting to learn more, to gain self-knowledge is, in my case, to do with the women who have helped form me: my grandmother who was so strong and determined, a tough Scot if ever there was one; and my mother – now I begin to understand what drives her.

Underneath it all, Tracy craves love: it is life to her, as necessary as air to breathe. In her long-standing boyfriend, Simon Lawrence, she finally believes she has found that love and that it can be made to last. Ironic, as she says, that she has travelled the world yet plans to marry the boy next door (when they first met that's where he was living).

Yet while before the end of the Race she was saying that after this Whitbread it would be marriage and then children, now she wants more – and the next Whitbread may well be part of the enlarged vision. No one who has listened to Tracy for more than five minutes at a time could be mistaken in hearing that siren voice of the wanderer, the eternal gipsy.

Simon has held his tongue – and bitten it in anguish, too – yet there is in him a quality of pure strength to hold on to what he cares for most, that has slowly, very slowly emerged. For him it has been a

Simon Lawrence: he got his girl.

lonely race. When he first met Tracy, and they fell in love, it was relatively easy. She had a dream – don't we all? Yet, as he came to realise she meant it, he found he first had to share his love with more than a dozen others, then with the world's press.

Perhaps worse than that, he found, as so many women have before, that the sea is a harsh mistress (or lover) who brooks no interference. Sailing with her crew, too, created a barrier which was hard enough for anyone to penetrate. Add to that the growth among *Maiden*'s skipper and crew that they were, indeed, making history and anyone not directly involved knew they were somewhere else. If not a world apart, then an ocean.

Curiously, one of Simon's strongest cards has been his lack of interest in sailing. For some of those in the project that disinterest was perceived to be a conceit, a simple but effective way of keeping his distance. But, like Tracy, it was less artifice, more artlessness. Simon wasn't interested in sailing; he was, however, interested in *Maiden*, most unashamedly, in her skipper.

His decisions, to by and large stay away from the race while it was on, were also correct. Tracy was single-tracked about the race. She missed Simon but she had decided she would do without. When he did turn up – in Fremantle – there was heartache and arguing.

What attracts us to this woman, this dream fulfilled, is that she espouses our hopes and fears so neatly. *Maiden* is a family project, someone once described it and Tracy set it up like that. After all, women understand family dynamics much better than men.

When people left the project, they felt deprived, cut off from this

Domestic bliss: well, one day, soon. Tracy and Simon can still smile about all the work ahead to complete their Hamble house.

family feeling. Some of us felt that way when we left stop-overs, or watched the yacht leave on its next leg.

Maybe, just maybe, it was a deeper dream she had realised, a return to the days of childhood when all her family were with her and she ruled as only a child can rule. In *Maiden*, maybe, she found again her lost childhood: this was her home, her hearth, embracing, as only she dared, the entire globe.

What most defies imagination is that she took a yacht and raced it for 33,000 miles in the worst conditions the seas and winds can deploy. She persuaded, in total, 13 other people that they could hold their fears to their faces and overcome them. She led those girls over nine months, taking a team into the teeth of a gale, into and out of the eye of the hurricane. It remains a unique achievement, a level of sheer guts few have matched.

In those lonely watches Tracy sat in her navigation station. She was 27 years old and she had, finally, discovered something most of us take a lifetime to unravel, and then, mostly, cannot decipher. She had found *herself*.

The crew should have the last word . . .

Dawn   If there is one thing I've got out of the Whitbread, I would have to say it is increased self-confidence. There is no way anyone could have gone through this experience as successfully as we have and not having a feeling of . . . We *can* do it . . . anything!

Watch out for the Maidens! We will be out there succeeding in our separate endeavours but we will also – always – be together.

Michèle   I like racing because all the time you push yourself and the boat. The Whitbread is the longest yacht race. For me, as well, there has been the challenge of going into the Southern Ocean, where none of us had been before. But that is what I like, that is the reason for going at all.

Jo   I've got confident – I *never* thought I would feel this good. I have also got some very dear friends, had some fantastic times – as well as some sad ones. I feel I have got to know myself and what I want out of life. I know I don't want to cook in a Whitbread again! What's next, I don't know but there is something out there . . .

Nancy   You have to risk a little but with some trust and a belief in what you are doing, lots of hard work, and some fun on the way, yes, dreams *do* come true.

Sally   Been there, done that – ticked it off and got the T-shirt!

Mikki   The challenge and dream of my life has come true. And, also, I have come to know 11 other people, all great personalities and beloved friends who are always going to be here for me – my family. We have something together that can not be taken away.

I got my peace of mind, too! And we didn't fall off the edge of the world, after all, did we?

Angela   A lovely warmth inside. Gone is that feeling of 'if only, if only'. Of course my sailing skill has tripled but there is that elusive determination now imprinted on me.

And I've done something huge in my life – conquered something I used to hold in awe. My love to all the Maidens for being life-long friends. I'll never forget.

Mandi   When I was ten years old my Whitbread began as a raindrop falling to earth. I became that drop of water, and over the years I found myself in a trickling stream, being fed and carried to a river that flowed, long and winding.

A year before the start of this Race my river became rapids, hard, rushing, and then I discovered that the Whitbread was the falls of Iguazu (the world's largest in South America).

I am totally in awe! I now lie at the bottom of those falls, ecstatic, tired, stunned, swirling around. I shall recover and journey out to the ocean.

Jeni   The first thing that springs to mind is the amount of self-satisfaction. The whole world behind you! Then, of course, there are friendships, strong close friends for life. A lot of laughing, a lot of miles, and an increase in self-confidence. Oh yes, I'll do it again!

Tanja   It was a very good and special experience which will always be with me. I learned that the world is big, round and that most of it is a beautiful ocean which gives all of us something from that beauty.

Claire   For me it has given one of the greatest senses of pride and achievement I have known, along with a realisation that I have nothing to prove to anyone.

I have also come away with lasting friendships, borne of total trust, respect and deep affection.

ACKNOWLEDGEMENTS

Many people have contributed towards the success of *Maiden*, but in particular I would like to pay tribute to the following . . .

King Hussein and Queen Noor of Jordan for believing in me: with faith, honour and courage anything is possible.

My brother, Trevor, Uncle Arthur, Auntie Edna and cousins Graeme and Gregor Bint, and all my family and friends whose love and support kept me going.

Simon Lawrence for his very special love before, during and after the race.

Peter, Daphne and Sacha Lawrence, my 'new' family.

Ali Ghandour for his belief.

All at Royal Jordanian in Amman and London.

Her Royal Highness the Duchess of York for christening our boat and becoming our Royal 'Maiden'.

Tricia McMahon for all the great advice through thick and thin.

Colin Moynihan, Minister of Sport, for recognising our worth among all the other sporting achievements he sees.

Rick Tomlinson, for friendship and photography (sometimes both at the same time).

Duncan Walker and Johnny LeBon, for putting *Maiden* together.

Keith Webb, for all the graphics we had printed and all the birthday cards and faxes that we couldn't.

Rear Admiral Charles Williams, the Race Chairman, for unstinting belief and sound advice.

The *Maiden* shore team – Howard Gibbons, for being there at the beginning, getting *Maiden* to the startline, and the finish, and putting up with me in between; Sarah-Jane Ingram for the brilliant job she did organising us ashore and her loyal friendship; Dee Ingles for the thankless task of running the office while we were off around the world, and for her help after the race; Pam Hale for being so much more than just a housewife from Netley; and Ian 'Poodle' Bruce for getting *Maiden* ready for each leg and for the safe delivery of our air and sea containers. Thanks to you each and every one of you.

And to Mike Corns and Janie Boysie, skipper and cook of my first boat, look what you got me into!

AND SPECIAL THANKS TO . . .

John Anson of Whitbread.

The Amin family of Hamble – Tony, Sheila, Miles and Alison – for loan of the tiger's claw and for working so hard on the fundraising (especially Captain Codpiece!).

Charm Eberle.

Fiona Edgecombe for her help in setting up Maiden Great Britain Ltd.

Paul Emmerson and colleagues at National Westminster Bank, Portsmouth.

Captain Brian Evans, Royal Naval Sailing Association.

Bob Fisher.

Alan Green and the Royal Ocean Racing Club.

Paul Greensmith and Paul Waite, the Ps in P and P Electronics.

Lizzie Gibbons.

Hamble and all our friends and supporters there.

Hamble Yacht Services Ltd.

Dave Hipwood for arranging the Albany Life insurance for *Maiden*'s crew.

The King and Queen, Hamble, our local pub.

Tim Jeffery.

Jol and Judy and the English Harbour Supporters Club, Antigua.

Roger Lean-Vercoe.

Lewmar Marine, Havant.

Gary Lovejoy, Gareth Evans and all at TVS Southampton, will the Big Match ever seem the same again?

Suzy Mayhew and the Gower Supporters Club, South Wales.

Ian Maiden and all at Arthur Maiden Ltd, London.

Jules Mantle.

Paddy McMahon.

Brian Merry

Peter Montgomery of Radio New Zealand, long live the maritime gladiators!

A. H. Moody and Sons Ltd, Swanwick.

Greg Murphy and Katherine Skellon, you were marvellous!

Hugh Myers

Denise Norman and everybody who worked on the TV Pool at the stopovers.

Barry Pickthall, David Branigan and all at the Pickthall Picture Library, Littlehampton.

David Pritchard-Barrett of Whitbread and his wife Joanie.

Chris Quinton and Terry Mills, for help with houses, cars and a famous Caribbean fundraising party.

Mike Richards, Hood Sails, Lymington.

Royal Southampton Yacht Club for the homecoming party.

Roger Sawell and Roni Roddis at Rainbow's End, Southampton.

Dave Crago at Southern Marine Coatings, Poole.

John Stelling.

Henri Strzelecki.

Barry Taylor and all at Testwood Motors, Southampton.

Linda Trumble.

223

Eddie Ward-Owen, Bruce Banks Sails, Lock's Heath.

David Earl at TV2 Northampton

Bob and Anne Houston at the Westhaven Motel, Auckland, for taking such good care of us.

And, last but not least, to our most generous but anonymous benefactor and all those people, too numerous to mention, who made donations to our funds or bought a T-shirt to keep us going. We could not have done it without you.

GREAT BRITAIN
THE SOLENT

Western
Approaches

Gulf Stream

Azores High

UNITED STATES
FORT LAUDERDALE

Atlantic Ocean

Northeast Trades

The Doldrums

Southeast
Trades

Pacific Ocean

South Atlantic H

URUGUAY
PUNT DEL ESTE

Prevailing Westerlies ▶

Brazil Current

Southern Ocean

Cape Horn

WHITBREAD

ROUND THE WORL

Antarctica

Leg 1. — **Start 2 Sept. '89**
        Arrive Punta Del Este 9-18 Oct.
Leg 2. — **Start 28 Oct. Arrive Fremantle 29 Nov.-10 Dec.**
Leg 3. — **Start 23 Dec. Arrive Auckland 12-16 Jan. '90.**
Leg 4. — **Start 4 Feb. Arrive Punta Del Este 28 Feb.-8 Mar.**
Leg 5. — **Start 17 Mar. Arrive Fort Lauderdale 13-21 Apr.**
Leg 6. — **Start 5 May Arrive Southampton 21-29 May.**